LEGEND OF THE BLACK ROSE

LEGEND OF THE BLACK ROSE 1

A.W. HART

WOLFPACK
PUBLISHING
— EST 2013 —

WOLFPACK
PUBLISHING
— EST 2013 —

Published in the United States by Wolfpack Publishing, Las Vegas

Wolfpack Publishing
6032 Wheat Penny Avenue
Las Vegas, NV 89122

wolfpackpublishing.com

Paperback ISBN: 978-1-64734-070-4
eBook ISBN: 978-1-64734-069-8

LEGEND OF THE BLACK ROSE

The fact death would come to Theresa and Aquiles Rivera was no surprise, for all are born to sin and while some die in the Lord and some die in vain, all mortals must pass. Some more violently than others. But it has been my experience since serving the Church here on the west Texas plains that such a savage decease may lead to new birth, in the next life naturally, but on earth too.

In no small way then, the sacking of Rancho Rivera that autumn and the devastation wrought on the adobes y jacales of the people of Santo Tomas contributed to the rise of the Black Rose and the fiesta de balas — the carnival of bullets — which was to follow.

CHAPTER ONE

On torn hands and chafed knees, Catalina Cristiana Rivera spattered the blazing white hardpan with blood and watched the scarlet blossoms shrivel coal black in the desert sun. She gagged on the iron taste of it, coughed once, twice, and again.

Eventually she forced her leaden arms to push herself up. Her legs trembled with the strain.

She would not cry out.

Veering into the narrow Chihuahua canyon with its sly outcroppings of black igneous rock and indifferent stands of lechuguilla had allowed them a moment of rest, but had ultimately been a mistake. A perilous misstep, — her own stumble-footed fault, — had caused her to fall among the boulders of the pass, tearing her forehead on thorns, bruising her cheek and the bridge of her nose. Blood mixed with sweat and grime to paint her face into a mask of rage and despair.

This morning, she had been beautiful.

A lifetime ago.

"Madre, tenemos que darnos…prisa," she said, urgency in her voice.

Mother, we must hurry.

A stone's throw behind her, Theresa Rivera, third descendent of the Contessa D'Mores of Madrid, matriarch and keeper of the New World Spanish porciano — the land grant to Rancho Rivera — clawed at the stone outcropping. Her withered fingers were ringed in gold, broken and exhausted.

"No peuedo ir…."

Catalina Cristiana Rivera gasped for breath as the sound of thundering hooves and high-pitched cries of delight lifted her face toward the horizon.

There, on the edge of her vision, a scarf of dust trailed a silhouette of four riders on horseback, low in their saddles. They charged across the vast tract of arid ground toward them like hounds on the hunt.

Closing in for the kill.

When the chase began, Lina and her mother had also been on horseback. But when Theresa fell from her old Andalusian mount at the limestone pass, Lina had abandoned her own mustang. In the furor, the Rivera steeds had galloped on, and Lina looked for a haven for her and her mother in the canyon.

Now, with her tan charro jacket caked with sand atop a ripped crimson blouse and her tight, gray jodhpurs torn at the knees, Lina held to the goal of reaching the village of Santo Tomas.

There would be help there from the sheriff, perhaps a posse of men.

She and her mother were Riveras, after all, and it was Rivera land they crossed. Rivera land all the way from the Rio Grande to their now-ruined estancia, thousands of acres of Texas grass and scrub, mountain and valley.

From the sky-lands to the sacred springs.

Land Catalina should have traveled without fear. Land ruthlessly violated this day with the breaking of a three year-old peace.

The riders continued their obscene shouting, ever so much closer now.

Four men, maybe more behind them, dressed in bandito rags.

Garcia's *chacales* (Jackals), enough to finish familia Rivera, and to end an era of prosperity for the entire region.

Without the Riveras — without their diligence — Garcia's raids would go unchecked. He and his Apache lieutenant, Denver Three-Moons, would bring pain and misery with them.

Lina crawled away from the boulders toward a *matorral*, a tangled blind of greasewood scrub and yellow pine.

A hiding place, perhaps.

But the tangled roots stopped her advance, and sharp yellow flowers dripped like poison from prickly stems. A long time ago, she had seen petals like these gathered together into a funeral bouquet.

The mustang riders yipped with bloodlust and insanity. Only seconds away.

Catalina still hoped to escape.

The riders bayed in triumph.

There was no escape.

Lina climbed to her full, muscular stature of six feet. Her shoulders were square, her slender hips poised and balanced. She would not meet hell on her belly like an insect.

"Lina, no. Save yourself," said Theresa.

Theresa's typically robust demeanor was now a gray husk in the brilliant sunlight. Her rich, fine pile of dark hair was a clotted snarl. She cradled her left arm at an awkward angle, her shoulder slumped impossibly low. Her blue trousers were stained black from hip to knee where a scuffed boot lay beneath her.

And there were other things wrong. Her speech was slurred. Blood pooled in one eye.

Catalina longed to kneel at her mother's side, to act upon the tender charity she felt deep within her breast.

There wasn't time for charity.

Theresa clawed at the inside of her jacket, frantic to retrieve something. "Madre de dios…quemado… quemado," she said, her words making no sense to her daughter.

Lina turned away, hooking a loose strand of raven black hair around the long braid at the base of her neck. The oath she spat was as filthy as the blood trickling along her lips and chin, her hate for the attackers no longer held in check.

She stripped off her jacket, letting it drop, while her fingers worked the grit-crusted buckle of the gleaming silver belt at her waist. This, then, was how it would end.

"They are now upon us," said Lina.

The chacales arrived in an explosion of joyful shouts and scattered sand.

Lina removed her belt with a flourish.

"Ah-ha," said a toothless bag of meat dressed in an open white jacket and dusky chaps, the forest of hair on his chest powdered alkaline gray. "I see you Riveras waste no time getting out of your pants—"

And then his words were drowned in a squeal of agony as his hands shot to his throat, his knobby fingers raking through torn skin and torrents of blood.

Lina cracked her belt again like a whip, and Toothless plunged from the saddle of his bucking steed. A wedge of flesh was sliced from his neck, and his severed carotid artery spouted like a geyser. He pounded into the earth with a gut-wrenching crunch.

Gripping the cylindrical hilt firmly in hand, Lina twisted her belt into a series of twirls and loops. The weapon's length of flat razor scales telescoped to eight feet, twelve, more. She flung herself forward with the momentum, like a dancer, shooing away the dead man's mustang, whirling between two more of the raiders.

She recognized the one on her right, a mustachioed creature named Fausto. The one on her left was a brawny Texan who often worked for Garcia. His name was Wes Stark.

Fausto's fat mitt fanned a Colt Army revolver, triggering it with a left hand.

Lina rolled away from the tongues of flame as the big man's seal brown mustang circled around her.

"Give it up, señorita," said Fausto. "You are all that's left, comprende? Your hermanos are dead. You don't want to die like your men?" The human animal bared his tobacco-stained teeth "Why die like a man when you can live like a woman?"

Lina lobbed a defiant wad of spit toward his face, and Fausto tossed off his last shot. She ducked, trailing the move with her whip-sword, slashing out at the gun's flaming barrel — a miss.

Fausto jerked his spent pistol away and ducked low in his sheepskin lined gaucho saddle, his enormous sombrero slipping from his head to hang on his back from a braided strap as he spurred his horse. A second flick of Lina's wrist snapped the tip of her weapon across the mustang's rump, sending it into a frenzied pace to buy her some time.

But now there was room for Stark to intrude. Lina spun to face him, her weapon recoiling across the sky, gleaming silver in the scalding sun.

The blonde Texan carried a Snakecharmer — a 12-guage short-barreled shotgun — but was slow on the uptake. His sloth earned him a bone-deep gash at the wrist. With a scream, he jerked the trigger of his gun, chucking an explosive blast high over Lina's head.

Even as she swung around again with the whip, Stark leaned into his roan stallion, aiming to trample her under the frothing animal's thrashing hooves.

Point blank, she refused to harm the charging animal with her weapon, choosing instead to dive and chew bleached gravel. She landed hard on her ribs, her flexible steel blade flung out beside her.

But still she gripped the urumi, letting the foreign name roll across her parched tongue, uttering it over again like a mantra through cracked lips. "Urumi," she whispered, and the word with all its import to her history gave her strength, reminded her of her training with her brothers Rivera in the caverns under their residence.

Urumi. The word called up the martial heritage so precariously slipping away this day under the barbaric cruelty of the horde.

Thunder peeled through bedrock toward her and with newfound power, Catalina flipped onto her back and stared directly into Fausto's replenished six-shooter. Leaning from his saddle, Fausto was a scorpion's strike away from filling Lina with lead when she viciously unfurled the urumi steel whip at his arms. The blade bit deep through his cotton shirt, and Lina arched her back, heaving the man from his horse, stripping flesh from bone as the weapon obediently returned.

Fausto landed with a crash, and Lina was immediately on her feet. Dizzy, wavering, but she stood above the screaming Mexican bandit whose bloody arms jerked in the shale like beached fish.

"Die like a man, chico," she said, putting a boot to his back.

Fausto rolled away from her in agony, his cries growing weaker as the shock of his injuries took hold. Lina picked up his spilled gun.

She aimed it at Wes Stark.

For his part, the Texan was clumsily trying to

reload his single shot scattergun. His spooky horse, still rattled from the Snakecharmer's first blast, galloped three different directions at once.

An easy target for an expert shot.

Catalina worked the trigger, and the boom echoed over the rock field where her mother lay whimpering.

Stark hit the ground like a sack of rain-soaked oats, and his mustang dragged him back toward the horizon.

Lina turned to face the fourth man, a curiosity who until now had shied away from the action.

Casually standing beside his horse, he gripped an iron .45 automatic in each hand. A smoking cheroot dangling from his lower lip, he wore a sweat-stained guayabera shirt, untucked over steel gray trousers. He carried a campaign sabre on his belt and wore a grim visage familiar to the peasants on both sides of the Rio Grande. The smug expression of the oppressor.

But this was not Garcia.

Under a battered cavalry hat with gold cord belonging to the old Confederate states of America, the man's white hair was cropped close to the skull. Likewise, his sword and iron scabbard were short and less curved than their Mexican counterparts.

Standing above the crumpled form of Theresa Rivera in relaxed triumph, he was old enough to be Lina's grandfather. He carried enough thin scars on his hands and knuckles, enough rocky caverns on his wind-pocked whiskered face, to prove it.

Lina held Fausto's Colt in her left hand, the urumi slack at her waist in her right. Keeping watch on the twin guns, her mother's mourning cry fueled the steam hammer rage in her heart. It was all Lina could do not to take off the devil's head with a flick of either wrist.

But one of the automatics was less than a foot away from Theresa Rivera's face. The slightest twitch of a finger might set it off.

"Drop the gun," said the man. "The whip too."

In her mind's eye, Lina saw this mornings' memory of her parents burning ranch house, the slaughtered cattle sprawled across the verdant meadow, the bodies of her father and brothers hemorrhaging in the paved carriage way.

When she thought she'd used up her quota of tears, a stray drop slipped down her cheek.

She didn't dare risk her mother's life too.

What was left of it.

She let go of the pistol and the urumi at the same time, and they plopped down into the sand.

"Who are you?" said Catalina.

The raider took a long pull from his smoke, then flicked it away with his tongue.

"Name's Carter Dawson. My friends call me Tut. I'd like you and me to be friends."

"State your demands," said Lina.

Exhaling with a throaty chuckle, Lina imagined Dawson could just as easily have been jawing with a neighbor over his back fence instead of addressing the last remnant of an innocent family slaughtered in an early morning raid.

"My demands? Are you kidding, girl?" The baritone voice rolled through sorghum and butter before it hit her ears, and Lina recognized the drawl of a Virginian. "See, there's the thing you Riveras don't understand. You with your primitive weapons and old-fashioned ways. Everything's so...*theatrical* with y'all. So romantic."

"Garcia has gone too far this time," said Lina. "As long as one of us still breathes—"

"Garcia?"

"Can go to hell. You tell him and his Indian you heard it from me. Tell them you heard it from Catalina Cristiana Rivera."

"Whatever you say, honey. I'll be sure to tell ol' Tony Garcia exactly what you said. Who's this Indian you're talking about?"

Lina paused, considering Dawson's words. Then she said, "Why are you doing this?"

Dawson chewed his answer like a drowned wad of tobacco. "Honey, I'll tell you the same thing I told your dad before I blew his brains out. This ain't nothin' but cuttin' a clear path. Don't you take it personal."

"Not...personal?"

"It ain't no different than pulling weeds in a garden." Dawson nodded at the urumi, limp in the sand. "What the hell's that thing supposed to be, anyhow?"

The urumi was a twelve-foot blade of flexible edged steel, wielded by warriors on the ancient Indian sub-continent and brought to Argentina in the 17th century where secretive sects of gauchos trained with it in tandem with the boleadoras.

"Family heirloom," said Lina, barely able to speak through her rage.

"Like I said, primitive." Dawson toed at Theresa's silent form with a silver-spurred boot, then brought his attention back to Lina. "Your ma's in rough shape. You say the word, I'll put her down. I'd do the same for any sick animal."

"Bastard," said Lina, the word seething from her raw throat.

"I'd have done it already, but I figured maybe you and me could come to an understanding."

Lina tried to keep her breathing calm, tried to quell the tremors of tension wracking her arms and legs.

"Here's what I propose," said Dawson. "You're a good lookin' filly. Getcha cleaned up, you'd be a respectable gal. I've always wanted a respectable gal on my arm. Given time, you and me could be right good friends." Dawson nodded toward Theresa. "You ride along with me and I'll spare your mother's life."

"Ride along where?"

"Today? Santo Tomas. Tonight, the hotel—the Casa del Poeta. Tomorrow?" Dawson shrugged with a twisted grin. "I try not to get ahead of myself."

His face was the coyote. His tongue belonged to the devil. "Por favor, señorita?" he said.

Lina's eyes burned at the still figure of her mother.

"Por favor?" said Dawson again. *Please?*

If she could get her mother to the Texas village, to the mission...there would be help with the nuns there.

They would know a doctor.

"My mother goes along to the village," said Catalina Cristiana Rivera. "You'll let me get her to the mission?"

"Naturally," said Dawson, "but afterwards, you

stick with me."

Lina swallowed the bile building up in her throat and answered. "I will do as you say."

"Gracias," said Dawson, lifting his left hand to tip the brim of his hat back with the barrel of his automatic. "I surely do appreciate—"

"No," cried Theresa Rivera, lurching to her knees, swiping out at Dawson's lax right hand, knocking the gun to the ground where it clattered across the bleached caliche.

"Son of bitch," said Dawson.

Then everything happened at the same time.

Dawson brought the pistol in his left hand around, pointed it at Theresa, and pulled the trigger twice. The loose, rocky footing caught him off balance, and the automatic's recoil bucked the shots astray. The blast was enough to send Theresa spasming backwards. Her head clunked into a standing boulder.

As her mother sagged into herself, Catalina snatched up the urumi and slung it forward with all her strength.

The weapon's bloody end struck home, peeling away a layer of Dawson's cheek and splitting the lobe of his ear. He slapped at the wound, shouting pain wracked obscenities.

The attack wasn't enough. Dawson was still on his feet, and now all his rage was directed at Lina.

"Damn you to hell," he said, marching forward, shoving the automatic in his left hand ahead of him, pulling the trigger with crazed malice.

The first shot grazed Lina's left shoulder in its sizzling passage, the second crossed her knee. Without conscious thought, propelled only by a lifetime of training, Lina's right-hand fingers clutched the urumi's hilt. With a twist the animated blade swiveled back and curved forward to strike, finding Dawson's gun hand, forcing him to drop the firearm as the steel slivered skin, muscle, and bone in its passage around his wrist.

The raider's roar was a wet mix of outrage and misery as he staggered to one knee. Clenching his jaw and with the urumi's edged blade buried deep in his fist, Dawson jerked the whip away from Lina's grip.

He howled in short-lived triumph, but Lina snatched up Fausto's Colt.

Through blurry, salt-stung eyes she tossed lead at the moving shape in front of her with only one purpose in mind.

To send Tut Dawson straight to hell.

She almost succeeded.

The devil sank to his hip and nearly went down.

With a last reckless assault, Lina emptied the gun, propelling Dawson into a reeling spin, knocking him over and leaving him stretched out and deathly still.

Lina tossed the pistol aside, careened toward her prostate mother. Tenderly she cradled the woman's head. "Madre," she said.

Theresa's eyes remained shut against the sun, her voice barely above a whisper.

"Vamos…save yourself."

"Mother, I can't leave you."

Lina half-dragged, half-carried her mother to Dawson's roan horse.

Again, Theresa worried the inside of her jacket. "Madre de dios...quemado...quemado," she said.

Lina had no idea what her mother was talking about. "Burned? What is burned?"

Theresa pulled something from inside the jacket's fine-stitched lining, lifted her closed hand and pressed it into Lina's palm.

Lina gazed at the charred thing she held. It was a cord of braided leather strung through a series of oblong wooden beads, ending in a knot with a burned black crucifix. The rosary smelled faintly of sandalwood and smoke, and a familiar spiced incense Lina couldn't place.

"What is this?"

"Go to the mission. Seek...the Sisters of Señora Maria." Theresa's breathing was labored, came in sloppy, heaving gasps. "Mother Mercy...knows..."

"What? What does Mother Mercy know?"

Theresa's face was an anguished grimace as she uttered her last words.

"The truth," she said.

CHAPTER TWO

From the plaza gardens outside the mission's west gate, Mother Mercy watched the lemon coloured sun sink behind ropey clouds fencing the west, a harbinger of sour evening vespers at the mission of Santo Tomas. Sister Sofia's laryngitis was hardly better, even though she had excused herself from the mid-day meal to rest, which left Adeline filling the soprano role in the psalmody.

Mercy paced along her row of wildflowers on the edge of the wading river. Through horn rimmed spectacles she watched a pair of prostate pilgrims dip their faces into the warm spring water, only a few inches deep.

Her fingers brushed against the petals of a yellow coneflower.

She'd stay here and skip vespers if she could.

Adeline was good for one vocal go-round before she'd start coughing and hacking and Ahem-ing her way through everything which followed, leaving

the Magnificat far from magnificent. The Sisters of
Señora Maria were sorely short on sopranos.

Mercy brushed her hands on her pleated blue
habit and straightened her veil and the heavy white
guimpe draped over her chest and shoulders.

One of the pilgrims—a middle aged mound of
bread dough with raisin eyes and too much makeup,
like colored cake frosting—noticed Mercy standing
next to the flowers and sat up. "Are you a nun from
the mission?" said the pasty pilgrim.

Mercy's response was polite. "Indeed I am."

The woman's companion, probably her husband,
sat up. He was as narrow as his wife was wide. At the
dry edge of the shallow watercourse, the man groped
for his Stetson and tugged it over his hairline. "You
ain't maybe seen this old Blue Nun we heard about?"
he said. "We come down from Iowa in the automobile. The wife here's got the miseries in her hip, and
we was hopin' to get the Blue Nun to cure us."

"We heard sipping the water helped bring her to us."

Mercy did her best to be patient with the travelers. "The Blue Nun works in her own way."

"Sister, you're not giving us much of an endorse-
ment," said the man. "We hoofed a long ways for
results. You ever seen this ghost, or spirit, or what-
ever-she-is?"

Mercy knelt down to the flower patch and cleared
a handful of creeping vines from the roots of a violet
desert willow bloom. She listened to the man with
half an ear as she freed a fiery red ocotillo stem from
encroaching grass. One step at a time, she told herself,

remembering the patience of Job. A garden didn't flourish or fail on a single day's labor, and neither did a convent rise and fall on an evening's vespers.

She realized the man had quit talking and the two were waiting for her to say something.

"I saw her," said Mercy. "Once. A long time ago."

"And?"

Mercy waited for the man to continue.

"Did the Blue Nun cure what was wrong with you?" he said.

The question caught Mercy off guard. She had no doubt she had seen the legendary blue apparition. But was it real, or a product of her prayerful imagination? She had never been sure. Had the vision cured what was wrong with her?

"She pointed me in a direction," said Mercy.

"Shucks, my old hound dog can do the same thing," said the man.

"Harold," chided the wife.

"It's true, ain't it?" said the man. "C'mon Hilda. Let's see if we can't find a second opinion."

The unsatisfied pilgrims stood up and brushed themselves off before wandering back toward the village market, squabbling the entire way.

Mercy found solace in the soil and continued to tend the garden.

She didn't like to think about the Blue Nun.

Instead, Mercy focused on the garden. Here she always found peace and a calm which normally eluded her. Maybe it was the pleasant sound of the water trickling over the rocks. Maybe it was something else.

She watched as another pilgrim rolled up her pantaloons and waded out into the water.

Since the coming of the railroad, there were more people visiting the springs than Mercy could count. Some to bottle the water they considered holy. Some to bathe and cure their aches and illness.

The 400 souls of Santo Tomas, including 24 at the mission, were surrounded by the warm, life-giving waters, more than a dozen pools and wading streams originating in gravel beds north and west of the village. From there, the water coursed above and below ground through a series of slews and caverns beneath the Rivera hacienda and into the smaller, more cramped cellars of the convent. Inside the mission walls, the nuns drew water directly from the underground spring system and considered themselves blessed with an endless supply.

There was no way one person could watch over the complex network of waterways, and so Mercy was glad for the Riveras and their holy cause in protecting the springs.

As she hummed quietly to herself, a rusty, striped bee hung over her fingers, trilling into the late-afternoon dusk—joining her in an impromptu two-party harmony. Mercy smiled, turning her welcoming palm up, and the winged tenor lit on her ring finger.

And stung.

Mercy snatched her hand back, put her pierced finger to her lips and a sudden gust of wind hurled the bee sideways even as a new chorus of voices crashed over her from inside the adobe walls of the mission.

She hurried to the tall brick wall and stepped through the gate into the plaza as the first gray-robed figure glided out from the common room. Her face covered in a long, dark hood, her hands wrapped around a gnarled crucifix of dry brush, the woman led the seven sisters of sorrow.

While Mercy nursed her finger, the horde moved as one in its haunting, solemn procession to the fenced campo santo—the black stone cemetery— whispering the Miserere in a ghostly chant.

Their appearance was an ill omen.

The seven sisters were drawn together by terrors beyond what even Mercy had experienced in life. Murder and miscarriage, disfigurement and rape, each was called by her own private terror. Each was locked in an eternal vow of darkness.

The gray ones shared little in the duties and daily routine of the convent, and Mercy liked it that way. Cloistered in a cellar under the other nuns' quarters, they shared nothing of their mystic rituals.

They only appeared outside to portend dire events.

They were prophets of doom.

Mercy shivered as she witnessed the arcane march.

And here was Andronicus poking his nose into things as usual.

"To what do we owe their not-so-pleasant appearance?" said the priest as he approached along the cobblestone walk, jabbing a thumb toward the seven sisters, the pallor of his skin as gray as the unkempt ruffle of hair around his liver-spotted pate. "I hope it isn't about Sofia? Still on her sickbed, poor lamb?"

Andronicus was dressed in an ankle-length black cassock as was usual for the autumn and winter season. This particular tunic was new, spotless enough to absorb all the surrounding light and reflect it back in the purple ornamental buttons and piping that announced his position as a Chaplain of His Holiness, Pius X.

"A few episodes of the sniffles, Monsignor, nothing more," said Mercy, forcing herself to look away from the gathered mass at the cemetery.

Andronicus caught her eye. He nodded toward the sisters of sorrow. "I certainly didn't think it was drastic enough for the witches to appear."

"The reason the Seven Sisters have graced us with their presence is a mystery," said Mercy.

"A most inopportune time for their histrionics, what with the train arriving tomorrow from the alpine country." The old man scowled. "I needn't remind you Charles McKenzie will be aboard, along with officials from the railroad traveling to Nuevo Piño. God's hand is leading all of Santo Tomas into the future. We mustn't appear to be superstitious simpletons."

Mercy replied with candor. "I don't take the Sisters appearance lightly."

Andronicus raised his arched eyebrow.

"You'd do well to contemplate such a practice, Mother. Once our new parish pastor is settled in, I intend to seek a personal audience with his Excellency Bishop Ward concerning your seven heretics."

"They are hardly mine."

Andronicus waved away the objection. "The Sisters of Señora Maria are privy to their secrets, Mercy. But all that transpires within the convent is under your jurisdiction. Rest assured you will be held accountable."

"As will we all before Christ our Lord, Reverend Monsignor."

Mercy didn't drop her eyes from the priest's gaze, and finally Andronicus looked away.

"Don't be late for vespers," he said, turning on his heel. Mercy watched him hurry across the dusty plaza for the church, head held high.

So important. So vain.

She couldn't help but smile as his loose shoelace flopped along in the dust.

Once Andronicus passed through the tall arched wooden doors, Mercy turned to walk back to her flowers, the whispering murmur of the Seven Sisters continuing on like a rush of winter, their Latin liturgy mixed with unfamiliar words and strange tongues.

Was the Monsignor right? Were the grey ones perpetuating blatant heresies inside the convent? Or were they, as Mercy always believed, the incarnate hand of the Holy Ghost, pulling back the curtain on tomorrow?

What a tomorrow it would be if Charles McKenzie had his way.

After months of building and construction, the once-weekly train was proving to be a boon for the citizens of rural Texas village long denied the luxuries shared by the rest of America. Charles McKenzie had promised to put Santo Tomas on the map, and he'd certainly delivered.

Grateful for all the good the train brought with it, Mercy was also wary.

Things were moving too fast. Expectations had ballooned beyond reason.

Progress brought predators, and with every rose there came more than one thorn.

Thorns of Greed.

The whispered story was Charlie Mac already wanted more, much more. Not content with his railroad into Mexico, there was talk about a second spur, one that would slice the town in two and devastate the springs. A spur backed by an affluent Mexican from Nuevo Piño .

A rapping sounded at the gate. Mercy answered the summons.

She pulled back the latch from its oak frame, opening the door to reveal a willowy mestizo dressed in white cotton serge di Nimes, a blue poncho, and wearing worn leather huaraches on his callused feet. His bronze head was shaved clean, as were his cheeks and chin, and his eyes were embedded chips of unseeing granite.

"How can I help you, señor?" said Mercy.

Wooden beads fell from the blind beggar's withered hand, but there were precious stones there too. One of the gems caught a ray of the setting sun, glinting scarlet and gold.

"Your rosary is beautiful," said Mercy. "Did you make it?"

The blind man smiled. "The past comes full circle, Louise."

Mercy flinched at the name. "Do I know you, old man?"

"With your vows, you became Mercy Justice, but Louise Byrne lives inside."

"What is it you want?"

"The past comes full circle."

Mercy blinked, and the beggar stepped aside to be replaced by the shambling form of a girl falling from a roan horse, struggling under the weight of a prostate woman. The girl's riding clothes were torn and stained, and her braided hair matted in fat clumps. Crippled by her ordeal, she stumbled once, twice, frantic to keep her burden from touching the ground.

Mercy hiked up her habit and ran past the rosary maker to the distressed pair, catching them both in mid-fall.

The girl's face was a mass of dried blood and sand—the woman she carried, equally soiled. Both were severely burned by sun and the cracked lips and swollen tongues spoke harshly of dehydration. It didn't take a second look to see the older woman had passed.

Mercy gently rolled the older woman's corpse over to its back.

Then she got a shoulder under the girl's arm and lifted. "Let's get you inside, señorita," she said, and was surprised to see the eyelids flutter, the lips forming words in response.

"The...truth," said the girl, her closed fingers falling open and limp.

Trailing a scorched, crumbling string of beads, an ebony cross landed at Mercy's feet.

Inside the mission, the Sisters of Sorrow reached the crescendo of their macabre hymn.

CHAPTER THREE

At first there was infinite black, like she was sliding on her back down a long underground tunnel in one of the caverns under the springs, pressed beneath the weight of a thousand anvils and smothered by snow. Catalina Cristiana Rivera tried to rub her arms against the cold, tried to raise her frost-bitten fingers to her lips to blow on them to feel warm again.

She had never seen snow, but had hoped to next winter on a trip with Carlos to the far away mountains.

Then she realized she wasn't breathing. She couldn't move her arms or legs.

Lina slid down the chute faster, tendrils of ice wrapping around her throat as she opened her mouth.

She tried to call out, to yell into the dark.

When her eyes snapped open, a concerned face held a hand up in front of her nose.

"How many fingers do you see?" said a voice, not her own.

Lina kept trying to talk, to ask for help, but she

couldn't make the words come.

Candlelight flickered on the soft rust-colored walls around her, and the concerned face was a chiaroscuro canvas painted in slabs of gold light and black shadow with eyes like slivers of blue ice.

Lina had never felt so cold in her life.

The fingers went away, replaced by a thick clay jar. Lina shook her head, and the face blurred, but the lip of the jar advanced steadily, touching her mouth. Liquid seeped over the edge, burnt the split skin of her lips, trickled over her swollen tongue.

It was acid. It was boiling oil.

Lina jerked away but her head was held firm, as in a vice.

"Shhh," said the voice. "It's just water from the springs. Sip it slow."

The springs?

Lina's mind raced back to the last thing she could remember.

*****

The alarm had come early, before dawn when she still lounged under the clean, white woven sheets of her bed. The cool high country air had flowed through an open north window, the tranquil cluck of chickens congregating outside and the soft lowing of the milk cows caressing her ears.

Then the cacophony of the bell, the clamor of ringing steel as Carlos ran his truncheon along the perimeter of the steel triangle hanging outside casa Rivera, the clamor of struck stone as iron shod

Andalusians were brought to the defense from the north pasture by her father.

"Raiders!"

But who would dare?

Booming explosions of gunfire thudded across the mountain plateau above the desert and echoed in the adobe buildings of the ranch. Bella, the cloud-white Pyrenees was spooked into barking, and the thunder hurled Catalina from her bed.

Aquiles Rivera shouted over the tumult, "Lucha por Dios y Rivera"—a warrior's call to arms. So it was a holy war.

The ranch was under attack.

Only Garcia would be so bold, only Denver Three-Moons so callous.

Innocuous at first, incursions by the pair and their horde of bandits across the border into Texas grew more violent over time. Eventually, the Riveras went to war and put a stop to it.

The Pax Rivera lasted three years.

Before she could finish dressing, she saw three of her brothers cut down by men wearing sweaters and oversized sombreros. David, Miguel, and Francisco, masters of the facon, the heavy Argentinian sword, were torn to ribbons in the lane by an army of riflemen on wild mustangs.

The peace was shattered.

Lina frantically watched as more riders poured over the hillock, down the lane and through the stand of buildings. The livery stable was set ablaze and all the horses of the remuda set loose through broken fences. The hired men's bunkhouse sagged under a torrent of gunfire.

She searched the horde for a glimpse of Garcia or Denver Three-Moons, but there were too many of them, riding too fast. When she saw her father on his black gelding, the breath caught in her throat.

Aquiles Rivera rode his horse in retreat.

He dashed across the lawn with Lina's brother Carlos and stopped beneath Lina's window. "Take your mother down the east slope," he said. "Find help in Santo Tomas."

Without a backwards glance, Lina had led Theresa, on horseback, down across the flat land.

She didn't dare question Aquiles' wisdom.

The Andalusians were strong. Her cause was just.

For three hundred years, the Riveras had worked the Spanish land grant, thousands of acres of open bunch grass and barren waste. For three centuries they stood in defense of the springs of Santo Tomas, sentries over the sacred waters whose miraculous healing ability gushed from the living rock in sprawling caverns beneath their hacienda.

The tributaries of those holy springs coursed through the cellars of the mission church at Santo Tomas and branched out into a dozen pools and coves. The waters fed small forests of trees and nourished the Rivera's ample herds of cattle and called to pilgrims of the Church from all over the world.

Sometimes Señora Maria, the Blue Nun herself, was rumored to appear in the water, though Lina had never seen the legendary spirit.

Religious practice was a foolish waste of time.

What was real was muscle and bone. As her brothers had taught her.

Rock and steel. As they had trained her in the caverns.

Faith was immaterial.

Hadn't her parents prayed to Sister Maria for a future filled with happiness?

What had it got them? Three years of peace? Raiders on their doorstep?

And yet...

There was something wrong.

Something nagged at Lina. Why now? Why would Garcia attack now? What did he have to gain?

The air smelled of wood smoke and spicy incense.

Abruptly Lina sat up in a narrow column of sun, motes of dust whirling around her face. She blinked against the light, recognizing it as morning.

A new day. But where?

She sat in the center of a cool bed, not her own, roughhewn from a pulpy wood and tied at the corners to make a basket for a straw-stuffed mattress. Her pillow was filled with goose-feather down, and the sheet lightly draped over her was made of tight, woven cotton.

Lina wore a light gown dyed the color of the sky. She had bare shoulders and nothing underneath. Her feet were bare.

But she was no longer cold.

The soft pillow and clean sheet proved there were luxuries in this place, but apparently they were few. The bed and its side table, along with one scuffed old piano stool, were the only pieces of furniture in the room. A tarnished silver hand mirror and matching hairbrush were the only accessories. The black, wooden rosary rested between them.

Above her, the open light was a diamond patch of blue centered in a ceiling of heavy wooden joists held up on tall columns of oak. The red adobe walls were dry, but deep red closer to the hardwood floor. It was damp in one corner where a patient porcelain bowl waited on a clay ledge cut out of the wall.

The sparkling water and white enamel cup called to her.

In her race to slack her burning thirst, Lina nearly tripped on the trailing sheet.

She put the cup to her lips, telling herself to sip slow. *It's just water from the springs. Sip it slow.*

Who had said that? Because, Lina was sure there had been a voice.

She put the cup down and looked around. There were two doors to the room, one wooden with a leather strap latch and pinpoints of sun showing through. The second, at the foot of the bed and perpendicular to the first, was likewise closed.

How many fingers do you see?

Lina wondered at the calm, feminine voice in her memory.

What had happened to her?

She felt a tugging at her shoulder, an itching at her knee.

Careful, inquisitive fingers found two plasters there. Lina moved to the bedside table and picked up the ornate silver hand mirror. Her cheeks were high and angular, her jawline smooth and scrubbed clean. Her hair had been set free of its braids, washed, and brushed. She pushed a stray lock away from her nose where indigo and red blemishes, like ripe raspberries marred the edges.

The pain was gone, and she could breath. She pushed at the plaster on her forehead.

The pain.

In a rush, the memory of the mad rush down the path from her home to the canyon came back to her.

Lina remembered her mother, Fausto, Stark, and Tut Dawson.

She had taken the old bastard down, blown him to kingdom come. She'd held Theresa in her arms, received the rosary. Black and charred.

She opened her callused palm.

Lina put her hand to her nose and found an oddly familiar smell. Sandalwood and something else, a scent like the flowers of the creosote bush after a torrential desert rain. She glanced at the table, between the brush and the mirror where the black rosary waited.

A last, mysterious gift from her mother.

At the creak of the interior door, Lina spun into a defensive crouch, pushing her back against the rough clay wall.

The woman who appeared was in her early 40s, short with copper blonde hair pulled back in a severe bun, spectacles perched on her nose. She wore a pleated blue habit with white guimpe draped over firm breasts. A gold and red rosary hung from her rope belt, and a wooden crucifix was around her high, bleached collar. The nun's head was bare.

When she spoke, it was with the voice of authority. "Up already? Aren't you full of surprises?"

Lina stayed quiet, letting her thoughts catch up to her pounding heart. She breathed in and out. Told herself to slow down. "What is this place?" she said.

"You're a guest of the Sisters of Señora Maria," said the nun. She carried a stack of pressed clothes, a blue dress and white undergarments.

"In Santo Tomas? Am I at the mission?"

The nun closed her eyes with a reassuring nod. "This is the mission of Santo Tomas. I'm Mother Mercy. I oversee the convent here." Mercy strode across the floor to the bowl of water, her quick feet encased in polished black leather shoes. "Let me get you some fresh water. Would you like a cup of tea? We have coffee as well." Her tone of voice was matter-of-fact. "Have you used the chamber pot?"

"I...that is—?"

"Under the bed."

Lina shook her head. "No, I haven't."

The bedside manner of a steam engine.

But Lina preferred it to a cloying, weak nanny.

"How did I get here?"

"Thereby is the tale," said Mercy. "I could ask you the same thing."

"I'm Catalina Cristiana Rivera. My ancestral home was attacked by armed raiders. My parents have been killed."

The nun took the information in without reaction. She stood with the bowl in her hands, nodding. Finally, she said, "Let me refresh your water at the pump outside."

"You need to go to the sheriff," said Lina. "We need to get him to form a posse. There were more than two dozen men. They're still out there. Maybe still at the ranch."

"Hush, child. One thing at a time."

"We must mount a response to this outrage."

Lina charged to the shuttered window and pulled it open. Mercy put the bowl back down.

Outside, the mission plaza was an empty panorama of cobblestone lined walking trails and gardens of short leafy trees and squat bushes, shadowy and secluded behind thick adobe brick walls.

Mercy followed Lina back across the room with her eyes. The same ice blue eyes from the night before.

"You brought me here?" said Lina. "Dressed my wounds?"

"We gave you this room and tended to you, yes. Sister Adeline and myself. But it wasn't us who brought you here. It was you who came to us. On a roan horse."

Lina had to admit she didn't remember much of what transpired after the fight with Dawson. "Was I alone? Did I have another woman with me?" said Lina, her eyes immediately full of tears.

"The woman in your arms was dead."

Lina recoiled as if struck. It wasn't the news of her mother's death that jolted her—that, she had been resigned to in the desert. Instead, it was the stoic way Mercy delivered the news. Cold, hinting at a hidden anger as deep and flourishing as Lina's own.

But anger for whom?

Lina showed Mercy her chin. "She was Theresa Estella Rivera. She was the granddaughter of Contessa D'Mores of Madrid."

"I'm sure she was."

Lina took the cavalier attitude as an insult.

"She was descended from royalty."

"May she feed the worms as well as they."

Lina's face flushed with indignation.

"You dare? I too, am royalty."

Mercy sat on the bed and put her hands on her knees with a sigh. "Forgive me. Since you appeared last night, I've had a lot on my mind."

Lina found she couldn't hold the Mother Superior's gaze. Nor did she have time to ponder the woman's odd behavior as a wave of exhaustion nearly swept her off her feet. She leaned heavily against the wall.

"There were four men," said Lina. "They followed us from the invasion of Rancho Rivera."

"Did you know these men?"

"One was Fausto, a local bandito who crosses the border for Garcia. A second jackal named Wes Stark. I don't know the third man. But the leader of the corrida was there."

"Manuel Michael Garcia?"

"No, I...no." Lina chewed her fingernail and let her memory lead her back to the sound of her own voice—*Garcia can go to hell. You tell him and his*

Indian you heard it from me. Tell them you heard it from Catalina Cristiana Rivera.

"The leader was an American," said Lina. "With a southern accent."

She heard his voice again in her head—*Sure thing, honey. I'll be sure to tell ol' Tony Garcia exactly what you said.*

"He acted as if he didn't know who Garcia was. He called him Tony."

Mercy nodded. "As far as I know, Manuel Michael Garcia has been called a lot of things. Never has he been called Tony. Are you sure Garcia was behind this attack?"

Lina had to admit she didn't know. "Perhaps...not."

"Maybe this American was thinking of Tony Garcia, the famous actor from New York."

Lina raised her eyebrows in surprise. "You know of such things as famous actors?"

"This is a holy convent," said Mercy, "not a prison." Then she asked about Dawson. "What happened to this American you're speaking of?"

"He was called Tut Dawson. I killed him," said Lina, without hesitation. She expected the nun to cross herself.

Instead, Mercy simply said, "Then you will need to rest."

She stood up and went to the open window. Outside, a pair of grasshopper sparrows flitted through the stocky branches of a scrub oak tree. "Crawl back into bed, and we'll check on you at noon."

"You will hand over my clothes, immediately,"

said Lina. "And my belt."

Mercy turned to leave. "In a few days. First you need rest."

"A few days?" Lina sprung forward, grabbed Mercy's arm to spin her around.

Impossibly, the short woman twisted back, got Lina's arm pinned behind her and shoved her to the ground where she landed hard on her backside.

Again, Lina was the first to blink.

And again, Mercy's voice betrayed her name.

"You're a guest here, dear. I expect you to behave accordingly."

Lina sneered into the hard blue eyes. "Guest? Or is this a prison after all, and I'm the prisoner?"

"That's going to be up to you," said Mother Mercy.

CHAPTER FOUR

Mercy waited until Catalina Rivera had succumbed to fatigue and was again asleep before leaving her new charge under the watchful eyes of Sister Adeline. Dressed in full, with white coif and blue bandeau falling over her shoulders, the Mother Superior left the mission through the south gate with its tile-covered portico and ventured into the village.

The street was busy as befitted a weekday morning, crowded with women and children carrying baskets to the market, full of men pulling wagons or leaning on hitching posts where they nodded in casual conversation.

Loose chickens and vagrant goats cleared the way as Mercy joined the stream of traffic.

At the frame doorway of the sturdy stucco mercantile building, a young man in a straw sombrero laughed out loud with his older, gray-haired friend. On the wooden boardwalk, an old woman covered in a striped woolen blanket clopped along with callused feet. Past the general store was a friendly barber's shop. On the other side piano music drifted out from the shadowy recess of Lloyd's Cantina.

Mercy had barely taken a dozen steps when she was accosted by a voice coated with cane sugar. "Como estas, Mother Mercy?"

She continued to walk, and the twelve year-old Apache caught up with her.

"What are you selling today, Paco?"

The boy's eyes were breakfast saucers of milk and feigned innocence. "I'm selling nothing today, Mother." His overbite showed a row of teeth too big for his lips to cover, and his close-cropped black hair was slick with gel, raised into a cockscomb at his forehead. "Today I'm collecting for the poor." His long white sleeves were buttoned and linked at the cuffs with silver, and he wore a gray vest with matching pants.

Mercy smirked at his robust declaration. "The day you work for the poor is the day our Lord returns, and I expect to see my Savior first."

"You wound me, Mother. You truly do. Why do you hurt Paco by saying such things?"

"Paco hurts himself by skipping mass three Sundays in a row."

"The Lord's work is never done, Mother. Don't you teach us as much in primary school?"

"And you're doing the Lord's work?"

Paco stopped on the pine walkway long enough to cross himself. "Every minute. Every day."

He continued to stroll along with Mercy as she crossed in front of a lazy mule and its two-wheeled wagon of hay. A bearded gent holding the creature's bridle tipped his battered derby hat. Mercy held up two fingers in blessing.

"There, you see," said Paco, prancing ahead of her, facing her so he moved in reverse on the walkway. "You would bless an old man whose life is over, but phooey on Paco."

His joyful complaint coaxed a smile from Mercy's lips. "I pray for you ceaselessly," she said.

"Then Paco walks in grace," said the boy.

"You do indeed," said Mercy.

At the far end of the street a crowd had gathered on the patio of the hotel Casa del Poeta directly across from the new train depot, its tall, polished glass windows glowing in the sun. As Mercy walked along the edge of the thoroughfare, the enormous steam locomotive parked there cut loose with a soaring whistle. The townsfolk cheered.

"Have you come out to see Charlie Mac's Big 705?" said Paco.

"There appears to be quite a crowd for the train."

"All the top boss men of the Sioux City and Orient railway are here this morning. Lander Sturgeon, Bill Greaves, Charlie Mac. Mrs. Sturgeon is also along for the ride."

"You know quite a lot."

"I know just about everything," said Paco.

On a temporary platform high above the gathering, a black clad trio with white moon faces and wearing silk stovepipe hats stood with a woman wearing a fancy dress and cap. One of the faces was encircled with a mane of bushy red whiskers and the pudgy fist next to it held a broad, black umbrella against the sun. "Isn't Charlie Mac grand?" said Paco. "One day Paco will grow a manly beard such as his."

When the 705 sent up its whistle again, a second cheer went up from the assembled villagers, and the officials waved.

Paco grasped Mercy's hand. "You must come see Charlie Mac's private car, Mother. They say it is trimmed with gold and full of wonders. Electric lights and leather chairs and fine rugs. Chandeliers and stockpiles of fine wine."

"I'm sure it's a wonder to behold." Mercy said, gently reclaiming her limb.

"Ordered direct from the Pullman company with all possible luxury. Never has such a car been seen." Paco waved his arms to emphasize the grandeur. "Since the mainline to Mexico is open, who knows what Charlie Mac's next project might be."

Mercy could understand the boy's enthusiasm, but she had an innate distrust of Charles McKenzie. The red-bearded baron had an endless purse and seemed to push men around like pieces on a chessboard, changing the rules of the game whenever he didn't have the upper hand.

She'd never met the man in person, but his beard and black umbrella were legendary.

Paco chattered on. "Some people say he'll find oil in Santo Tomas. If anybody can, he's the man to do it. He's gifted that way, Mother. He's like King Midas in the stories. I bet he will for sure find oil. Ned

Sedgewick says Charlie Mac has the mineral rights just about sewed up." Paco put his finger to his nose. "Viva la revolucian!"

"Repeating gossip is a sin," said Mercy. "And the Mexican revolution—or talk of mineral rights—shouldn't concern twelve year-old boys."

"Oil is the future, ma'am."

"I've heard nothing about it."

"Charlie Mac knows. You'll know when he is ready."

"Paco, you may admire this affluent cowboy," said Mercy. "But be careful your trust isn't ill-founded"

"Come see the car with me?"

"I have business here," said Mercy.

"You have until tomorrow morning. Then Charlie Mac will take his fancy coach across el Rio Bravo del Norte."

"En Estado Unidos, we call it the Rio Grande," said Mercy.

A pair of young men walked from the cantina, and Mercy waited in front of the mercantile for them to pass before changing the subject with Paco. "What news from Rancho Rivera?"

"I don't think it's wise to ask about Rancho Rivera, Mother," said Paco.

Mercy lowered her eyebrows. "I'm asking."

"You'll hear nothing from me," said Paco.

"You're a cousin of the Riveras, are you not?"

"I am a cousin of many peoples," said Paco. "Jicarilla and Spanish, Americans and pirates of the high seas."

"Pirates?"

"Are you sure you can't walk with me to the train?"

Mercy had never seen Paco so evasive. She put her hand on the boy's shoulder. "If the Riveras need our help, we should lend it. They have always cared for the people of Santo Tomas."

Paco glanced in the direction Mercy's feet were pointed. "You're not going to old Constable Ned?"

"He's the only law we've got."

Once more, Paco reached for Mercy's hand, but this time his grip was frantic. "Don't be involved, Mother." He was genuinely concerned.

"Be careful, Paco, your heart is showing."

"Law in Estados Unidos is not law for Rivera land."

Mercy brushed past him. "This is what I'm afraid of."

Paco raced ahead and planted himself on the boardwalk between Mercy and the cantina. He folded his arms. "Either way, you should not go into such a place."

"What if I told you I once lived in such a place?"

"I would not believe you."

"Proof you don't know *everything*, after all." She patted his shoulder and pushed open one of the swinging doors. "Vayo con dios, Paco."

"You forgot my dime, Mother."

Mercy stopped at the threshold. "What dime?"

"I told you, I am out collecting for the poor."

"Give them your shoes," said Mercy.

Paco looked down at his bare feet. "I have no shoes, Mother."

"Then you'll have to think of something else."

Mercy turned her back and walked into the shadow of the cantina.

CHAPTER FIVE

The adobe room was cool, its sticky tile floor littered with popcorn hulls and stained with spilled liquor. A long, old-fashioned walnut counter faced her, leading her gaze down the length of its brass rail as her eyes adjusted to the light. The hawkish man behind the counter curled his head sideways, welcoming her with faint scorn. "Not your usual watering hole. Lose something, Mercy?"

"Nothing I can't find in prayer. How about you, Sloan?"

"I got nothing to confess. Get you something to drink?"

Mercy declined. "I won't be here long."

She moved along the bar, resisting the urge to let her fingers trail along the lip of polished trim. The liquid smooth surface was a mirror, reflecting a golden array of amber bottles on shelves stacked on the rear wall and the sensual wood grain, buffed by a thousand hands, lured her in.

To climb onto a stool was like getting back onto a horse. You never forget how to ride.

The pull of grain and hops. The heat pouring down her throat.

Sheriff Ned Sedgewick sat where he always did, at a square table to the far right of the counter, a half-full tumbler and an empty bottle in front of him. Next to him sat the mayor of Santo Tomas, Pip Carlyle.

Mercy pulled out a backless stool from beneath the table and sat down across from the men. She did her best to ignore the raw aroma of rye.

"Sister Mother of Mercy," said Sedgewick. "What brings you to my humble office this bright, God-forsaken morning?" He burped. "Sorry," he said.

The sheriff wore clean denim work jeans, cuffed over polished black boots and his flour sack of a stomach lapped over his belt. On one hip he wore a holster with a Navy revolver, and on the opposite side, a leather-sheathed knife with an ivory handle. His gray shirt was rumpled and unbuttoned at the collar. The tin star pinned loose on his chest hung low in a fold of loose flannel. Anything could've been inscribed on it.

Sheriff.

Constable.

Town drunk.

"Hello, Mother," said Carlyle. With a rumpled tie and wrinkled suit coat, Carlyle's attire wasn't much above Sedgewick's, but at least he was sober. Mercy acknowledged him with a curt nod. "Mayor."

"It's that god-damned crowd gathered for the

train, ain't it?" said Sedgewick. "I knew there'd be trouble." He picked up his drink and consumed half of it. "Who was the owlhoot, and what's he done?"

"It's nothing to do with the train. Or the crowd."

"Mr. McKenzie won't stand for nobody harassing your girls. Neither will I."

"I should say not," said Carlyle.

"The sisters are currently occupied with chores and morning devotions. It's not what you're thinking."

"I seen your Father Whats-his-name stroll down there," said the Sheriff.

"Andronicus," said the mayor.

"Maybe he'll take care of it?" said the sheriff.

Sedgewick waved at Gus and the barkeep carried over a fresh brown bottle.

"Monsignor Andronicus is forever the social butterfly. I imagine he'll be with the crowd for most of the morning," said Mercy.

"Where else would you find a physician, but with the sick?" said Carlyle with a satisfied smile. "I read that in the Bible."

Sedgewick clapped a fat, liver-spotted hand to his face and let it fall, dragging his flabby jowls partway to the table top. "I'm a Methodist, myself," he said.

Carlyle patted the sheriff's shoulder and pushed his chair back. "Speaking of crowds, I'd best do my part in the day's festivities."

"Don't wanna keep Charlie waiting," said Mercy.

"No, Mother, we don't," said the mayor. He nodded his goodbyes.

As Carlyle went out the door, Sedgewick sat up

to focus on the new bottle and poured a healthy measure into the glass. He swallowed some, and looked straight at Mercy for the first time since she sat down. "What's it you want to see me about?"

"Something important," said Mercy. "Something happened yesterday at the Rivera hacienda."

The sheriff let himself fall against the back of his chair like a pile of soggy laundry. "Is that a fact?"

"I wondered if you knew anything about it?"

"Nobody tells me anything. Lawman's always the last to know." He burped. "You should've asked the mayor. He prolly knows all 'bout it."

"There was a raid of some kind. I think the place has been sacked."

"I doubt it very much."

"Will you look into it?"

Sedgewick tossed a thumb over his shoulder in the direction of the train station. "I gotta stay here and watch the train."

"I imagine you might assign a deputy to handle it."

"Deputies are busy with the train."

"Then you can go yourself."

"This here's just a short coffee break."

"I suppose then you'll be back, hard at work?"

Sedgewick nodded slow. "I suppose I will."

Mercy felt the muscles in her neck and shoulders cramp with tension.

"At least call together a posse of men to ride out to the sky-country and see about the Riveras."

"Now, you know I'm not on the best of terms with that clan."

"It doesn't matter," said Mercy. "I'm asking you to do your job."

"I don't think Carlyle would like it. I don't think Mr. McKenzie would approve."

"What's Mr. McKenzie got to do with it?"

Sedgewick blinked in polite surprise. "What doesn't Mr. McKenzie have to do with?" Sedgewick drained his glass for a second time. "In case you don't know the facts of life—and begging your pardon, ma'am, I wouldn't expect you to—Charles McKenzie owns most of everything between here and Alpine. Before the year's up he'll own the town and everything south and west to the ocean—across the border too." He put his finger to his nose. "It's all in the works."

"Which has little to do with—"

Sedgewick waved away Mercy's protestations. "Mr. McKenzie asked for complete security in town today, and I'm here to make sure he gets it."

It took all of Mercy's willpower not to snatch up the bottle of rye, drain the contents and drop the empty bottle on the sheriff's head.

"What about all the good the Riveras have done for Santo Tomas? For the springs?"

Sedgewick's lip curled into a snarl.

"That backwoods bunch of gauchos hasn't done spit for this community compared to what the railroad is doing. We're talking cattle, mining, real economic development." He leaned down and peered into Mercy's face. "And there's more to come. Imagine the added cropland once we outfit the springs for irrigation."

Mercy ran her hands along the sides of her habit,

wishing she could wipe away Sedgewick's words as easy as the physical signs of her frustration. She pushed herself back from the table.

"We have different ideas about the future," said Mercy.

"Mark my words, Mother. The Riveras' time is done."

"Have you ever heard of a man named Tut Dawson?"

The sheriff wiped his lips on his shirt sleeve, and for a second the concern in his eyes was equal to Paco's. He said, "Don't get involved with this, Mercy."

Mercy stood up. "I should've known not to waste your time, Sheriff."

Sedgewick seemed to ponder the words, then he dropped his eyes.

"Yeah." He nodded. "You likely should have."

A thousand appropriate replies leapt to her tongue, half of them blasphemous, none of them worthy of her vows. She bit her lip and marched out into the daylight.

Sister Adeline waited on the boardwalk.

Mercy's voice was low, such that only her sister could hear. "Ride to the Rivera hacienda. Take Sofia with you. Be wary. Watch for trouble. Report what you find."

"Sofia has only just recovered her voice."

"Then the fresh air will do her good." Mercy turned to the post office. "I need to send a telegram."

"Mother?"

"Vayo con dios, Adeline," said Mother Mercy.
Go with God.
She prayed He wouldn't let her down.
Again.

CHAPTER SIX

Catalina Rivera awoke to a flickering lamp on the table next to her bed and the sound of hushed conversation and tin cutlery on ceramic plates. The smell of roast beef smothered in onions and stewed tomatoes, garlic and potatoes and fresh bread wafted through the open window, urging her to quickly dress in the clothes Mercy left for her.

After a long day's sleep, Lina's aches and pains had faded with the daylight, and she was starving.

Tired of being cooped up, she pushed up the latch, cracking open her room's side door into a long, open space furnished with three oak slabs and enough chairs to surround them. At the table closest to the door, three nuns with bare heads finished a common meal, passing serving trays of food, drinking from tin cups. One of them was the Mother Superior she had met before, the one called Mercy.

The heady, thick aroma of hot coffee made Lina's head swoon.

"And you say there was nothing left of the estancia—the residence?" said Mercy.

"Nothing," said the buxom one next to her. "Sofia and I explored the hacienda for more than an hour. If anyone was left alive, they've escaped or gone into hiding." The heavy nun spread a smear of whipped butter onto a fat slice of bread. She took a bite and talked around her chewing. "Nothing left of the house but a pile of rubble and a pole with an iron triangle."

Lina held her breath. Almost certainly the nuns were talking about Rancho Rivera.

"What about the raiders? Wasn't there any sign of the men who did this? Maybe you saw a clue to their identity?"

The big nun, Adeline, hesitated before she answered. "There was the imprint of many horses."

"The revolutionaries are always riding across the border to plunder."

"The shoes on Garcia's horses make a familiar imprint," said Adeline. "I did not see Garcia's print today. Nor the cowhide shoe prints of the renegade border Apache."

"It's the times we live in," said the third nun. She was a slender girl with a slight cough. Adeline called her Sofia. "Revolution at the border, the Germans building an empire in Europe. Rumors of war."

"And ye shall hear of wars and rumors of wars; see that ye be not troubled," said Mercy. "Matthew 24, verse 6."

"No rumors," said Adeline, with firm conviction. "The remains I saw today told of a great battle. The tin wall of one haybarn caught at least a hundred bullets."

"What about the dead, Adeline? Did you see any bodies?"

"Odd thing," said Adeline. "With so much destruction, I was sure we would find the remains of—"

"Oh," said Mercy, looking straight at the crack in the door Lina peered through.

She had been discovered.

"Come in, child," said the nun. As Lina padded into the room, Mercy introduced the other two nuns. This is Sofia and Adeline. They've only just returned from a journey."

Sofia stood up and pulled out the chair next to her. "Would you like something to eat?"

Lina didn't need to be asked twice. With a nod of gratitude, she sat down next to Sofia and watched with eager anticipation as her hosts filled her plate with slabs of roast, bread, and a mountain of potatoes.

"It all smells wonderful," she said as the food landed in front of her.

From a corner pot, Mercy poured a full helping of coffee into a fresh cup before carrying it to Lina's side. "We're happy to share," said the nun.

Lina had cleaned up half of everything before coming up for air.

All three nuns were staring at her with bemused expressions.

Adeline peered at Lina like a circus attraction. "I've not seen such an appetite since I grilled ten ducks for Teddy and crew—"

"She's referring to Mr. Roosevelt," said Sofia.

Mercy explained, "Adeline is fond of regaling us

with stories of her sordid frontier youth."

"Mr. President, that's seven for you and three for everybody else." Adeline recited the lines of her story from memory. "Of course, back then, he wasn't the president yet, but I had a hunch."

Lina continued to eat as the women talked, and with her second cup of coffee, she began to feel human again.

It had been a long couple of days.

"When I came in, you were talking about my home?"

Mercy nodded. "I asked the sisters to ride out to your ranch."

"I'm so sorry, Catalina," said Adeline. "We didn't find any sign of your family."

"Perhaps they escaped into the caverns of the spring?" said Mercy.

"We looked there, of course," said Adeline.

Lina held a napkin to her mouth. "What of the remuda? My father had more than a dozen horses in the stable."

"We found no remains," said Adeline. "I would assume your animals were set free or escaped the fire on their own."

"Thank heavens," said Mercy.

Before Lina could ask any more questions, a knock came at the room's window. Perturbed, Mercy hurried over with more than a little impatience. She opened the window and a sprightly form leapt into the room. At the cheerful sight of even one of her family, Lina felt a weight hurl itself from her shoulders. She jumped up to meet him.

"Hola, señora y señoritas," said Paco. "Hello, Catalina Cristiana."

A wash of joy rushed Lina to her knees where she embraced Paco at eye level. She felt her lips pull back in a smile, and her face flushed with happiness and relief. "Some of us have survived, eh, primo?"

"Si, Catalina," said Paco, but he whispered in her ear as she hugged him again. "But beware. We are still hunted by the Virginian. I will come to you again in an hour."

The Virginian? He couldn't mean Tut Dawson?

Lina had killed Dawson.

Hadn't she?

Lina climbed back into her chair and watched her cousin dig inside the pocket of his wool trousers. When his hand came out, it clutched a block of factory chocolate. He put the treat on the table in front of Adeline. "Paco is as good as his word."

"What's this, Adeline?" said Mercy.

"Spoils from the outside world."

"It came in on the train. Along with a million other wonders," said Paco. "Teas and coffees and books. A whole shop full of clothes and an eye doctor from Missouri. One of the cars carried a theater group. This chocolate from the stores of confectionaries, a gift from your humble servant."

"A gift is it? Why am I suspicious?" said Mercy.

"My vows of poverty never included chocolate," said Adeline, reaching for the sweet treat.

Lina watched the ease with which the sisters conversed, with Paco and with each other, but her eyes kept seeing Tut Dawson's face. Kept hearing his slow drawl in her mind.

She was sure she had misunderstood her cousin. The raider was dead.

In saving herself, she had avenged her family. The ordeal was over, and once she fulfilled any debt she owed the mission, she would return to Rancho Rivera and start over. Paco would help.

And there was always the chance one or more of her brothers yet lived.

"Would you like some chocolate, Catalina?" Paco asked?

Lina shook her head as if coming out of a dream.

"Thank you, Paco," she said, accepting a piece of the sticky candy.

He nodded toward her room, then silently mouthed the words, "One hour."

She nodded to show she understood him.

Lina put a hand to the plaster on her forehead. "I think perhaps I should rest some more," she said.

Immediately at her side, Mercy helped her back to her room.

"Good night to each of you, and thank you," said Catalina.

The nuns gave her reassuring looks, and Lina stepped through the door. She stood with a weary posture next to her bed.

Mercy squeezed her arm, then closed the door as she left.

Lina felt a fire spring up inside her breast when the Mother Superior turned the lock.

She remembered Paco's words.

But beware.

CHAPTER SEVEN

It was more than an hour later when Paco scratched at her window.

"Where have you been?" said Lina. "It's almost midnight."

Paco carried an enormous canvas warbag hanging from a strap over his shoulder. "I had to wait until the Monsignor turned in. He's been talking with somebody, outside."

Paco's burden was awkward as he climbed through the window, but before Lina could help him, he crawled out from under it and pitched it toward her bed. The sack landed with a light thump. Not too heavy at all.

"What do you have there?" she said.

Paco took her hand and sat next to her on the bed. "You must not be seen outside the walls of the mission, prima. Tut Dawson lives."

"I saw him go down," said Lina. "I shot him."

"Shhh," hushed Paco. "You mustn't speak of murder inside a church. Even a failed attempt."

"I seek the Lord's vengeance," said Lina.

"So does Tut Dawson."

"He knows I'm here?"

"He knows you're in Santo Tomas. He found his horse, the one you rode here, at the livery."

"Do you know where he is now?"

"Si, he's at the hotel. The Casa del Poeta."

Lina recalled the Virginian's salacious invitation. "Just as he said he would be," she said.

"There is more you should know," said Paco. "At the hotel there is a saloon, much more elegant than Lloyd's cantina. The train men eat there and have meetings with the mayor."

"The train men?"

Paco eagerly told Catalina about Charles McKenzie and his luxury car, about the railroad officials and their silk hats, about plans for a new spur and the oil and mineral rights.

"Slow down, slow down," said Lina. "One thing at a time. What does any of this have to do with Tut Dawson?"

Paco rediscovered the thread of his narrative and took a deep breath. "I saw the Virginia man there too. Drinking at the bar with one of the railroad men."

"How did you come to be in the room?"

"I was selling a pocket watch to a skinny pilgrim from Iowa."

"You believe Dawson and this rail man are acquainted?"

Paco shrugged. "Quien sabe?" he said. *Who knows?*

"What did they talk about?"

"There's to be a huge gathering in Nuevo Piño, a

wedding celebration, but also business to conduct with the Mexicans and a German! This is when I heard the villain tell about his horse."

Lina remembered how her urumi had sliced into Dawson's cheek, cut his hand and wrist. "What about his injuries?"

Paco's reply was uncertain. "He is bandaged, and favors his hand a bit."

"Nothing else? I was certain I'd shot him."

"He's an evil man, Lina. I could tell from the smell of him, though I believe he has bathed at the hotel. He has a darkness around him. And the stink of death." Paco's voice dropped an octave as he revealed a final choice morsel of information. "He spoke to me."

"What did he say?"

"He asked if I had seen a beautiful señorita with raven black hair and curves smooth as the rio."

Lina felt her face flush.

"He is looking for you, Lina. You must not be seen."

"If what you say is true, Dawson and I have unfinished business. I must go to him."

"I knew you would think so," said Paco. "Which is why once more, I come bearing gifts." The boy pulled the canvas sack into place between them and unlaced the top.

Lina pulled out a long, black cloak with a flared, attached hood. "A disguise?"

"It will help you blend into the night."

Paco moved to the corner of the room and retrieved a cup of water from the enamel pan while Lina explored the contents of sack. A black tunic with wood carved clasps, scarlet piping and button loops, flared sleeves and laced leather gauntlets. Black leather pants with nickel conchas and leather tassels running down the outer seams. Knee-high, lace-up boots. "Where did you find all this?" said Lina.

"The theater group from the train," said Paco. "Their car is full of trunks and standing wardrobes, and the wardrobes are full of costumes."

"They have yet to unpack?"

"They're traveling on with the train across the border. They are part of the wedding celebration."

"You are a good judge of size," said Lina, holding up the tunic.

"I have an eye for the señoritas," said Paco proudly.

"And I will put your eyes out if you try to watch me undress," said Lina.

Paco poked out his lower lip. "To suggest I would try such a thing dishonors Paco."

Lina leaned over and wrapped her arms around the boy. "I am teasing you, chico." She kissed him on the cheek. "Now it's time you found your bed. I hate to think what Mercy or the Monsignor would say if they found you here with me at this hour."

"I will wait for you on the boardwalk near the hotel."

"You will not," said Lina. "I have deadly work to do this night."

Paco smiled. "I almost forgot." He unbuttoned a side pouch on the sack. Inside was Lina's steel urumi. "I found it in the Mother Superior's office."

"What were you doing in the—? Never mind," said Lina. "What else?"

In his hand, Paco held a flat, rectangular tin with a snap lid. He popped it open and a few grains of slick, black powder spilled out onto the bed. Inside the tray were two compartments. One was filled with a greasy black tallow, the other's contents were blood red.

Paco plunged his fingers into the black side, scooping up an ebony wad and drew the sign of the cross on Lina's face, from forehead to chin and then across the bridge of her nose and closed eyes. "Make up?" said Lina.

"Not makeup," said Paco. "This is from the Apache."

Lina tasted mesquite on her lips and the faint smell of bacon fat.

Paco filled in the spaces at her temples and forehead and the tops of her cheeks with crimson.

"No longer Catalina Cristiana Rivera," said Paco.

"This is war paint," she said.

"And you are the warrior," said Paco.

******

She stole into the night, her cloak wrapped tightly around her lithe frame. After being closed up in the mission for two days, it felt glorious to be outside, breathing the cool desert night air.

Embedded above the mission bell was a cross of stone in a lighter color than the bricks making up the edifice of the tall campanero. The cross was lit by the dim sliver of moonlight, and once out of the tower's shadow, Lina saw nothing but stars.

How many nights had she spent perched on a cliff's edge, patiently trying to count those white points of light, wondering if anybody could ever map them all?

Gravity no longer held her, and she crossed the mission plaza in quick, silent steps, launching herself up to where she planted a toe on the mud wall, then another step, and over.

She landed in the village street, just across the way from the livery barn. She imagined Tut Dawson's roan sleeping in there, nickering softly, growing fat and lazy on its feedbag. She was grateful to the horse for carrying her and Theresa to safety, but his presence had given her away, forced her to wear a disguise.

As she ducked across the street, first to the alley behind the stable, then to the side of the brick Landowner's bank next-door to the hotel, she once more felt a wave of gratitude to the roan. He had helped Paco to see her need for the cape and hood. The roan had helped her to be free in the shadows.

Because under the cloak, she felt like a different person.

No longer a mourning girl, but a spirit of vengeance. Not the last of her family, but for the first time, a night creature, powerful and alone.

Someone who always had been alone, and always would be.

When vengeance came to Tut Dawson, it wouldn't come from Catalina Rivera, but it would be for her. Revenge for the girl whose hopes and dreams died along with her family.

She touched the urumi wrapped tight around her waist. Revenge would strike like lightning from the storm, splitting Dawson down the middle like a hollowed tree, exposing his rotten insides.

The bank was a three story building with pro-truding brick corners—a ladder to the sky. Like lightning, she would strike from above.

Lina reached out to grip the first brick, to pull herself up, when a voice full of drunken lust hissed behind here. "Lookee what we got here, Shane. A pretty circus bird."

"I likes circus birds, Clem. How's about we bag her up and keep her as a pet?"

Lina turned to face the two men. Somehow, during her reverie about freedom and the night, they had slipped up behind her.

The foolish musings of a schoolgirl had neatly exposed her to two of Santo Tomas's worst.

Shane Ricketts and Clem Ruiz.

Often she had heard her brothers mention these two walking piles of garbage. Suspects in a number of unsolved crimes, including cattle rustling and the rape of a young Apache girl, they traveled as a pair and carried big bowie knives next to their six-shoot-ers. Clem wore a tall, beige ten-gallon hat. Shane's hat hung at the back of his neck on a loose leather cord.

They were mean as any two men could be, and tricky. Best not to dally.

"You boys have mistaken me for somebody who tolerates your stench," said Lina. "I suggest you walk away and find more bawdy company."

"Did she just say we smell bad?" said Clem.

"I believe she did," said Shane.

"She ain't very polite," said Clem.

In the bank shadow, Lina's voice was low. "You'll

smell worse moldering in the grave."

"Why don't you step out here in the moonlight where we can see you better?"

"Get her, Clem," said Shane.

Clem took a step forward, his arm snaking out with a greedy, groping hand.

Lina's fingers wrapped around his wrist like steel clamps, jerking him ahead even as she launched her boot into a high arc and rocked his head back like it sat on a spring. He staggered off to one side, and Lina followed through with a fast punch to the Adam's apple.

Clem hit the clay and rolled onto his back, clutching at his throat.

Shane looked at his friend, then back at Lina as she slid in close, her hood falling back.

"Y-your face," he stammered. Startled by the macabre sight, Shane went for his big knife too late. Lina jacked her bent elbow into the flat of his nose, causing a sloppy wet crunch and a quick cry of agony.

Too loud.

She would have to learn to be more circumspect.

Grabbing a handful of Shane's oily hair, she jerked him forward, swinging her weight around at the last minute to sling his head into the brick wall of the bank.

Thud.

That ought to keep him quiet.

As fast as she could, she dragged the two men into the shadows behind the bank.

Then, pulling herself up on the bricks, she quickly scaled the side of the building and disappeared over the rooftop.

CHAPTER EIGHT

She crouched brooding on the hotel roof, peering down through a glass skylight into the open stairway, waiting for Tut Dawson to leave the bar and make his way to his room. Once she saw him pass under her in the dim gas light, she planned to open the hatch, slip through the skylight and come up behind him as he opened the door to his room.

Then she would break his neck, just as her brothers had taught her.

Quick, cold, and efficient.

This time, she would be sure to put Tut Dawson down. *Just as she would any sick animal.*

Further up the street, a drunken stumblebum singing a Mexican love song staggered down the boardwalk from Lloyd's Cantina to the railroad track. Lina thought she saw a glimmer of moonlight reflect off a tin star on his shirt, but she must've been mistaken.

There was no possibility such a wretch could be the sheriff.

Then she heard a familiar voice from earlier in the night. Clem Ruiz.

She craned her chin up, watching over the false front of the hotel as Clem Ruiz shuffled toward the singer, calling him by his title. "Quick, sheriff, we need to find a doctor for mi compadre. For…Shane."

Sheriff? The drunken buffoon was the sheriff after all.

"Where'sthe trouble, ol' buddy. What can ol' Ned Sedgewick do for you?"

Sedgewick was sober enough to recognize Clem, but not sober enough to understand the request.

"Shane and me were walking back to the hotel from the cantina when we were attacked."

"'Tacked? By…hoo…whom?"

"A hoo-doo. A haint. Hell, I don't know. I thought it was a woman, but there ain't no way. I mean, she took Shane and me like we were rag dolls."

"Ah-ha," said Sedgewick. "I knew it all…along." The sheriff paused to burp. "A woman of the night."

"You no comprende, amigo. This woman, she is not of the night. She is the night. Scarlet and ebony, like the rose and its deadly thorn. Blood red and dark as death."

"Bad as all that, is it?"

"I think Shane is dead."

"You better show me," said Sedgewick, shoving Clem back in the direction he came from, toward the back of the bank building.

Lina would've rolled her eyes if they weren't glued back down to the landing under the hotel skylight. Unless he'd choked on his own vomit, Shane wasn't dead. She made sure he was still breathing before climbing to the top of the bank and crossing over the rooftops to the hotel. How long the toad would sleep was anybody's guess.

But she hadn't killed him.

Scarlet and ebony, like the rose and its deadly thorn. Blood red and dark as death.

She had certainly frightened Shane Ruiz.

Good for Lina, she thought.

No.

Good for the *Black Rose*.

Then Tut Dawson appeared on the hotel landing under the skylight, and distractions burnt away like morning river mist under a scorching sun.

For the Black Rose, the only two creatures in existence were her and the man who had taken everything from her. Soon, only one would remain.

She flung open the skylight and dropped into the hotel hallway, her cloak spreading out behind her.

At the sound of her landing, Tut Dawson half-turned.

The Black Rose slammed into his lower back and sent him hurling toward the door at the end of the hall. He hit hard, bounced back into a spin, arms up, fists raised. He shook his head furiously at the surprise attack, tried to focus on his new opponent. One of his hands was wrapped in strips of heavy wool pinned just below his elbow.

The hall was open to a three-tiered teardrop electric chandelier and the dim, lamp-lit lobby below. A picketed oak balustrade was the only barrier to a fifteen foot drop. The Black Rose closed on her prey.

Dawson wobbled, took a step and swung a wide haymaker through thin air with his good arm. The Black Rose ducked, surged forward and snapped a kick at his ribs while he was off balance. The man was all iron-hard meat and gristle and she didn't dare give him an edge. He teetered against the railing, pushed himself upright as she pummeled the side of his neck with a closed fist—like hitting hickory wood.

She spun just out of the reach of Dawson's second wild punch. He sputtered, "Stand still, damn you," then charged like a bull with both of his long arms open wide. She rolled low, sweeping out with her legs, knocking one of his pins out from under him. Dawson keeled into the railing, but quickly steadied himself. This time, he stayed still, waiting for the Black Rose to press her attack.

Her element of surprise was wasted.

Now it would be a contest of fighting skill alone. Dawson was fuzzy with liquor and handicapped with a hurt right hand, but the Black Rose too had yet to fully recover from her desert trek.

A doorway on the other side of the main staircase opened. A head poked out, followed by a voice, "Pipe down out there. People are trying to sleep."

Dawson took advantage of the distraction. More sure of his footing, he shuffled in like a boxer, swaying to the left, feigning right, landing a crack to the head. The Black Rose heard a ringing in her ears and lurched into the wall, pulling her leathered forearms up in front of her face. She blinked twice.

It would take more than a single blow to bring down a warrior trained by the brothers Rivera.

But Dawson doubled down, cranking a fist to the belly, then another. "Show you what it means to jump ol' Tut in the dark," he seethed. "See how much of this you can take."

Catalina Rivera had learned to live with pain. Since the start of her training, she'd endured muscle spasms and pulls, bone fractures and sprains. Her brothers had been ruthless, especially Carlos who told her that to go easy in training was to lose hard in life. He'd worked on her behalf to best her, and she learned to return the favor.

She'd learned to encapsulate the agony, enclose it in a red ball, then push it aside in her mind to deal with later. When the white hot ache below her ribs screamed for release, she wrapped it with empathy, but deliberately thrust it aside.

Could Tut Dawson do the same?

He was cudgeling her with his left hand, protecting his bandaged right. Darting out, the Black Rose snatched the injured appendage and drove it down, into the cap of her knee.

Dawson's scream was thick and primal.

Not letting up for an instant, the Black Rose attacked with skilled hands, clutching the sides of Dawson's sweating slick head, driving her thumbs like rail spikes into his eye sockets. He lurched backwards, roaring with rage, but she wouldn't let go. They careened across the hall, colliding again with the bannister.

Dawson brought a knee up hard, hammering the Black Rose between her legs. He gripped her right wrist, trying to rip her hand from his face. But his right hand was useless, and she wouldn't let go.

They skidded along the railing, Dawson cursing between grunts of exertion, the Black Rose silent and focused. Another two guest doors opened and three sleepy residents wandered out to watch the brawl. "Why, land sakes," said a wide flour sack of a woman, "it's a girl he's fighting."

With his greater weight, Dawson swung them around and thrust himself on top of the Black Rose, bending her over the rail. "You'll send both of us to hell, Dawson," she said.

"I'm already there, sweetie."

Dawson's right hand was half-way unwrapped and he groaned as he used it to grip. With both hands he dragged her fingers down his face, and when the Black Rose was forced to let go, he managed to get both arms under her, clutch her around the waist, and press her away with one powerful shrug. She went crashing to the floor at the top of the stairway.

The Black Rose rolled and climbed to her feet. She was beginning to tire. The hall was filling with people.

Dawson wiped at his eyes, blinking, maybe seeing double? The Black Rose jabbed at his face, lancing a hard right across his nose. He swung wild, clouted the side of her head with the force of a steam hammer. For an instant, everything went sideways, and she felt the impact of the floor.

Flat on her back, Dawson leapt to smother her.

The Black Rose arched up to meet him and slapped his attack aside, but the momentum sent them both off-balance. They rolled down the open stairway to the second story banister.

Hitting it with a wood-splitting crack, they broke through into space.

The shock of their landing knocked the breath out of both of them, but the Black Rose recovered first. She spiraled into a fighting stance, waiting for Dawson to move, glancing to the left and right. The hotel lobby was spacious, but already more doors were opening, more people filing in to watch the spectacle. She couldn't risk unleashing the urumi in such a setting.

No matter how much she wanted revenge, she wouldn't spill the blood of innocents to get it.

With a flourish of her cloak, she rushed for the exit and pushed it aside.

But Dawson was ready to clash again, tackling her from behind. Together they plummeted across the threshold and into the dusty street.

The pulled apart, each giving ground, then circled one another.

The Black Rose felt her heart toil like a blacksmith, hammering the sides of her torso with a heavy maul, each rush of blood crashing through her pain-wracked system. She wasn't sure how much more she could take.

But she took solace knowing Dawson was also hurt. He kept slapping the meat of his palms into his eyes, and when he shook his head it was obvious he couldn't see straight. He shambled sideways, focusing his gaze high and to the right.

The Black Rose came in low, from the left with a blitz that crunched into Dawson's jaw. She was rewarded with a howl of surprise.

He pitched a half-hearted counter attack, waving his arms and hoping he'd land a blow, but she wasn't where he thought she was.

"You've lost, Dawson," said the Black Rose. "I can go all night, but you're not man enough to continue. But then, I suppose you hear that pretty often." She smiled at her verbal stab, knowing it hit him in the manhood where he lived.

He screamed at her in defiance, then called her a filthy name—once in English, once in Spanish. He finished with a warning. "I'll kill you, wench. Whoever you are, I'll kill you."

Whoever you are.

Could it be Dawson didn't realize her identity?

The Black Rose chewed on the possibility. Paco had said Dawson was looking for her.

She had assumed during the course of their battle her opponent would have realized who she was. The fact he didn't seem to know now was an unexpected surprise, but ultimately disappointing.

She worked the buckle of her belt, unlatching the urumi.

Dawson would need to be told. In his last minutes of life, he needed to know who had bested him. He needed to hear the Riveras had been avenged.

The Black Rose prepared to strike.

"Peace be with you, sister," said Mother Mercy from the boardwalk in front of the hotel. "Peace upon you, brother."

Dammit, thought the Black Rose. Not now. Not when she was so close.

Mercy walked casually down the steps and into the street. Dawson turned to face the nun, "Stay away from this, witch."

"Don't you think you've had enough?" said Mercy. She turned with a patronizing look. "And you?"

The Black Rose backed away, crouching low.

Mercy stepped between them and spoke to Dawson a second time. "Let it go, son. It's over."

"Git outta my way," he said. "Or I'll move you myself."

"Or not," said Mercy.

Dawson shuffled, took two steps and backed up like he'd been hit with a fly swatter.

The Black Rose watched as Mother Mercy moved in one fluid motion, gripping the wooden crucifix on her breast, pulling it apart to reveal a short, hidden dagger she aimed at Dawson's astonished face.

"One more outburst and I'll slit you open from bun to brisket," said Mercy. "Let it go."

The Black Rose circled around, careful to keep her painted face under the shadow of her hood.

"And you," said Mercy, addressing her directly, but keeping watch over Dawson. "I should think a lady would have better places to be than wandering the streets at night."

Dawson glanced in her direction, then at the onlookers gathered at the hotel door. Men and women, pilgrims and travelers.

Paco stood with them, and the sight of him caught her heart in mid-stride. She'd told him to go to bed, but he'd insisted he would meet her.

What if he'd been caught up in the frey? What if he'd been hurt?

Again, Mercy told Dawson to stand down. "I won't ask you again," she said.

Dawson shrugged in a reluctant truce.

"Hell with it," he said, letting his shoulders slump.

Holding his good hand to his face, Dawson limped back to the boardwalk and climbed the stairs. "Somebody get me a drink?" he said to the crowd.

Then he disappeared inside while Mercy watched from the street with the dagger still in hand.

If the Mother Superior said another word, The Black Rose didn't hear it as she fled into the shadows of the night.

CHAPTER NINE

The Black Rose didn't let herself feel the pain until she slid through the window of her quarters at the mission. She landed on the floor, sat spraddle-legged against the wall beneath the open pane, her arms wrapped around her bruised midsection. She need-ed to get up, wash her face, change out of her clothes before Mercy returned.

But she couldn't make herself stand.

She did her best to push herself up, and before she could fall back, Adeline was there to catch her. "Mercy said you'd gone out," she fumed. "She's out looking for you now."

A compact kerosene lantern waited on the table beside the bed, and Adeline lit it. "We'd best get you cleaned up."

Then the nun led the Black Rose to the bed and helped her strip the cloak and dark clothing away from her battered body.

Catalina unwrapped the urumi, coiled it back

into a tight roll, snapped the buckle latch firmly in place and hid it under her pillow. Then she walked to the rear wall and fell against the adobe shelf to let Adeline sponge away the accumulated grime and Apache paint.

"You're bruised up decent enough," said Adeline. "Though, I dare say Teddy had it worse one night in Dakota after he wrestled a bear."

"Teddy?" Lina struggled to hear over the intermittent bells going off in her head. "Oh, the president," she said. "I forgot."

"Of course it wasn't a grizzly, if that's what you're thinking. No man alive wrestles a griz and lives. No, this was your garden-variety black bear, though still a heavy-duty menace for any rough and tumble hombre." Adeline squeezed the sponge out in the white enamel pan and the water was colored pink. "Not to say your opposition was a lightweight."

Lina flinched as the nun poked her ribs. "You're gonna have a pretty rainbow of color here," she said. "Let me get my salve."

Adeline hurried from the room, leaving Lina beside the pan, half naked and chilled in the crisp night air. She never understood how the desert could stay so hot during the day, even during winter months, yet dip to such freezing temperatures overnight. Like the number of stars, it was a mystery no one seemed able to explain, but Lina wouldn't ignore.

She liked mysteries. Liked to roll them around her mind and ponder them during the free minutes between routine tasks. Mysteries of science and mathematics. Of history and battles.

Criminal mysteries.

Like the one in which Tut Dawson was surely embroiled.

Her eye caught sight of the rosary on her side table. Another mystery for sure, and one she was committed to asking Mercy about the next time they met.

Adeline walked back in with a black satchel in hand, still chattering on like she'd never left. "My doctor's bag," she said, lifting it high. "I did a bit of boxing myself, you know. But of course you couldn't know, how could you?"

Lina couldn't help but be amused. In spite of her aches and the physical exhaustion, she enjoyed listening to Adeline talk. She found herself liking the big nun more than anyone she'd met in a long time.

"I'm not sure I can imagine a lady boxer," said Lina.

"Look in the mirror, my lovely."

"I meant as a sport. In public. It seems like there would be little support."

"You'd be surprised."

Lina grit her teeth as Adeline smeared a dollop of brown balm across her ribs. The smell was somewhere between a strong tincture of iodine and a rancid stocking. "I'm guessing your remedies are homemade?"

"This was my grandma's solution," said Adeline, "but I cook it with the spring water for extra healing."

"What is it about the springs that heals people, Adeline?"

The older woman stepped back. Her face showed surprise at the question as she cleaned her hands on an off-white towel with an embroidered edge. "Why, it's the Holy Ghost of course."

"I know, but I mean actually."

"Actually, it's the Holy Ghost."

"Scientifically then."

Adeline pursed her lips. "The heat, the minerals in the water, some sort of geographic chemistry nobody understands." She whispered again, "The Holy Ghost."

Whatever the origin, the spring water had undeniable power. As did Adeline's salve. Lina relaxed as each of her wounds was cleaned and inspected, her cuts and scrapes cleaned, her body wrapped and bandaged. "Come morning you'll be plenty stove up," said Adeline. "Nothing to do about it but get on with your chores." She fished a pocket watch out from a pocket in her habit. "See you in a few hours. Mercy's got you down for breakfast duty at four-thirty."

"I don't eat breakfast," said Lina.

"Suit yourself," said Adeline, "but the rest of the sisters do. Boy, oh, boy. You'd better be ready to cook."

"I don't know how to cook."

Adeline put her hands on her hips. "What exactly did you do on that ranch of yours?"

"Father had a cook from Madrid who prepared all our meals."

Adeline's laugh was loud as a donkey and twice as annoying. She carried the small lantern to the side table, then helped Lina get dressed in her plain nightgown. She pulled back the sheets and Lina collapsed into the bed.

"Then Mercy put you in the right place for an education. Personally, I'm on evening duty this month, so you'll be up before me." Her face was full of mischief. "For the record, I like my eggs scrambled. But then, I've never been picky."

Lina nodded with only a partial understanding. The soft mattress was pulling her down and into its embrace. The dark swirled around her.

"God keep you, Sister Catalina," said Adeline, as she blew out the lantern and carried her bag out the door.

The word reverberated through Lina's dreaming mind.

Sister?

******

Mercy might've had Lina scheduled for breakfast duty, but when she awoke, the sun's afternoon place showed her she'd once again slept away most of the day. She crawled out of bed, a clanking machinery of misery. She stretched with caution, taking the measure of each muscle, coaxing her body past the discomfort to assume a beginner's fighting stance. With a silent count, she pushed through the martial forms she had first learned in childhood, exercising body and mind in a series of fluid movements.

Lina was careful not to strain herself, working around the dull thickness of each injury, accepting each warning twinge, noting her sore spots, and moving on.

When she was done, her body was covered in a thin film of perspiration, and her breathing was slow and controlled.

She rinsed off at a pan of recently refreshed water and had just finished dressing in the white bra, underpants, long shirt and blue habit of the convent when Mercy knocked on her door.

Lina invited her in with reluctance, steeling herself in expectation. She was sure to be chastised for her previous night's adventure.

Instead, Mercy sat on the bed, patting the spot next to her.

The Mother Superior was dressed in the same manner as she'd been the night before. Lina was tempted to ask if Mercy slept in her sturdy black shoes and blue habit.

Her curiosity got the better of her, and she decided on a more pertinent question. "Last night at the hotel, why did you interfere?"

Mercy continued to pat the mattress. "Sit down," she said.

"I'll stand, thank you."

"It's hard to have a pleasant conversation when one of us isn't being pleasant."

"I had the bastard," said Lina, holding her thumb and forefinger a fraction of an inch apart. "I was *so close* to retribution."

"You were close to being tossed into jail. Or worse. Ned Sedgewick was in the crowd. Drunk out of his mind or not, he's still the law in this town. He might've chosen to draw down on you both."

"If it meant Dawson's demise, I'd gladly have given my life."

"If you'll excuse me saying so, Miss Rivera, you're

spouting a bunch of horse apples. Machismo may have played well with your brothers, but around here we consider it base stupidity."

"I don't care about your consideration."

"We've already established as much."

"You didn't answer my question. Why did you interfere?"

"The honest answer? I need you alive and free, not dead or in jail."

"You need me?"

Mercy nodded. "I do. We all do. The Sisters of Señora Maria. The people of Santo Tomas."

Lina denied the words. "I am nothing. It's my family you need, not me."

Mercy seemed to consider her words, then agreed. "You're right. It's not *you* we need at all."

It wasn't the answer Lina expected, and she complained. "Muchas gracias, señora," she said. "I'm sure I appreciate your sentiments very much." She put her hand on her hip. "May I go now?"

"Of course, you're free to leave at any time. But you don't have a horse."

"I'll buy one."

"With what?"

"I have credit in this town."

"Not anymore. Not since word's gotten around about the raid on your hacienda."

Lina hadn't considered that. What good was a family name without property and wealth to go with it?

"I'll work. I can earn enough to buy a horse."

"Doing what? Adeline tells me you can't even

scramble an egg."

Lina felt her face get hot as the Mother Superior gracefully punctured each of her defenses.

It simply wasn't fair.

Against a man like Tut Dawson or Fausto the bandito, she was nigh invincible. Her fighting skills were a match for any man.

Against a short, dumpy woman of advanced age, Lina was helpless.

God's blood!—she thought—this matron had to be nearly 40 years old, and there was nothing she could say to shake the biddy's supreme confidence.

Finally she gave in, and sat on the mattress, discouraged.

"You're forgiven, sister," said Mercy.

"I didn't ask to be forgiven," said Lina.

She was discouraged but not defeated.

They sat together, side by side and silent, for more than a few minutes. Finally, Mercy sighed and said,

"A dead man was found this morning in the village."

"I'm sorry," said Lina.

They sat a while more, and Mercy continued. "This man gave confession last night to the Monsignor."

"Then he entered heaven with a clear conscious."

"I don't think so. Nothing Andronicus said seemed to please him. The man was tormented by his recent actions."

"How do you know? You said he confessed to the Monsignor, not to you."

"The walls in this place are thinner in some places than in others. Especially when a sinner is compelled by strong emotions to express his guilt loudly."

Lina studied Mercy's face, her posture. "It's weighing heavily on you, isn't it? This man's confession?"

Mercy agreed. "He was one of the raiders who took your ranch."

Lina's interest was piqued, and suddenly she had a thousand questions. "Who was he? Did he say who he worked for? Did he explain why they rode against us?"

Mercy shook her head. "Yes and no. Not exactly."

"But you learned something?"

"When I said we didn't need you, may I explain what I meant?"

Even though the Mother Superior seemed to be changing the subject, Lina acquiesced.

"Let me tell you about Catalina Cristiana Rivera," said Mercy. "Let me tell you about who she is today, and who she will be. She was driven from her ranch, you understand. She was lost and alone."

"You make me sound like a child," said Lina.

"Catalina joined the holy Sisters of Señora Maria as a novitiate," said Mercy. "That is, she became a novice in the order, a candidate for the vows."

"I have no interest in your vows."

"You and I know this. Your enemies do not."

"My enemies are my own business."

"Not exclusively," said Mercy. "We have enemies in common. When I took my vows here at the convent, I swore a sacred oath to protect the holy springs. This duty belongs as much to the convent as it does your family."

"What about the priesthood? Does the duty belong to the Monsignor as well?"

Mercy's voice dropped to a whisper. "When it comes to the springs, Andronicus and the Sisters have different opinions."

"You don't trust him, do you?"

"The Sisters of Sorrow have appeared. Then you showed up at the gate. A man involved with the raid on your ranch is dead but only after he rid himself of a terrible burden. I fear our mission is in for something of a...what's the new expression? A shake-up."

Lina didn't know who the Sisters of Sorrow were, nor did she understand why her own appearance would mean anything important to the future of the mission. What she did understand was the dead man had told Andronicus something vital, something Mercy learned through her eavesdropping.

"You need to know I want Catalina Rivera here with us," said Mercy.

Then the nun reached back to the bedside table and retrieved the burned black rosary. "But at the same time, I want *her*, out there, engaging the enemy before he gets a foothold."

"Her?"

Mercy pressed the rosary into Lina's hand. "The hooded woman I saw in the street last night. The woman who caught the imagination of the people in town. The woman the villagers are now calling the Black Rose."

Lina held the black rosary up into the light. "My mother gave me this. She said you would tell me the truth. How did this come to be burned?"

"When you were born, there was a fire. I was there, in the middle of it. You are, quite literally, a child of the fire."

Lina was skeptical. "My mother never told me about a fire?"

"There are many facets to your story. For now, you must accept this is as a part of your heritage." She pressed the rosary into Lina's hand. "Keep the rosary with you at all times. More importantly, keep it with *her*, when she dons her cloak."

"Please tell me the rest? About the fire and my mother?"

Mercy laid her hand on top of Lina's. "I will, once you get back from your journey."

"Journey? What journey?"

"You didn't think I'd let Dawson get away with what he's done? Especially not now. Not after what I learned from the dead man's confession."

"But why go on a journey?"

"Charles McKenzie and his damned umbrella left on the 705 this morning, bound for Nuevo Piño. Dawson was seen following the train on his horse."

Lina's hopes, so quickly raised high, were dashed back down. "Across the border? Then he is lost to us."

"You're going after him," said Mercy.

"Me?"

"And Adeline." Mercy stood up. "The dead man didn't tell us much, but he said enough. Since your family is out of the way, the stage is set for the next step in their plan to overtake Santo Tomas and the springs."

"Paco overheard Dawson talk about a wedding

and some sort of meeting with a Mexican and a German," said Lina.

"Dawson works for Charles McKenzie," said Mercy.

McKenzie.

Lina recalled all she had ever heard about the millionaire cattle-baron. Ruthless in business, but benevolent when it came to helping the poor. Ambitious, but altruistic. Her father had met with him once, but Lina assumed the conversation to be a friendly one. As she recalled, the cattleman had asked about buying some land.

Aquiles had politely rebuffed the man's offer. The Rivera's land was not for sale.

Apparently McKenzie didn't take no for an answer and had employed Dawson to take it.

It made sense. In her heart, Lina knew it was true.

The attack hadn't come from Garcia and Denver Three-Moons after all.

"I wonder if the confessor's loose lips contributed to his death," said Lina. "If you overheard his confession, maybe somebody else did too?"

"Or he may have continued to talk after leaving here," said Mercy. "There are men at the cantina with big ears. I have no proof of anything."

Lina put the puzzle together in her mind, but there were still pieces missing. "What is McKenzie planning to do?"

Mercy didn't know. "It's what the Black Rose must find out."

"And likely stop," said Lina.

"Ostensibly, you'll be going to Nuevo Piño to assess the well-being of the children there. While Catalina Rivera visits the young, the Black Rose can find answers."

Lina made up her mind. "On one condition," she said.

Mercy waited for the caveat.

"When the time comes for Tut Dawson to die, I don't want any interference. I will have my vengeance."

Mercy replied, "Vengeance is mine, says the Lord."

"Then the Lord and I share the same goals," said Lina.

"Perhaps you will work as His right hand," agreed Mercy.

"And His terrible sword," said the Black Rose.

CHAPTER TEN

Charles McKenzie swirled the aged Scotch whiskey around the inside of his cut glass tumbler and raised it to his lips with one hand while he fingered the ivory handle of his closed umbrella with the other.

He drained the glass.

As he let the glowing amber liquid flow into his throat he closed his eyes to the window of his private Pullman car. Leaning back, doing his best to relax into the supple leather covered fainting couch, he turned his face sunward and assured himself the details of his life were coming together, warm and bright. With the muffled click-clack of each passing tie-plate the future rushed to meet him.

Too fast.

The big 705 was the first in a new line of steamers. His was the first luxury car to traverse the distance to the railhead in Nuevo Piño.

But he couldn't enjoy it.

Ever since his first undertaking was complete, he

couldn't stop thinking about the next one, a spur line through Rivera land and the middle of Santo Tomas then running across the border, before going all the way to the Pacific Ocean. His plan was for his line to encompass the entire north of Chihuahua. With the abundance of spring water and mineral wealth he thought was available, they would all be set for life.

But this Chihuahua Spur was a bitter pill.

Because Charlie Mac had a problem.

He was flat broke.

The railroad men expected results, especially now, after the success of the line he was riding on, and so he was forced to be somewhat…reckless with his plans.

He consoled himself knowing the Riveras never would have sold out.

On the other hand, the people of Santo Tomas would certainly acquiesce.

With Fino's money backing him, how could they refuse? He'd give them five times what their pitiable dry land was worth.

He played with his umbrella and assured himself of his plan for the Chihuahua Spur.

Charlie Mac had a railway line into Mexico and fingers crossed. He had the backing of Porfirio Diaz's top military governor and a blessing from the German emperor.

He sipped again, coughed as the expensive liquor slipped down the wrong way, and raised a linen handkerchief to his heavy red beard. His second cough was a roar, shaking his two-hundred pound frame, bringing him half-way off his chair, and sloshing whiskey onto the sleeve of his tailored white, silk shirt. He consumed the rest of the drink, and walked across the moving car to the wet bar, keeping himself steady with an outstretched hand.

The bar, like the rest of the car, was courtesy of the Sioux City and Orient railroad men who had originally funded Charlie Mac's dream. He still owed them all a tidy sum for pulling the salient strings in Washington, pushing the right men into the most desirable directions to get his Texas branch line to the border and beyond. He was well pleased with the efforts.

But now, at the pinnacle of his vision, some of them seemed utterly lacking in patience. They wanted to see profits.

Interest in the new Chihuahua Spur seemed to rely on spreadsheets and dollar signs. Details rather than Charlie's grand vision. Landers wanted to know how soon the ground would break. Sturgeon was hounding him about how efficiently the springs could be diverted. They all demanded to know how quickly the people of Santo Tomas could be bought out and moved out of the way.

And what about that damned mission church and its convent of hens?

Such a harried response was disappointing, especially since the first phase was already complete. He'd spent the last of his own money to get the Riveras out of the way forever.

Charlie Mac resumed his position on the couch with a fresh Scotch in hand, and closing his eyes, told himself everything was going to work out.

The train began to slow, and he opened his eyes.

Outside, the sandy plain was busy with mesquite and sagebrush, and a lonely back road wound down from a far blue mountain range, like someone had roped a bank of thunderclouds and tied them to the horizon. At the intersection of the winding way and the railroad track, a man on a boney bay horse rested in his saddle, one leg hooked over the horn. He wore a battered Confederate campaign cap, a loose tan blouse, and ragged denim pants. His right hand was bandaged with heavy wool. A crooked thin cigarillo hung from his lips.

The train stopped and the man dismounted.

Charlie Mac watched as a second man, a short Mexican wearing a sombrero, disembarked from a forward car and walked to meet the first. The two briefly conversed, then the second man handed the first one an envelope. He waited while the first man rifled through the paper contents with his thumb, then they nodded once at one another and the second man picked up the reins of the horse and led it away, up the road toward the highlands, away from the rail.

The first man climbed on board the train.

Before it started moving, he stepped inside Charlie Mac's car.

"Have a drink," said McKenzie, nodding at the sideboard with its gleaming bottles and tumblers. "Whatever he gave you for that nag was too much."

Tut Dawson poured a measure of dark, spiced rum into a glass and hooked a lime onto the lip. Clenched between his teeth, his cigarillo bounced up and down when he spoke. "I don't see why I had to ride hell to breakfast all the way out here to meet up with you."

He carried his drink to a green velvet upholstered chair with polished walnut arms and legs. He let himself collapse as the train lurched forward, the big steel couplers grabbing one onto the next with a jarring, booming clatter.

"I could've smuggled myself on board last night in Santo Tomas without anybody seeing me." He raised his glass. "Skol."

"After the spectacle you made of yourself?" McKenzie raised his glass in return. "Everybody had eyes on you. Lawmen included."

"Lawmen?" Dawson plucked the cigarillo from his lips and, spitting out a stray leaf, balanced it on the arm of the chair. His quick laugh was the yipping of a coyote. "You don't mean Sedgewick? He's nothing but an old rumpot." Dawson leaned forward and aimed his index finger at McKenzie's chest. "Do you know his official office is a back table in Lloyd's cantina?"

"I was referring to a U. S. marshal, actually. I don't have his name."

Dawson pulled a face, sat back in his chair and sucked on the wedge of lime, then sipped from his glass. Finally, he said, "Never heard anything about no marshal."

"If he wasn't there last night, he will be today. One of the nuns wired Fort Bliss for him. Yesterday."

"La Noria mesa's a long ride away."

"By horse. What about automobile?"

"Automobile?" Dawson looked like he'd never heard the word.

"I don't pay attention to automobiles." Dawson finished his drink and placed the tumbler on a side table. "Why'd the nun call for a marshal?"

McKenzie held Dawson's eyes through the cloud of cigar smoke. "Why, indeed?"

"You think it's because of our raid on the Rivera's?" Dawson laughed a second time and rubbed the back of his neck. "A nun you say? And she called for a marshal?"

"You're a wanted man in Texas. You're lucky nobody recognized you."

"We ain't in Texas anymore."

"A determined marshal might try to follow you."

"Determined marshals end up dead. Now you're just borrowing trouble in order to needle me. Is that what you're trying to do? Needle me?"

"Who was the girl in the hotel last night?"

Dawson finished his smoke and dropped it into the backwash of his tumbler. It sizzled for an instant, and he replied. "I can't say for sure, but I've got an idea."

"I'm waiting."

"I think it was the Rivera girl. I'm not sure of her name."

"Catalina Cristiana," said McKenzie. "Her father called her Lina. You were supposed to make sure there were no survivors."

Dawson narrowed his eyes. "You ever weed a garden, Charlie. Sometimes one of the little buggers gets through."

"I wonder where she learned to fight. Who taught her how to do all those moves?"

"I don't have any idea."

"The point is you drew unwanted attention to yourself. Which is why you get on board the train here. Which is why you don't come back with us on the return trip. As it is, you're lucky to be paid."

"Which reminds me," said Dawson. "I'm waiting on my final installment." He rubbed his thumb and fingers together.

"Have another drink," said McKenzie. "You'll get paid when I get paid. As soon as we reach Nuevo Piño."

"Before or after the wedding?"

Charlie Mac shrugged. "Either way, you're invited to enjoy yourself. This is an international occasion--with all the trimmings. Food, drink." He sat back on the couch. "Women."

"Who's getting married?"

McKenzie told him.

"You're making friends in high places," said Dawson.

"When a man has grand aspirations, it's vital he connect with the polite society."

"I'm not much for polite society."

"Like I said, there'll be plenty of recreational opportunities."

Dawson got up and fixed himself another drink.

"In Nuevo Piño, you can have your pick of the females," said McKenzie. "I understand there's eight or nine bridesmaids, and a score of cousins."

"I like my belles blonde and from Dixie."

"They're all the same in the dark, my friend. And some are better. Don't let your last night's misadventure color your opinion of the species as a whole."

McKenzie held out his empty glass. "Fetch me another, will you?"

Dawson tossed back his fresh helping of rum before he yanked McKenzie's glass away and hurled it down the length of the car where it smashed against an oak chest of drawers. Before McKenzie could react, Dawson was on him, using his good hand to grab a fistful of the cattle man's shirt and twist.

The fine silk collar tightened around his neck like rawhide drying in the sun, and Charlie Mac remembered a story he'd heard about the Apaches, how they would soak down strips of leather in salt water, wrap them around your naked frame, and leave you out in the desert sun. The shrinking, drying rawhide crushing your bones, squeezing the life from you over days and days. "Un-unhand m-me," he sputtered.

Dawson twisted his wrist. With his air cut off, all McKenzie could do was listen.

"Don't you treat me like your house boy, Charlie, and don't you lecture me on women. You and me both know you're nothing but a two-bit cow scalper who kissed the right bunch of ass to get into this railroad deal."

"Y-you're ch-choking me."

"Don't ever talk down to me again."

Dawson finally let him go, the bastard shoving him hard into the back of the couch.

Charlie looked past him, through the window over the bar, just beyond Dawson's shoulder. A horseman rode alongside the train, and was quickly joined by others. At first he thought it was Garcia and Denver Three-Moons, and he felt he throat constricting once more.

Dawson's idea of hiring some of the revolutionary landowner's more ambivalent soldiers to join in the Rivera raid was inspired. The anti-Diaz faction made perfect scapegoats, and besides, Charlie Mac had certain assurances Garcia would be dealt with in short order.

Assurances from "friends in high places" as Dawson said.

The lead man steered his big bay closer to the tracks to wave at the long Pullman car. Charlie Mac let loose a sigh of relief. The man was dressed in the steel gray jacket of Porfirio's rurales, a wide felt sombrero and a red necktie. He carried a Mexican army rifle, as did his fellows.

"There, you see," McKenzie told Dawson, "we're getting a right proper escort. Like I said, there's nothing to worry about."

"Funny, I don't recall you saying anything," said Dawson.

"If I didn't say it before, I'm saying it now."

"There's where you and me differ, Charlie," said Dawson. He scratched a lucifer to light on the heel of his boot and rolled the end of a fresh cigar in the flame. "I figure there's always something to worry about."

CHAPTER ELEVEN

By the third day of her convalescence, Catalina was chafing at the drudgery of convent life. She had helped Adeline scrub and polish the tables in the common room, split wood with Caroline to keep the cookstoves going, mended habits and veils with Clara, spackled a chunk of broken plaster with Sofia, and even spent four hours in the livery stable across town, grooming the seven mission horses with Paco.

Lina's hands and feet were blistered in fresh places, and her muscles ached continuously from the near ceaseless labor.

"How much longer until we undertake our journey? Surely we've cleaned every surface in the convent and darned every darn garment." Outside the south walls of the mission, the morning market bustled with activity and Lina impatiently fiddled with the plain length of rope around her habit and adjusted her novitiate's veil.

She would never admit it to Mercy as they walked along the boardwalk beside the mercantile in Santo

Tomas, but hard work had been the best remedy for her mind and spirit.

It hadn't eliminated her grief or taken away her ongoing sense of loss. But it had helped give her something else to focus on.

"You will leave when I deem it's the proper time," said Mercy, "but now you must quickly face front."

Andronicus strode along the boardwalk on an intercept course.

Mercy's voice grew with volume and was drowned in honey enough to cover her disdain. "Good morning, Monsignor," said Mercy and Lina nodded at the priest.

"Ah, good day, good day," said Andronicus, "and who do we have here? Ah, if it isn't the lovely Catalina Rivera." He reached out with his gnarled hands and took her fingers in his own. "I'm simply beside myself to hear you're choosing a life of service with us. In these ever-changing times there's such a need for the church and the church is in sore need of willing hands."

Lina bowed in feigned obedience and Andronicus placed his hand on her head in blessing. His hand remained a fraction too long, stroking her hair with fingers which assumed too much familiarity and it was all Lina could do not to pull away.

"I look forward to knowing you better, daughter."

Turning to Mercy, the priest said, "What's your business in town today?"

"A variety of errands. Checking on the children. Visiting shut-ins. I thought Catalina might enjoy meeting old Mrs. Lopez."

Andronicus nodded. "I would have been more than happy to occupy our new prospect while you performed your duties," he said, showing Lina his straight, white teeth. "Next time you walk to the market, I hope you'll do me the honor of an afternoon's company."

Lina's voice was pleasant. "I am old enough to not need a chaperone when walking to the market, Monsignor."

The priest's lips curled into a forced smile, but his eyes betrayed his anger.

"At any rate, God be with you both," he said.

Once the priest was out of earshot, Lina voiced her opinion of him aloud. "He's quite unpleasant, isn't he?"

"You taunt the Monsignor at your own peril," said Mercy.

"The reverse is also true," said Lina.

"At least think about the role you're attempting to play. You're supposed to be a humbled heiress preparing herself to become the bride of Christ."

"I agreed to go along with the charade, Mercy. I'm willing to sacrifice the truth for the cause, but I won't sacrifice my dignity on top of it."

Mercy harrumphed, and they continued along the street, nodding to pedestrians and side-stepping the occasional cow pie.

What must it be like to work day in and day out with a man like Andronicus? To hide one's true nature, stifle one's opinion. Lina imagined the thousands of petty slights and regular sacrifices Mercy must have endured. When she spoke again, her voice softened. "We will both need to be more careful where Andronicus is concerned."

"Agreed," said Mercy. "Now—"

An apparition wearing the white cotton clothes and the toeless shoes of a peasant stepped between them. "Una momento," he said.

Startled, Lina instinctively reached for the belt at her waist. Her urumi was back at the convent. The rope she wore was comparatively useless.

Mercy reached out to touch Lina's arm. "A friend," she said. "I think…."

The man's bald head was dark and wind burnt, his eyes, flat and unseeing. With a warning tone, he said, "The righteous is cautious in friendship."

Then he held up his fist and opened his wrinkled fingers. A charred, black cross trailing a string of wooden beads streamed from his fingers. It looked exactly like the rosary Lina had received in the desert from her mother.

"Where did you find this, old man?" said Lina.

"The maker strengthens those who receive the rosary, just as iron strengthens iron, and one who has great faith strengthens another."

"You made it?" said Lina.

The rosary maker dropped the ebony treasure into Mercy's grasp. "This is for Mary Rosetta," he said.

He turned his head toward the boardwalk where a girl with a dark, flat brimmed hat with a colorful beaded band bustled from the door of the mercantile. Her thicket of hair was the color of a harvest moon, her figure equally full, straining against her shoulder less lime blouse and ankle-length skirt of forest green. Her chin was bruised.

As Lina watched, she aimed herself downtown, then turned toward the mission. Mercy swallowed loudly.

The girl clutched a tartan handbag with gold clasps, and her lace up boots clicked on the pine boards when she walked.

When she saw Lina and Mercy, she put one of her hands between her ample breasts.

"Oh, holy hell," she said.

"Can we help you, dear?"

She tipped her hat. "I've done got myself lost as a seed-tick in a sandbox. Which way's the hotel?"

"The Casa de Poeta is on the next block, across the street," said Mercy. "What brings you to our village?"

The ginger-haired girl jumped from the board-walk with girlish athleticism. "I'm Mary Rosetta," said the girl with an out-thrust hand.

Lina ignored the girl, turning in every direction. The rosary maker was gone.

"He tends to come and go rather quickly," whispered Mercy. She shook Mary's hand. "It's a pleasure to meet you."

"What's this?" said Mary, as Mercy pressed the black rosary into her hand.

"A gift especially for you."

Mary poked out her lower lip, appraising the craftmanship of the piece. "Handmade is it?" She nodded her thanks and unsnapped her purse. The rosary disappeared inside. "Wonder where I might get a bite to eat? You say the hotel is this way?" She pointed in the wrong direction.

"How did you happen to come to town so early in the morning?" said Lina.

Mary's fair complexion couldn't hide the pink blush glowing behind her freckles.

"You're asking a ticklish question," said Mary. "How about you tell me your name instead, sister?"

"Señorita." Lina told Mary her name.

"You're a nun?"

"The Señorita has not yet taken her vows," said Mercy.

Mary was skeptical. "So it's like you're playing nun for a while to see if you like it? Trying on the habit to see how it fits?"

"If you like," said Lina.

Mary was gobsmacked. "Lordy me, I didn't know you could try out to be a nun." Her emerald eyes twinkled. "You get free room and board as long as you're at it?"

"Are you asking if you might stay at the convent with us?" said Mercy.

A man on horseback rounded the corner at a gallop, and Mary looked over her shoulder. "Hell, yeah." Her fingers shot to her lips. "Oops. Sorry."

The man streaked past, and Mary said, "Let's go then. Let's be on our way."

Lina smiled to herself. This Mary Rosetta was sassy and had the makings of an ally.

"I think our rosary maker would appreciate it if we offered you the invitation," said Mercy.

Mary clapped her hands. "Hot damn."

"I would ask you to have a care with your language."

The redhead put pinched fingers to her lips and turned. "Under lock and key." But Lina saw the woman cross the fingers on her other hand. Perhaps this Mary was a woman after her own heart.

"Do you have any other belongings? A valise? A change of clothes?"

Again, Mary's cheeks flushed. "None to speak of," she admitted.

"Fear not, Mary," said Mercy, turning toward the mission, and putting her hand on Mercy's bare shoulder, "like you, Catalina only just arrived with the clothes on her...uh, back."

Mary bustled across the street ahead of them, and as they made their way to the gate, Lina tried to see the mission through the young woman's eyes.

The long south wall of pink adobe mud, baked in a natural oven for centuries, cracked and crumbled, spackled and repaired, supported a gate of ornate carved oak, strapped and hinged with steel. East of the gate, the majestic facade of the holy sanctuary rose up to watch over the street before it, and stretching along the top of the wall beside it, an arched walkway leading to the convent garden.

Crowning the face of the church, the four-eyed espadana—the bell gable—rose into the sky and showed crystal blue through its four semi-circular arches. Each opening housed a single brass bell on its individual headstock with ropes falling down from wheels to a raised platform inside the mission.

"I've loved the sound of the bells since I was a child,"

Mary told Lina as they walked into the cool afternoon shadow of the structure. "How often do they ring?"

"Morning and evening," said Mercy, "as a call to devotions."

"And for warning," said Lina.

"Warning? Goodness," said Mary. "It's hard to believe a peaceful little village like this would have any need for warnings." Again, her actions betrayed her words as she glanced behind them.

Lina thought Mary was all too familiar with warning signs. In fact, she seemed to be especially nervous. The purpled welt on her chin was fresh, certainly not more than a day old.

"The summer droughts bring the danger of fire," said Mercy.

"And too, there are the raids," said Lina.

"Raids?" said Mary.

Annoyed, Mercy explained, "Sister Lina exaggerates. Positioned as we are on the border, we've had an occasional incursion of Revolutionarios Mexicanos cross the border to visit Lloyd's Cantina. Nothing more."

Lina ignored the Mother Superior's chastising glare and pressed on. "If you make a home with us, your courage will certainly be tested."

"In what ways, señorita?"

Just then a chestnut Morab with a Mexican saddle loped up behind them.

The man driving the compact horse wore a loose-fitting linsey shirt and hairy chaps over his jeans. He carried a short cat o' nine tails and grimaced under a narrow, waxed mustache as he addressed Mary Rosetta. "I expected to find you here, wench. If not in such mannered company."

Mary's jaw twitched involuntarily, and Lina caught the slightest of trembles at her bare shoulders. But the redhead stood her ground, her reply sounding strong and sure.

"I told you I'd leave if you struck me once again, Ansel. When you did—I did."

Lina again took note of the bruise on Mary's chin and decided she would never question the woman's courage again.

Ansel's tone was demanding. "Now you will come back to me," he said.

Lina stepped between them. "Who is this man, Mary?"

"Ansel Blanchet," said Mary. "My husband, and the man who is most likely to kill me."

Blanchet dismounted, and Mary flinched as he cracked his short whip. "You will be silent, woman."

Lina couldn't help but smile. "Oh, I don't think so, chico. I don't think so, at all."

CHAPTER TWELVE

At the mission gate, beside the community bell's drooping rope, a smiling beggar with no shirt and an open dish sat next to a short mestizo who had a day's growth of whiskers and a shock of black hair hanging over his forehead. The mestizo held the reins of a speckled donkey in one hand, and gripped a tall hickory walking pole with the other. He was dressed in black, wearing a clay-colored charro jacket and riding boots. He smelled like a distillery.

As Blanchet advanced on the three holy sisters, Lina moved to intercept him, but not before Mary could act. Slipping past the cat o' nine tails, she queried the mestizo with her eyes and a slant of her head, holding out an eager hand.

The mestizo tossed her the wood pole.

At the same time, the beggar reached out with amusement and gave the bell rope an energetic yank. At the loud, clanging peel, Blanchet whipped his head around and up to look at the bell.

Holding on with both hands, Mary hit her husband with the wooden pole.

Blanchet recoiled with a grunt, but held onto his whip. Shaking off the blow, his expression was a weird mixture of joy and outrage. "You always liked it rough, eh cheri? Plus les choeses changent, plus ells restent les mêmes."

"What did he say?" said Mercy.

"The more things change, the more they stay the same." Mary sneered, sweeping the stick around toward Blanchet again. "Oui, monsieur. Aller aux enfers."

Blanchet ducked and flicked the whip, but Mary was just out of range.

Overconfident, he rushed in, and she slammed the end of the pole into his eye.

Then another jab smashed into his chin, drawing blood.

A third jarring blow bruised his throat.

Mary pulled back, twirling her weapon like an enormous baton, bringing it back into play as Blanchet staggered toward her. Like a pendulum, the length of wood arched up, Mary's enraged weight behind it. The pole sailed through the air, cracking into Blanchet's chin a second time, putting him down on the brick paved street.

While Mercy knelt over the stunned Frenchman, Lina complimented Mary's skill. "Well done," she said. "Very well done, indeed."

Her face and shoulders wet with sweat, Mary leaned on the pole, nodded and caught her breath. "Thanks," she said.

"Where did you learn to joust?"

Mary nodded toward her husband. "From Ansel. When we were young."

"You're still young, dear," said Mother Mercy. "You both are."

"You speak French?" said Lina.

"Oui," said Mary. "And a bunch more. Spanish, German, a bit of Portuguese. It's sort of a hobby."

Lina spoke to Mercy concerning Blanchet. "He's not seriously injured?"

"He'll be sore for a while," said Mercy. "Help me drag him into the shade of the mission."

Mary carried the pole back to the man with the donkey.

After Mercy and Lina had Blanchet situated against the adobe wall, they returned to where Mary was standing next to the donkey.

As they walked toward the trio, the donkey pinned back its ears, curled its lips, and started to bray.

"Hush, hush, Diablo," said the man. "It is the Mother Superior. You must be respectful." The animal twitched its ears but remained silent.

Mercy stopped a healthy distance away from the angry burro.

"Diablo?" said Lina.

"Si, si. He is a good friend, but he can be quite trying at times." The man moved his fingers back and forth between himself and the nervous beast. "Still, we are good for each other though, no? We make each other strong. Like iron on iron."

The same words as the rosary maker.

Lina shot Mercy a glance, and she gave a quick nod in response.

The man bowed, showing a smooth patch of skin at the crown of his skull, surrounded by a thinning crop of hair. "Raul Antonio Cassidy, am honored to make your acquaintance. I enjoyed watching your scuffle. An amazing display of martial prowess."

Mercy wrinkled her nose at the smell of rum on his breath.

"Do you have business with the mission, Señor Cassidy?"

A shiny silver flask appeared from Cassidy's hip pocket, and he took a long pull.

"Indeed, I do, Mother," he said. He flipped back the lapel of his jacket to show her a gleaming five-pointed star set inside a circle of gold. "I am a deputy United States Marshal. You called for me?"

******

"I don't know, Catalina," said Mary. "I've never been across the border."

"You must come with us," said Lina. "Tell her, Adeline."

The big nun passed along the sentiment. "It's the Mother Superior's decision."

Mercy poured a measure of boiling water from her kettle into each of four ceramic mugs before answering. "Mary must decide for herself. If she joins you, it needs to be of her own free will."

Mercy carried the kettle back into the kitchen before rejoining Lina, Mary, Adeline, and Raul Cassidy at their table in the common room.

Lina saw Cassidy admiring a faded painting of a Spanish conquistador, its surface a fine craquelure maze.

"He is Don Cicero Da Costa," said Lina. "In 1690, Santo Tomas was born of his doomed expedition to La Junta de los Rios—the junction of the rivers."

The marshal poured a measure of foul liquid from his flask into the tea. "And who is the priest who stands behind him?"

"Father Lopez, a Franciscan. The village was named in honor of Lopez's benefactor, St. Thomas of Villanova, a champion of the poor. It was Lopez who discovered the springs."

"After more than two centuries, you are still here," said Cassidy.

"Unlike other missions of the time, Santo Tomas was never abandoned after support from Spain was withdrawn in the 1700s," said Adeline. "Instead, the church held on as a haven for pilgrims, seeking the legendary power of the springs."

"And you have lived in peace with the natives all this time? With the Apache and the Commanche?"

"Thanks in no small part to the Riveras," said Adeline.

"My ancestors were given a Spanish land grant," said Lina. "We've held it for two-hundred years."

"Until now," said Adeline.

"Until now."

"I have no objection to crossing the border in pursuit of this man, Dawson, as you have suggested," said Cassidy. "But I would prefer to do so alone."

"Half-asleep with liquor?" said Lina. "Riding on

a cantankerous ass?"

"You insult Diablo?"

"You didn't ride him all the way down here?"

"Of course not," said Cassidy. "We only just received the reverend Mother's summons."

"How did you get to Santo Tomas?" said Mercy.

"Diablo and I rode in on one of Señor McKenzie's farm trucks," said Cassidy with a sly grin. "If this man, Dawson, works for McKenzie as you've told me, the irony is great, yes?"

"It is indeed," said Mercy.

"And so, Diablo and I hunt down this devil alone," said Cassidy. "And I am not asleep. And I am also not drunk."

"You don't carry a gun," said Lina.

"I don't like guns."

"Will you subdue Dawson with your walking stick?"

"If need be."

Lina's sigh was long and drawn out, and when she spoke her words came slow and deliberate. "And so you will need me to watch over you, amigo."

"Adeline is my right hand," said Mercy. "She too will go."

"Ay-yi-yi," said Cassidy, stroking the shadow of his beard. "To travel with two women..."

"Three," said Lina. "Paco said something about a German being involved with all of this," said Lina. "Mary's language skills might be helpful."

Mercy nodded. "Mary?"

The redhead bowed her head. "You gave me a swell black rosary to carry. If the Almighty's with us, who can be against us?"

"Una momento," said Cassidy. "Let's hold on, here. I need to check in with your pastor," said Cassidy. "I was told a Mr. Andronicus was in charge?"

The room was silent.

Finally, Mercy cleared her throat. "The Monsignor oversees the mission as a whole, but I am responsible for the convent," said Mercy.

"This business belongs to the convent," said Adeline.

"Exclusively convent business," Mercy confirmed.

Cassidy's face questioned each of the quiet women in turn, then smoothed out in understanding.

"You don't want him to know about this trip?"

"He knows about our mission trip to the children of Nuevo Piño. It's you I don't want him to know about," said Mercy.

Cassidy's eyebrows crawled down to meet over his nose. "Why not? Surely he's interested in justice?"

The women held their silence.

"All right, then," said Cassidy. Once more he opened the flask and poured out its contents.

Mary wrinkled her nose. "If you're gonna drink, at least drink something worthwhile. Your bugjuice smells like paint cleaner than something fit to drink," she said.

"For your journey, you will wear the garb of a priest," said Mercy. "Lina and Mary, like Adeline, will dress in the blue habit and dark veil of the Sisters of Señora Maria. You will attend the wedding of Ferdinand Angel Fino and his bride, Alejandra."

"Fino?" said Catalina. "Adrian Felipe Fino?"

Mercy's face filled with curiosity. "You recognize the name?"

"From long ago. My brothers spoke of him. He ranks high in the Federales. A personal friend of El Presidente, Porfirio Díaz."

"Federales," said Cassidy. "More and more, I don't like it."

"This doesn't mean I can't still enjoy myself, though?" said Mary. "Weddings usually mean food, drinks, and men."

"Your mission is sacrosanct, Mary Rosetta. You may not be a bride of Christ, but you're still a married woman," said Mercy.

"Actually, no. Not in the eyes of the church. Ansel and I were together…but, well the thing is, I called him *husband* and he called me *wife* because it made things easier in certain situations. We didn't want to have to answer a bunch of questions, you see…"

Her words died on her lips.

"You see?" said Cassidy. "You see? This is what I was afraid of." The marshal stood up to his full five foot height and wagged his finger. "I'm not shepherding a gaggle of hens to a festival of debauchery. Food, drinks, and men. Bah! How do I know this one won't be underfoot when the time comes for action?"

"I rather think Mary has proved herself under fire," said Mercy.

"And Adeline holds her own as a pugilist," said Lina.

Cassidy didn't seem convinced. "What about you, Catalina? What particular skills do you possess?"

A rush of heat flooded Lina's response, but was

immediately stemmed by Mercy.

"I am—"

"You're quite right, Marshal," said Mercy. "Our Catalina is the weakest of the three. But, shall we say, her *enthusiasm* makes up for what she lacks in skill."

Mercy's pronouncement may have been for the benefit of keeping the identity of the Black Rose a secret, but it didn't stop Lina from clenching her teeth.

Finally, she said, "Of us four, I'm the only one who can recognize Tut Dawson."

Cassidy's reply said he was resigned to the plan. "Dawson is wanted in Wyoming and Nebraska for rustling. Also, there's a Colorado warrant on him for robbing a train. Here in Texas, he's wanted for murder and kidnapping. This is the first chance we've had to nab him for quite a spell."

"It would certainly be a feather in your cap," said Mercy, "not to mention a jewel in your heavenly crown."

"You can keep your heavenly crowns," said Cassidy. "I'll be satisfied to stay in one piece."

"What will be, will be His will," said Mercy.

"¡Ojalá! *One would hope so.*" He finished his tea and leaned across the table. "In this heat, it is best to travel at night. We leave after your evening vespers."

Lina raised her cup to her lips as Cassidy turned to face her.

"Unless the young wildflowers' delicate sensibilities won't allow them to camp on the ground tonight?"

Lina deliberately spilled her tea in Cassidy's lap.

CHAPTER THIRTEEN

The four travelers set out for the river after a hearty supper of eggs and sour-milk pancakes, cured ham and thick slabs of bread with molasses. They carried with them a canteen of water each, lard sandwiches wrapped in wax paper, smoked bacon, and four cans of peaches—one for each of them. They were dressed in the uniforms of the church—a priest in black cassock with a flat brimmed black hat and three nuns in blue habits and veils.

Lina rode a black mare only half the size of her lost Andalusian, but she liked the animal's smooth gait, and the horse seemed to appreciate her steady hand. Adeline rode a buckskin gelding. Mary sat on the back of a sweet bay, and Marshal Cassidy used a Spanish saddle on Diablo and carried his walking stick across his lap.

In case it was needed, a lever-action Winchester 1873 rifle waited in his leather boot.

Mercy had insisted.

The sun was low in the west, casting light in orange rays through thick dabs of wet pink and indigo clouds, heavy on the horizon, threatening far off storms. Across the open desert valley, a ribbon of glimmering silver threaded its way through the clay plains and gray bosquecillos.

When they arrived at the border, the burro touched its nose to water and kicked up its heels. Ahead, the road coursed along the edge of a gently sloping terrace. "Calmate, Diablo, calm down," said Cassidy.

"What's got him spooked?" said Lina as the marshal urged his beast through the knee high current.

"Who can tell? The water may be too warm. It may be too cold. It might be because it is Thursday. This one has his own reasons for everything, and he doesn't always share."

"What do you have against a good horse?"

"It isn't the horse I have anything against. It is a fondness for Diablo, in spite of his hard-headed ways. He and I have been through much together. As I said at the mission. We make each other strong."

"I remember what you said," said Lina. "Iron on iron."

After the initial drive, Lina was sweltering in the long traveling habit, split in the middle for riding, wrapped with a rope at her waist. The coif and veil made her forehead itch. Underneath, she wore a light blouse, secured in the middle by her steel whip-sword.

She would not be caught off guard again as she was by Ansel Blanchet in front of the mission. Lina intended to keep her urumi close at hand for the duration of the journey.

Mary Rosetta appeared equally uncomfortable in the garb of the sisters. She splashed through the river at Lina's right, a loose strand of limp red hair drooping from under her veil. The black wood rosary hung from her belt.

Lina wondered how the rosary maker had known Mary's name before they did? How did he know she would cross paths with her and Mercy?

Lina steered her steed close to Mary. "I've been meaning to ask. Before we met you, did you see a blind man in the village? Maybe you spoke to him?"

"You and Mercy were the first people I spoke to after leaving my horse in the livery."

"You came from the cantina."

Mary agreed. "Washing out the road dust. To busy drinking to talk."

"This blind man, he's the one who made the rosary Mercy gave you."

"Never saw him before in my life. But maybe you can tell me—why all the hoopla over a hunk of jewelry?"

"Be sure to mind your language around Adeline," warned Lina, "or she'll take you to task as fast as the Mother Superior."

"I just don't understand what all the fuss is about."

"It's a rosary. Sometimes it takes the form of a knotted cord. The knots—or beads in this case—are a practical way for remembering a certain sequence of prayers."

"Like keeping score in billiards? You slide them along?"

"I hadn't thought of it quite like that."

"It's pretty obvious I've never been much of a

church girl."

Ahead of them, Cassidy and Adeline had cleared the river's edge and picked their way through a patch of brambles, the stickers nagging at their mounts' legs, causing them to high step and whiney.

Mary clucked her tongue. "I wonder what my old mom would say if she saw me wearing clothes like this? She'd prob'ly fall over in a cold faint."

The lead animals were increasingly restless, and as just as Cassidy seemed to have Diablo under control, Adeline's buckskin reared up in an explosive panic. Eyes wide and puffing, the frightened horse nearly hurled its rider into the briar-filled underbrush, but Adeline held the reins close and tight. She brought the horse into a pivot and his hooves hit the ground at the same time Lina heard the unmistakable vibration of the rattler.

Catching wind of the danger ahead, Lina's mare flared its nostrils and nosed into the path of Mary's bay. Meanwhile, Diablo had bounced Cassidy ten yards away from the snake in the opposite direction from Adeline, but still the warning clattered.

Cassidy had whirled the donkey around and was holding his Winchester level with one arm. He triggered the rifle, bent low to crank another round into the chamber with his left hand, then fired again at the snake as spattering shards of debris pelted Lina's habit and nicked her cheeks. With another shot in quick succession, the snake exploded into view, a writhing conduit of meat torn apart behind its impossibly wide-open mouth.

For a man who didn't like guns, his aim was true.

The dead snake spasmed and twitched, and Lina let her horse give it a wide birth as they left the water.

"Now we see why your donkey didn't want to cross," she told Cassidy. "It was a difficult shot, especially when made from the back of an upset burro."

"You're surprised at my marksmanship?"

"I am impressed."

"Don't get used to it," said Cassidy, jamming the rifle back into the boot.

Not sure how to respond, Lina asked about the burro. "Is Diablo well?"

"Old Billy No-shoulders didn't bite him."

"Billy No-shoulders?"

"Si, si, the snake. He has no shoulders, you see?"

"Let us hope Billy was an only child. I would not like to meet his brothers and sisters."

"Is everybody okay?" said Adeline, her buckskin back under control. Mary reined in behind her.

"I've been better," said Cassidy. The marshal's black cassock and flat brimmed hat had him sweating as much Lina. Looking at the white collar around his neck, she felt ten degrees hotter.

"*Billy No-shoulders* is beheaded, sister," said Lina. "There's nothing to fear."

"It's not the snake we should be afraid of," said Cassidy.

Lina turned to see the brow of the hill above them even as Diablo once more started to kick its heels.

The true reasons for the donkey's nervous disposition were evident in a row of a dozen strong pinto horses standing at the crest. Each carried an armed rider on its back. Lina recognized the Apache chief Denver Three-Moons, with his combed dark hair, streaked with silver, falling over shoulders sloped with age. He was old, but was still Garcia's right hand man.

Three-Moons wore a leather jacket two sizes too big for him, and loose canvas trousers. Next to him, Adolfo Stark, brother to Wes, the man she had killed in Dawson's raid less than a week before, sat with a rifle balanced perpendicular to his upright frame.

As Denver Three-Moons spurred his horse down the incline toward them, Lina's first hope was Stark didn't yet know what had happened to his brother.

Her second hope was if he did, he wouldn't recognize her.

The old Indian bypassed Cassidy like he wasn't there, driving his brown and white paint into the face of Lina's horse. He tilted his head one way, then another. Amused, he circled the mare as Lina whispered calming platitudes into its ear.

Three-Moons addressed her as *Sister.*

"We heard your gunfire. We came to be of assistance," he said.

"Your concern is appreciated, Denver Three-Moons."

"You know me?" His hand was big and rough, like it had been carved from petrified wood. He let his fingers play across this chin.

"Who doesn't know the exiled chief? Greatest of the Apache nations?"

A look of recognition passed over the chief's face.

"Catalina Cristiana Rivera," he said, his wide lips

parting into an expression of mirth. "Child of the holy waters. I certainly wouldn't expect to find you here, riding out in the open." The chief lowered his head and spoke low. "Especially not after the recent incident at your rancho. Señor Garcia sends his sympathies."

"What can you tell me about the incident at my rancho?"

Denver Three-Moon's voice was barely above a whisper, he mouth mere inches from Lina's ear. The smell of his bay rum hair tonic and tanned leather coat filled her head. "I'll give you fair warning, chiquita. Do you see the man up there, second from the end? The man wearing an open blouse of blood red, with the ivory knife handle at this belt? This man is Adolfo Stark, brother to Wesley Stark. He knows you killed his brother."

"We are on a mission from the church to Nuevo Piño, Three-Moons. We don't want any trouble."

"There doesn't have to be trouble." Denver Three-Moons wiped his mouth with the back of his hand and gave a half smile. "To have Catalina Rivera in my debt appeals to me."

"To be in your debt, does not appeal to me, Three-Moons."

Three-Moons waved the comment away. "Then I can't help if Stark recognizes you."

"Does Stark ride for Garcia?"

"He rides for me."

"But you ride for Garcia."

"Let's say I have an agreement with Garcia. My people have no love for the federales in Chihuahua.

They are cruel and full of themselves. Garcia is different. He has been kind to the people, worked with us to build homes, get medicine for our children…"

"Garcia and the Riveras have been at peace for years," said Lina. "As we have been with you and your people. If you had no part in the raid on my family home, say so now." She gazed into the deep-set brown eyes of the elderly man. "I will accept your word."

"I didn't know of it until the late afternoon on the day it happened." Three-Moons' voice was as calm and smooth as the glassy surface of the river behind them. The temperature must've been nearing 100 degrees, and the man's skin was as dry as his declarations. "I had nothing to do with it. Neither did Garcia."

Lina felt the first cooling breeze of night across her brow. She searched the old man's eyes, looking for any sign of untruth.

"I believe you," she said.

Three-Moons smiled and put his hand on Lina's shoulder.

She returned the gesture of friendship, but her voice was hard. "We will continue on our journey now. But know this, Denver Three-Moons. If your man Stark makes one move toward me, my friend with the long gun will put a bullet through his head. And if you break the Pax Rivera, there won't be enough sand in this entire desert to soak up the blood."

There was no fear in the chief's face when he replied, but neither was there a tone of defiance. He simply nodded, and said, "Stark's actions are his own."

"You won't back him up?"

"I have said what I have said," said Three-Moons. With a fast series of yips, he rode in a circle around Catalina and galloped away from her party to rejoin his company of soldiers.

The dust from his passing had yet to settle when Cassidy rode Diablo to Lina's mare. "What were you two talking about?" he said. "Will they let us pass?"

Lina turned her face to the men on the ridge. Stark had jockeyed himself into a new position beside Three-Moons, the backside of his horse turned toward the river. The men appeared to be conversing.

"Best be ready with the carbine," said Lina. "The one talking to the chief? His name is Stark. He doesn't like me much. If he makes a run for us, shoot him in the head."

Cassidy studied the row of men. "If he doesn't like you, it is good you are wearing a disguise then, no?"

"I think the chief is revealing my identity right now."

"I thought you two were friends."

"We are. But apparently those two are not."

As Cassidy turned, Adolfo Stark came marauding down the hill, a six-gun booming in each hand.

CHAPTER FOURTEEN

Lead smacked pell-mell into the earth around Catalina's horse as Stark poured on the gunfire. The mare reared up, and Lina drove her to the right.

Stark corkscrewed toward them on his painted horse with its fancy vaquero saddle, guns held high, spitting death. Adeline and Mary wheeled their horses back toward the river and Cassidy held his ground, fumbling his carbine.

Stark swerved toward Lina, more careful now, drawing a bead with one open eye on the iron sites, his tongue between his lips. There was an explosive boom, followed by a quick wind at her left ear. Too close!

Catalina leaned low across her mare's withers, spurring her into a gallop, hoping to lead Stark away from her companions. This was her fight, and she didn't want anyone else hurt because of it.

Stark fired again, screaming above the percussive din. Something about revenge and fornication. If only she could get to her urumi.

But Stark's horse was gaining, and behind him was Mary Rosetta.

Lina waved the girl way. "Mary, no!" But her words were carried away by the wind.

She reached beneath her habit and grasped the hilt of her steel belt only to stop when a rifle blast clapped through the air. In the periphery, Stark slumped over and his horse went the opposite direction.

The gunman's body spilled onto the ground where it rolled like a tumbleweed. The paint pounded on in the opposite direction toward the Rio.

Lina kept her eyes on Three-Moon's soldiers in the distance. One by one, they turned away from the scene and disappeared behind the hillcrest. Lina knew by the time she and her friends rode around the terrace there would be no sign of them.

She raised her hand, and Three-Moons returned the salute before he too vanished.

The rotten son-of-a-bitch.

Lina spun around and reined in above Adolfo Stark's corpse. Dismounting, she met Mary and the marshal.

"Three-Moons deliberately sent Stark to his death," said Lina, keeping her eyes on the now-vacant ridge. "I don't like a man who gets somebody else to do his killing for him."

"Is that a fact?" said Cassidy. "Well, what do you call what you just did?"

He slid off Diablo and, slamming his Winchester back into its satchel, marched over to the sprawled out body.

They stood over the corpse, Cassidy cursing

softly under his breath.

Lina shook her head. "No different than the snake, Marshal."

"Different," said Cassidy. He had his flask out and swallowed a good quarter of its contents. Then he caught her sidelong glance. "I came to your village because Mercy called. I agreed to go after Tut Dawson." He faced Lina squarely. "My intent has always been to take him alive."

"Then you're a fool."

"I don't like killing," he said, wiping his mouth on the sleeve of his cassock. "I've had to do it before. I didn't like it then, and I don't like killing this boy today."

Lina poked the corpse with her toe.

Adolfo Stark's blonde hair was the same bleached white color of the sand, and the breeze picked it up and laid it down on a whim. His face was twisted in a final grimace of rage.

A boy was he? A liar, a rapist, a hard-boiled killer. All of those and a thousand more black marked names. But not a boy.

Never a boy.

Mary bent over and picked up one of Stark's spilled pistols.

Cassidy slapped it out of her hand. "Leave it," he said.

"We may need it," said Mary.

"I'll carry it inside my saddle bag," said Lina.

Cassidy shook his head. "I said no. Bad enough we're traveling with a rifle. That much can be argued away as protection against coyotes. Mercy wanted us to travel as a priest and three nuns, then dammit, we better start acting like a priest and three nuns."

"I agree," said Adeline, as she joined them over Stark's body. "But the first thing we'll do is give this boy a Christian burial."

This boy.

Sweat ran down Catalina's back like a torrential rain. The hair under her veil was clotted and wet, and her face and neck were far too hot. She struggled to control her temper.

Finally Lina said, "We mustn't labor in this heat, sister. And we mustn't tarry. There's shade up ahead at the grove of trees. Best we rest and then move along."

"Do as you will," said Adeline. "I've sworn allegiance to the Giver of Life. I won't let Him down, even in the proper sending-off of one such as this."

"Are you out of your cotton-pickin' mind?" said Mary. "Let the vultures have him. The good Lord made them with occasions like this in mind."

"I won't," said Adeline.

"Jesus Christ," said Mary.

Adeline whirled faster than the eye could follow and shot out a hard right, rapping Mary across the mouth.

The slim young redhead hit the ground with a plume of dust.

"Don't you ever take misuse His name in front of me," said Adeline.

After a moment of silence, Lina helped Mary to her feet. "Have it your way, nun."

Adeline's eyes picked out each of them in turn. "Who wants to carry the body?"

******

A hollowed out arroyo in the side of the sandy hill near a twisted huddle of mesquites made a convenient cubby hole for the corpse, and Lina rolled Stark up in Adeline's saddle blanket.

Cassidy used his walking stick to pull soil from above down onto the dead man, trading off with Lina and Adeline to complete the job.

After they finished with the makeshift grave, Mary fashioned a crucifix of branches bound together with the barbiquejo—the braid—of her flat brimmed hat. Adeline said a few words from the Bible she carried in her saddle-bag. Then they all moved to the far side of the gloomy oasis to sip water and chew flavorless sandwiches under the crooked, bone white trees. They sat in a square, Catalina across from the marshal, Adeline facing Mary.

"We are more than three hours behind our schedule," said Lina. "I had hoped to camp farther out and reach Nuevo Piño before noon tomorrow."

Cassidy washed down a piece of jerky with a splash from his steel flask. "Any more enemies you want to tell us about?" he said. "Any Commanche war parties, by chance? Maybe just a rowdy band of drunks you took a shine to back in the village? Appreciate you tellin' us now rather than after the shootin'."

"Don't you think you've had enough to drink?" said Lina.

"No. Not like it's any of your business. Or did I misunderstand you?" He held the flask out at arm's length. "Were you asking for a drink?"

"I'll take one," said Adeline. She put the flask to her lips and took a healthy pull. Then she handed it to Mary who did likewise.

"Lina?"

Catalina declined the offer, and Cassidy retrieved the flask, stuffing it into his canvas sack.

The marshal's question about enemies hung in the air between them.

"The Rivera name is both treasured and feared," she said. "I have nothing to apologize for."

Lina took in the ghostly, moonlit expression on her companion's faces, careful not to linger on any one of them.

What she saw in the individual, she saw in all. They were wary, maybe even afraid.

It was clear they didn't trust her.

Surrounded all her life by conflict and skirmish, she sometimes forgot other people had been raised differently. It was true each of the three people sitting with her had experience in battle, but only Catalina Cristiana Rivera had been born to it.

What would it be like to be raised without a threat of violence?

What had Mercy told her? Catalina was a child of fire.

"I didn't know we would run into Stark," she said.

"We're lucky the Indian liked you."

"My family is well respected by peoples on both sides of the border. As I said, we have friends as well as enemies."

"How about in Nuevo Piño?" said Cassidy. "Got

any friends there? More important, do you have any enemies? I for one would like to know what we're going to find when we ride into town?"

Lina thought about it, then said, "The Riveras are not so well known in that region. For some reason, my mother and father never traveled there. Or, if they did, they went without me."

"You've never been to Nuevo Piño?" said Mary.

"I have not. Have you, Adeline?"

The nun shook her head.

"Then it's unanimous," said Cassidy. "We'll all be strangers in town. Like babes in the woods. Easy pickin's for any kind of buzzard." He spat, then climbed to his feet. "Great. Just great."

In the distance, a coyote howled, as Cassidy said, "Shall we be on our way?"

Without a word, the four travelers packed their gear and pressed on.

The road was adequately marked, if not maintained well. At one point, where a wide curve traversed a steep valley, a rockslide forced them to walk on the only open road there was—the railroad tracks.

Here the steel rail had been flung out over a wide gorge, and the footing seemed soft and chalky. Lina imagined her horse would punch through the soil between the ties at any second, and they would plummet to their death in the canyon below. She had to remind herself McKenzie's 705 had recently crossed the same track, and its passage certainly strained rock and steel more than the four travelers.

The chill night air was prematurely cold for

autumn, and they wrapped themselves in blankets. Adeline's blanket warmed the dead back at the arroyo. Cassidy shared a striped poncho.

The miles wore on and on.

Once, Lina thought she caught a whiff of fresh pipe smoke—an apple-flavored blend of tobacco like her father had used. Then it was gone, and try as she might, she couldn't find it again.

She almost convinced herself she was imagining things.

Almost.

Then she smelled the pipe again.

Above them, a whorl of pin lights circled the north star. The familiar constellations tracked their way across the dome of night as expected, and Lina's unerring sense of direction followed suit. They rode with the solemn massed peaks of the sierra madres to their left, and open scrub range on their right.

The marshal continued nursing his flask.

Ahead of them, craggy lone plateaus anchored the buffalo grass to earth and the fickle road carried them up arid slopes, then down through dewlapped valleys.

They stopped at an ancient, unoccupied way station called Lohman Siding to sip canteen water and warm themselves in a shack behind walls of greasy tar paper and cracked wood siding.

A candle, melted to a stub in its holder gave their respite a dim light around a three-legged wood table. A wrinkled sepia tone of Porfirio Diaz hung lopsided on a wall stud from a bent nail, and tin cans of tomatoes waited on broken shelves, blossoms of gray mold squeezing out through rusty holes.

Adeline counted seven kangaroo rats under a paper sack of rancid cornmeal crumbs.

"You catch 'em, I'll fry 'em up for supper," said Cassidy.

The marshal was quite inebriated.

"We are being followed," Lina told her companions. The stinging cold wind whistling through the walls gave the words a haunting tone.

"How many?" said Adeline.

"Two at least. Maybe three."

"How far back?"

Lina closed her eyes and breathed in the night smells of yucca plant and cactus, rancid cigarette smoke, and the smell of a fresh lit pipe burning an apple-flavored blend. "Close," said Lina. "Just outside, now."

Somebody kicked open the door, and a gun went off, spitting fire.

CHAPTER FIFTEEN

The bullet sizzled through the air and slapped the back of the cabin, putting Lina behind the door on the floor next to Adeline. Mary dived into a huddle under the shelves, and Cassidy upended his chair. Lina heard him crack his head on the side of the table even as he sagged and rolled underneath.

She shot to her feet and put all her weight behind the door, slamming it shut on their assailant before he loosed another round.

Adeline immediately lent her substantial mass to the effort, and Lina lowered a hard oak bolt into its catch, latching it tight at the door jamb.

Three more shots tore at the door, splintering the frame.

Siege!

Lina blew out the candle, and they waited.

The only sound Lina heard was her own quick breath and that of her companions, as well as the rush of blood in her ears. She crept to the back of the dark, windowless.

"We can't even fight back," hissed Mary. "The guns are outside on Diablo."

"Boxed like Christmas fruit bread," said Adeline. "They can hold us in here until we rot."

"I've tasted your convent fruit bread," said Lina. "Rot is an apt descriptor."

"Talk like yours is the reason you have more enemies than friends," said Adeline.

"Who's this after us now?" said Mary.

Lina put her eye to a knothole in the wall no bigger than her thumb. "The cabin backs up on a rocky plateau," she said. "Mary, check on Cassidy. Is he still unconscious?"

Mary slipped away, then returned. "Yes," she said. "He's wearing a duck's egg crown."

Catalina jerked the veil from her head and asked Adeline to doubly secure her braided hair.

"My satchel," she said, and Mary slid the leather bag across the floor.

Lina reached inside and pulled out the rectangular tin with its snap lid. Quickly she dragged her fingers through the black Apache paint, drawing a cross on her face. Then she swiped two smears of red across her forehead.

"See if you can pry the tar paper loose, Mary," said the Black Rose as she donned her cloak.

Adeline looked around the cabin. "I'll use this," she said, plucking the Diaz portrait from its nail. Quickly she disassembled the tin frame and, folding it over, jammed an edge into the corner of the shack.

A fat chunk of rotted paper drooped away from the outer wall, revealing the shack's splintered siding.

"Keep working until the back of the cabin is clear."

"What are you going to do?" said Mary.

"I saw two men in front of the shack beside our horses," said the Black Rose. "Are they still there?"

Mary put her eye to the peep hole. "Yes. One of them is smoking a pipe."

"They have guns?"

"Yes."

Adeline had a large section of tar paper torn away from the rear wall, revealing a series of horizontal slats nailed to the frame. Blue-white moonlight striped the interior of the shack.

The Black Rose pressed her hand against the siding and it immediately popped free of its rusty nails. Working quickly, she soon had two boards flapping in the wind, enough to crawl through.

"Watch over Cassidy," she said. "Unless he wakes up, stay put."

Cautiously, she crept out onto a patio of rock leading away and up the side of a steep incline slick with loose rocks and creosote bush. Her fingers found a wandering root from the trees far above, and her feet found a place in the jagged hill. Slow, judicious, she crawled away from the shack, careful to be quiet.

Time inched ahead.

Moving in the shadows of rocky protrusions and deep crevices, the Black Rose mounted the next plateau, a barren landscape under the late crescent of a waning moon. There were trees here, old mesquite and sickly big tooth maple. The stone floor was level, sprinkled with gravel and loose sand, decorated with desert chaff.

A rabbit skittered away through loose shale and somewhere in the distance, a coyote howled.

The dry bosquecillo rustled in the breeze.

All of her senses alert, The Black Rose slipped deep into the thicket without a sound.

When she heard the first feeble cry, she mistook it for the coo of an Inca dove. The second anguished groan was all too human and nearly underfoot. A black shape, huddled against a broken stump.

Her nostrils flared at the scent of bay rum.

"Denver Three-Moons," she whispered, kneeling beside the boney leather-clad pile.

The Apache coughed, sputtered out two words. "Must...warn."

"Warn?"

Three-Moons made an effort to move and the Black Rose rolled him onto his back.

At the sight of her macabre face, his eyes bulged round and white like spring toadstools.

"What are you?"

"I'm called many things."

The Apache chief worked to catch his breath, his chest rattling like an empty paper sack as his eyes slipped shut.

The Black Rose gripped the lapels of his coat, propped him up against the stump. Though the sky's light was dim, the ragged gash above the Apache's left ear was clear. He had been struck from behind.

"These are your men, Three-Moons?"

Eyelids fluttered open. "Catalina...Rivera?"

"You would betray us after all?" said the Black Rose.

"No...no," said Three-Moons, catching her wrist in a worried talon. "I would not betray you. I wanted...to warn you."

"Who are these men?"

"Friends..."

"Your friends?"

Three-Moons shook his head. No.

"Friends of Stark," he said.

Typical.

"Had you not set Stark upon us, we both would be more comfortable now. Me under a blanket on my horse, you at home with your wine and your wives."

"Stark was a problem for us. Too...ambitious." Three-Moons worked to sit up, and Lina helped him prop himself against a broken stump of mesquite. He blinked a few times and his breath came in a more even rhythm.

With a little rest, he would certainly recover.

"I grow weary of petty squabbles between men, Three-Moons. Thanks to the solution to your problem, three innocent lives might still be forfeit. How many of Stark's friends are there?"

"Three. Trask, Weiss, and Cain."

The way his voice squeaked when he pronounced the last name raised the bumps on her arms. "Cain? Do you mean Ben Cain?"

He nodded. "The same."

Ben Cain was one of the most vile bandits in the Rio Grande valley. Called Benito Khan on this side of the border, he made his reputation through terror and intimidation. His enemies numbered in the dozens and included Garcia and the Riveras both. If Stark and Cain were allies, it was no wonder Three-Moons felt threatened.

No wonder he didn't kill Stark himself. Cain's vengeance would be terrible.

Was terrible.

Sucking in her breath, the Black Rose wanted to strangle the Apache chief.

"You got us in the soup good, old man. Assuming I get out, you will owe me your life, and then some."

Helpless, Denver Three-Moons nodded.

There was nothing to be done but fight.

The Black Rose recalled all she'd ever heard about Cain. His reputation was firmly established. If his mission was retribution, there was nothing to could stop him from making the kill. Not gold or silver, not women nor words.

A holy white collar and blue convent habits wouldn't register on Cain's conscious. He'd cut them down without a second thought.

Only death could stop him, and only the Black Rose stood in his way.

Which was something Cain didn't yet know.

She had that much of an edge.

Leaving Three-Moons to contemplate his sins, the Black Rose circled around the perimeter of the bluff above the shack until she found a flat outcropping. From this elevation, the railroads' dark tracks were a severe line etched in the silver surface of the world, stretching away from the rough country across the plain to Nuevo Piño's line of firefly lights.

Nothing moved on the vast range.

Below, the three horses from Santo Tomas were still tied to a pair of painted hitching posts with Diablo the speckled hell donkey. Lina's black mare nickered softly, sensing its rider's presence.

As if she could calm the horse by thought alone, the Black Rose pictured herself stroking the soft muzzle, scratching the tall ears. The mare snorted aloud.

If the two men at the front of the shack noticed the mare's agitation, they didn't show it. Instead, they stood casually smoking. One had a short cigarette butt stuck to his lower lip, the other chewed the pipe Catalina had smelled. Each of them gripped a modified rifle with a custom lever-action loop.

Their mounts were close-by, not tied but left free to roam.

Her black cloak billowing across the starlit void like raptor wings, the Black Rose perched above them, waiting for the right moment to strike.

The air was still, and the man with the pipe had a deep, husky voice which carried clearly. "I told you before, you got to wait until Cain gets back here."

The second man was more fidgety than the first, bouncing on one leg, then the other. The leather of his chaps creaked in the night, making his knees seem like springs in need of a good oiling. He scratched a match tip aflame with his thumb and pitched it toward the front of the shack. The fire winked out in mid-flight.

The first man scolded him. "You got to wait, Weiss."

The second man paid no attention, lit another match, and tossed it. His laugh was like the grunting of a randy boar pig. "Huh-huh-huh."

So the firebug was Weiss, which meant the man with the pipe was Trask.

Strangers to the Black Rose.

Weiss and Trask held their rifles like lazy schoolboys with loose garden hoses.

"Cain ought to be back any time," said Trask. "There ain't no sense wastin' matches."

Now her eyes were accustomed to the dark, making it easy for the Black Rose to quickly search the ground at her feet and locate a melon-sized rock with rounded edges.

Weiss kicked a tangled ball of dried sage against the front corner of the shack. "Hell, I'm tired of standing around. I'm gonna smoke them bitches out of there."

He struck a match and dropped it into the tumbleweed.

"Aw, Weezer, I told you to wait."

The sound of her movement masked by the men's conversation, The Black Rose hefted the rock over the edge of the precipice. They liked hitting people from behind, did they?

She let gravity do its work. Down went the rock, like a shell shot from a silent cannon.

The rock smashed into the back of Weezer's neck, dropping him to the ground with a sickening grunt even as the kindling at the shack erupted into a flickering orange cone.

Hungry tongues of flame licked at the dry wood siding, eagerly climbing the walls of the shack.

Trask whirled around with his gun at the ready. "Who the hell's up there? Cain, is that you?"

The Black Rose crouched low, below Trask's field of vision. She eyed the flame, wondering if Adeline and Mary had stayed put like she told them.

If Cassidy woke up, the three of them might readily escape through the back hatchway. But if the marshal was still out cold, the two women would have the devil's own time getting him out quietly through the narrow space.

The Black Rose came back up to her feet, slipping the urumi from her waist and squeezed the hilt as it uncoiled around her legs.

Awful as it was, the fire was the perfect distraction.

If only her companions could hold out against the smoke.

"Are you up there, Cain?"

A twig snapped. Before the Black Rose could turn, her skull exploded into a thousand shards of crimson agony, and a new voice followed her into the abyss.

"I'm here, Trask. But who the hell is this?"

CHAPTER SIXTEEN

Struck from behind, the Black Rose staggered, fell, and rolled with the momentum of the blow. She landed hard in a thicket of prickly cactus, struggling to shove back crushing walls of darkness. She cursed her foolishness and arrogance, knowing Cain's craven attack had caught her completely off guard.

A rush of blood thrummed through her ears and her head weighed a thousand pounds. Dark oblivion came in waves of sleep followed by aching wakefulness.

To give into the numbing black abyss now was to doom the occupants of the shack.

Her carelessness was inexcusable.

Feeling for the base of her neck, her fingers lingered on a duck's egg welt and came away sticky wet, and she cursed herself. If only she could stand.

Willing her eyes to open was triumph enough.

Columns of smoke were crawling along the sideboards as the flames danced and grew.

She had to save her friends. Somehow.

Above the din of crackling wood, Trask yelled into the night. "Dammit, Cain. They got Weezer."

"Take care of him," said the new voice. "I got one of 'em up here."

"We still got some of 'em trapped inside. You want me to come up?"

"Stay where you are. Take care of the boy," said Cain. "Watch the shack. Anybody sticks a nose out, you shoot it off."

"Damn right, I will."

Then Cain's voice came again to the Black Rose, masculine and gruff, demanding an answer. "What kind of get-up you got on, girl? You supposed to be some sort of Indian?"

The blurry outline of her attacker wore tall boots, jeans, and a loose linsey shirt. He came at her, snatched up her wrist in a merciless claw and lifted her to her feet.

The ghost face came into focus. It was cruel, with a wide open range of forehead sloping between hollow black eyes into a hook nose. The thick liquid voice dripped from pursed lips. "C'mere honey. Come to Papa Cain."

The Black Rose raised her knee to kick, lost her balance, and fell over sideways. Shoulder met granite with a splintering crunch. The urumi jumped free of her grip, clattering to the ground beside her.

Cain gathered a fistful of the black cape and again jerked her up, this time into a sitting position. "Gads, you're ugly," he said.

She forced herself to go limp like a possum, and

she held the pain at bay. Slowly, she regained her senses. Under the cloak, her fingers searched the earth for the hilt she had dropped.

Cain stepped backwards, hitched his thumbs into his gun belt. His rig was a sight to behold with tooled leather scrolling, hammered florets, and custom stitched bullet loops. Two big .44s fit backwards in fat holsters for the cross-draw, their ivory grips gleaming in the firelight.

Somewhere, the young Catalina had heard Benito Kahn once ruled an entire Mexican village with those guns and his fast action.

While her fingers slowly raked the ground, searching for the urumi, the Black Rose controlled her breathing. If she wanted to get out of this meeting alive, she would have to be as careful as she'd ever been in her life. Using ancient techniques learned in childhood, she slowed her heartbeat. Picturing the jangling clamor of pain inside her skull as a ball of bright red, she quietly dulled the hurt along with the color. Scarlet to pink, pink to white, white to transparent. As the ball washed away, the pain traveled with it.

"I sincerely hope your friends in the shack are praying for you," said Cain. "Maybe pray for an angel to swoop down out of heaven and carry all of you off. Ain't that what you church-goers believe in? Guardian angels?"

"I don't have any friends. I'm here alone."

"Confession time, little girl. I thought your type believed in confession, too."

"I don't know what you're talking about."

"Oh, honey. Papa Cain always knows when a little girl fibs." Cain whistled with disdain. "Wes Stark was my old saddle pard. You kill a man, least thing you can do is be decent enough to admit it. Now to be fair I don't I think you pulled the trigger on him. At least, not the way I heard it."

Below them, the front corner of the shack was an inferno, the wood popping under the mad orange fire.

"I imagine Wesley's killer is inside this shed right now -- getting it good, too. By God, I've seen burned flesh, and it ain't a pretty sight." Cain sniffed the air, watched for a reaction. "Yes sir, I do believe I smell a roast padre and some three blue chickens on the side."

The Black Rose snatched up her urumi and snapped out the blade into a whistling arc just missing Cain's shoulder.

A mistake she'd pay for. She was more groggy from the blow on her head than she'd imagined.

Cain's draw was swift, but he didn't pull the .44's trigger.

Not yet. Which was his mistake.

A second flash of the blade struck deep in his right shoulder. Both guns went off.

The Black Rose launched herself into the air, high and off the jagged crag of rock. Darting lines of hot lead spun under one arm and between her legs, drilling holes into her cloak, tugging at her decent.

She landed on her knees, flat on the flame engulfed roof of the shack.

Through smoke and shimmering waves of heat, Cain squared off and pointed both of his guns at her.

Under her weight, the roof gave way.

Twin explosions ripped the night air, hurtling death just over top her head.

The fall was less than ten feet, but she landed on her back, smashing into the table where she'd had supper less than an hour ago. The crack-up was enough to crush the breath from her lungs. She rolled to the floor gasping for air.

Then she was suspended between Mary and Adeline, and how she got there, she didn't know. She could only have been out for seconds. She coughed and a lance of white hot steel pierced both lungs.

Adeline bent low and crawled out of the tinderbox, turning around to help Mary pull the Black Rose through the split wood passage to the rocks outside.

They stretched her out under the stars next to Cassidy's inert frame.

"Goin' someplace, ladies?" said a familiar voice. Trask stood at the rear corner of the shack, his rifle held with both arms in an ineffective cradle carry. The Black Rose strained to rise to her feet. Within seconds Cain would arrive from the plateau above.

"You all stand real still," said Trask.

"Maybe some other time," said Adeline, "but not tonight." She outweighed the man by several pounds, had the height and reach over him. Trask's face blanched as she mashed an iron right into his guts, then walloped him with a hard left. A fast right uppercut to the jaw put him on the ground even as Cain skittered down the stone incline with both guns drawn.

"Gawd-almighty, you done it now," he said.

Striking a pose in a flat place between two scruffy pine shrubs, Cain was seconds away from pressing twin triggers. The Black Rose climbed to her feet and stood between Adeline and Mary. Their attacker was well out of reach, and her urumi was lost somewhere on the perch above. "I'm gonna do each one of you in the guts and leave you to die slow. But before I do, I want to tell you about Wes Stark, the boy you gunned down today. See, me and Wes, we—"

Cain's features stiffened and his jaw dropped with a silent oath as the guns fell from his suddenly inert fingers. His eyes rolled back in his head just before he pitched over onto his face. His last words were a muddy gurgle from deep in his throat.

Looking down at her feet, the Black Rose saw Cain's body, spread-eagle on the ground, a seven inch knife blade protruding from his back.

In the red blaze of the fire, Denver Three-Moons stepped from behind one of the bushes and joined the women. Aloof, detached, he planted a moccasin on Cain's belt and bent over to retrieve his knife. Pulling it slowly from its place in Cain's back, he said, "Dumb bastard always did talk too much."

CHAPTER SEVENTEEN

On the splintered wood of the rancho's boardwalk, Charles McKenzie kicked at the sand fleas flitting toward his gray wool trousers. He clutched the cracked handle of his valise tightly in his right hand. In the afternoon heat, his sweaty left hand held his closed umbrella.

With a lavender vest and light suit coat he was the picture of the wealthy Americano, here in the Nuevo Piño countryside to do business with a military aristocracy all too eager to flex its muscle on an international level.

Charlie Mac stood alone, waiting for Fino's man to lead him to the big house on the hill.

Claustrophobic and filthy, the northernmost boundary of the Fino-El Espolón ranch was a series of slumping sod huts and misshapen driftwood fence corrals crowded along a dry creek bed, its brushy banks gray, beige and brown.

Drops of sweat beaded up on McKenzie's neck. Of course, he wasn't dressed for direct sunlight.

Inside one of the corrals, a man opened a gate, and six or seven big cows funneled into a holding pen where two other men and a boy waited.

While McKenzie watched, the cowboys darted back and forth while the animals pounded circles around the perimeter.

Clouds of dirt flew with curse words attached.

"Vamanose!"

"Hup!"

One of the men yipped like a dog.

"Bisoño."

McKenzie sniffed hard, feeling the heat behind the word, though it wasn't aimed at him. He smelled sagebrush, cow flop, and his own desperation.

He'd left Dawson and the others behind in the cool third floor breeze of the city hotel to ride out early on a rented horse, to meet Fino and the German alone, before the wedding celebration as they had agreed the week before.

"Bisoño." *Greenhorn.*

A tentacleof red dust crawled with the breeze across the boardwalk, braking against McKenzie's city-polished shoes, and a hot gust kicked grit into his lowered eyes.

Tenderfoot.

The men continued to hoot while outside the corral fence, a beet-colored man, all cheese curds and applesauce stuffed into shirt and pants and sloppy boots, slouched away from the rail.

"You are Señor McKenzie?" said the cowboy.

Charlie Mac nodded, his tongue rough and still.

Like a dead mouse.

"Tully, Fino's brazo derecho. His, uh…right hand man." Tully shoved his stubby calloused hand forward when he got near. "Fino said you'd be in on one of the wagons."

He swiped his ragged hat off a balding scalp and wiped the sweat away with his long shirt sleeve. "I take y'r bag?"

McKenzie handed his case to Tully but kept hold of his umbrella. Holding it tight was like holding his last tie to civilization.

From the corral came another string of cursing.

Tully looked at the corral, then back at McKenzie.

"You ain't gonna need a bumbershoot. Ain't rained in Nuevo Piño for thirteen weeks. Likely won't for thirteen more."

"I like to be prepared." It was all he could think to say.

"I see from the way you're dressed. Reckon you're ready for the wedding." Tully cleared his throat and lobbed a ball of phlegm into the rusty sand. "We get fewer them than rain."

He nodded back toward the cow pen.

"Them boys are cutting out a blind cow."

McKenzie smiled politely, then nodded toward the corral. "I've got cows of my own back home. May I watch?"

"Belly up to the rail. Such as it is."

McKenzie thanked him and deliberately walked to the fence.

Inside the circle, a tall man with a blue shirt, dark

jeans, and black hat was in charge, dodging left and right behind a polled tan heifer, her course hair thick with flies.

"Ciudado," said the tall man, and a black haired boy pulled open a flimsy gate of barbed wire strung between three broken cedar poles.

"Okay, Miguel," said the kid.

The heifer spun but Miguel jumped in front of her. "Yah! Yah! Yah!"

The animal's left eye was almost completely blocked with a pinkish blob, a tumor.

McKenzie hoped the men weren't planning to keep her. Those things grew inside as well as out. He knew because his mother had died from the cancer.

The heifer put her head down, backed up one step, and turned clumsily away from the opening.

Miguel shot toward her with a yell, followed by a second man.

The heifer tromped past the kid and into a holding area off to the side of the corral.

Once the gate was secure, Miguel turned his attention to the other stand of cows.

"Let's get the next one," he said in English.

Shirts painted dark with sweat and dabbed with filth, the cowboys were all business, ignoring life outside the rough arena.

McKenzie gazed down, behind the grassy south pasture, to where the Fino - El Espolon's main house and buildings stood, the bunks, the stores of hay described in his letter of invitation. He reminded himself that these line shacks and corrals were only the northernmost edge.

The wedding celebration was to be held in an open meadow in front of the residence.

He breathed more easily as he watched the men in the corral, their methodical partnership as they cut out two black white-faced heifers, their steady hands and learned competence. These were professionals, as schooled in their art as the men McKenzie employed back home.

They knew cows and calves and nature. They cared for it in ways McKenzie could only imagine. He was a cattleman, but he only knew the business from one side. The side of sales receipts and auction slips.

These were caretakers.

Except all three men had firearms at their hip.

McKenzie swung the umbrella to his right shoulder and put one foot on the lowest fence rail.

From what remained of the winded beeves, Miguel singled out a young bull, slightly smaller than the others, the only black white-face left in the pen. Methodically the men took their positions, and the bull loped counter clockwise along the fence away from McKenzie, jackknifing back at the last minute toward the towhead.

Off guard, the kid stumbled and fell flat in the dust, the bull kicking and bucking as it drove past.

When it was clear the boy wasn't hurt, the men laughed and the towhead laughed too as the bull got close to the fence and started wheeling back around.

Sweat streamed down under McKenzie's collar.

He opened the umbrella against the sun with a snap.

The bull stopped at the noise, at the sudden flower-ing shape, startled, pawed the dirt, and spun in a circle.

"What the hell?" said Miguel.

Now the other cows saw the bull on the run from the umbrella and bolted away from Charlie Mac, past the cowboys, gathering into a heavy crowd at the far end of the pen. One bellowed out, then another, and the girls hit the fence, heaving against the barbed wire gate, then past it, the bull joining them in their increasingly frantic rush.

"The umbrella!" said the kid.

"What?" said McKenzie.

The cowboys spun on their heels, and the beeves broke loose onto the grassy south range.

"What?"

"Dammit, we lost 'em."

The man with the scarred eyebrow flung a stubby fin-ger toward McKenzie. "Shut-up your damned umbrella."

Before the shout could die, Miguel pulled an enormous iron barrel free from his belt. "Damn it all," he said.

Fire poured from the gun, and with three more rap-id explosions Charlie Mac's fine, black umbrella burst into a dizzy array of fabric tatters and shredded pine.

McKenzie's hold on America fell to the ground like a piñata at the end of a long day, broken and shredded. The wire tying him to civilization severed.

For his part, the cattle baron fell backwards, stumbling in his slick-soled shoes, landing with a thump, knocking the breath from his lungs. He gasped and crawled backward like a crab.

Tully got to him first, then Miguel and the man with the scar hovered like a solar eclipse, blocking out the light.

"Best dust yourself off," said Tully. "Fino is coming."

They reached down and pulled Charlie Mac to his feet just in time. An automobile with two highly-decorated militants in the front bounced down the white rock road from the main house. The open carriage with its flared fenders and sweeping engine cowl was painted brick red, and its barrel headlights and square mounted radiator, trimmed in glistening brass.

The red wood-spoked wheels stopped turning a scant ten feet from the trio of men. The driver shut off the engine and stood up from his black leather upholstered bench seat to reveal a broad navy chest splashed with medals. His thick stack of white hair was combed back into a curl which brushed his uniform's collar, and his big mustache might've been carved from whale bone. He leaned across the polished gold steering wheel.

"I am Fino, Military Governor. My companion is Gündelfinger, of the German Command. Join us."

Fino opened his hand.

Until now, McKenzie's communication with Fino had been handled by secretaries. This was their first time meeting in person.

Charlie Mac felt compelled to bow.

CHAPTER EIGHTEEN

Single file, the nuns and Father Cassidy wound down the gnarled market street at Nuevo Piño, waving away flies. Catalina Cristiana Rivera imagined they made a splendid picture against the squalid backdrop. Sister Adeline went first on her buckskin gelding, its black mane glistening in the desert sun. Then came Mary on the bay, cursing in French. She was followed by Catalina on her wiry black mare. Finally, as if emulating the Savior himself, the padre rode a humble donkey, his hands clasped together on the reins, his head lowered in faux prayer.

Or he was asleep. Looking over her shoulder, Lina wasn't sure which.

The morning's ride had provided a welcome respite for all of them. A rare school of rainclouds had played cat and mouse with the sun, giving them shade on the ride from Lohman's Siding.

Providing each of them a chance to sleep, if even for a few minutes in the saddle.

It had been simple work to gag Trask and Weezer and bind their hands together, but Adeline's continued insistence on last rites and proper burials had kept them busy with Cain for more than an hour. Naturally, Cassidy had been next to worthless, and as she watched him now, she wondered about his bottomless flask, held tight to his torso even in sleep. What demons did the liquor help him keep at bay?

For their part, the horses seemed to know the way across the range to Nuevo Piño.

Maybe they smelled water and were led by the nose to the wells of the Fino-Espolón estate. Maybe instinct told them to walk beside the rails. Catalina wasn't ready to buy into Cain's suggestion of a guardian angel. Only dumb luck had saved them last night — luck and an old friendship.

When bad things happened, Lina had always been taught to blame herself first. In this case, she'd been too sure of herself. Taken too many chances.

Maybe the Black Rose still had much to learn?

Whatever the case, she knew she wouldn't make the same mistakes again.

Lina pushed the unpleasant thoughts from her mind even as Mary's voice carried her back to the present. "I've never seen a more awful place in my life," she said.

The town was an ancient ruin on four or five acres of bedrock and blowing sand.

An open gutter of trickling sewage ran along the shoulder of the road, and children played in the muddy excrement. Through clouds of gnats, Lina saw centuries-old adobe dwellings, connected with crumbling walkways and wooden ladders.

She held her breath against the smell.

There were greasy, tattered rags hanging in a few windows, a sign announcing nickel beer in another. Open wagons fronted some of the dwellings with clumps of peppers and piles of flat fried bread. Flies gathered in twitching hordes on slabs of raw pork hanging in open doorways. A rawboned girl with scarred arms and a ripped tunic held a baby to her exposed breast. Father or husband, a stick of a man with a crop of white hair and a single front tooth leaned against a bullet-smashed brick wall in a yard littered with empty tin cans. His hand raised up as they passed, pulled by a heavenly string.

The opposite side of the street was dominated by a two-story brown brick building. The Royal Bank of Nuevo Piño was painted in English on the interior side of a sheet glass window and an easel was propped up just inside, showing off a tall, framed portrait.

The man in the picture wore an indigo tunic with red piping and fringed shoulder epaulets. His chest was a vast field of scattered stars — five and six point medals of all shapes and sizes with ribbons of blood red and ochre. He wore a waxed snarl of a mustache above his lantern jaw, and his hair seemed carved from a block of dirty marble.

Generalissimo Adrian Felipe Fino of the Federal Army.

Military Governor.

Three frame houses with white-washed siding

and black square windows were nestled in the bank's shadow like suckling pigs, one to the north, two to the south.

Pigs, or enormous dice, thought Lina, smirking at the allusion. Certainly any business dealings here were a gamble.

Behind the third house, she saw Charles McKenzie's 705 steamer, its tender loaded full of split wood, already turned around, with seven box cars parked behind the forest green luxury Pullman and a second passenger car. Even without smoke from its massive funnel stack or steam curling away in front of its stoic iron wheels, the train seemed impatient to move. Facing back along the tracks in the direction of Santo Tomas, the engine might leap to life at any second.

Watching the train, Lina half-ways expected it.

Just past the end of the adobe ruins, Adeline had reined her horse up to a broken hitching rail. Lina and Mary followed suit, staying in their saddles as the big nun crawled down from her horse. "Are you sure we're in the right place?" she said. "We didn't get turned around?"

With a lifted chin, Lina indicated the line of newly constructed rail, the sign in the bank window. She pointed at the strings of multi-colored paper triangles zig-zagging across the street above their heads and said, "Wedding decorations."

The garish flags flapped like bats in the dry wind, and the rainbow colors matched a painted wood sandwich sign at the corner of the bank. "La Boda." An arrow pointing the way out of town.

Somewhere in the adobe houses a baby cried and a child, not older than four or five, waddled through the stream of filth to tug at Adeline's habit. "Como estas?" she squawked. Adeline plucked the little girl from the stream of waste and cradled her in both arms.

"¿Cuál es su nobre?" she said.

"Verónica," said the child.

"You are a pretty girl," said Adeline. "Are you hungry?"

Up until now, Cassidy had remained still, taking in their surroundings, watching as Adeline picked up the emaciated girl. "Place seems mostly deserted," he said.

"They're all at the wedding," said Mary.

"Whether they want to be, or not," said Cassidy.

The road ahead led past a broken down barn wood hovel patched with slabs of rusted tin. A bent smokestack, wired together, bowed over the threshold where a venerable old soul in a moth-eaten blue coat and trousers stepped into daylight. Three scrawny children followed behind, dressed in flour sack dresses and brown canvas shirts.

"Not everybody's at the wedding," said Adeline.

Without another word, Cassidy spurred Diablo in the elder's direction.

At the same time, the gaunt woman from the open-doored adobe joined them, the skeletal baby still latched onto its sagging supply of nourishment. "Sister?" said the woman with a heavy accent.

"My name is Adeline."

The woman bowed but kept her distance from the nun. "Come, Verónica."

"Verónica es bonita."

The woman ignored the compliment and raked the air, reaching for her older child even as she struggled to balance the baby she held. And still more offspring appeared from the adobe home.

A family of stick and bone, though Lina.

Adeline's face filled with compassion. Kneeling at the river of waste, she put Verónica on her feet, and drew her mother down next to them. "Mary, hand me some bread?"

"You think we ought to?"

"Fine," she said, standing up to step directly into the sewage. "I'll do it myself."

"No, let me," said Mary, dismounting.

"We will need to be on our way," said Lina. "We must arrive at the Fino wedding before it begins, lest we draw undue attention to ourselves."

"I just love the way you talk," said Mary as she rummaged through her saddle bag. "*Lest we draw undue attention*, so on and so forth," she said. "Here, Addy." She handed Adeline a golden brown brick of unsliced bread.

Lina turned to Cassidy as Diablo returned. Stopping next to her mare, he said, "We were correct. Most of the town has gone to the wedding."

"Is the old man going?"

"He's hoping I'll give him a ride."

"As if Diablo would allow it."

"I'm hoping you will give him a ride."

Catalina exhaled with disgust. "I didn't ride all this way to be a Samaritan," she said.

"No," said Adeline. "You rode all this way to be a killer. Maybe our Father has a different plan for you."

Lina felt her face turn to stone and her eyes bore down on the nun. "My father is dead."

She turned to Cassidy. "Your peon has all afternoon. Let him walk."

Lina urged the mare forward without a backwards look.

******

With Mary and Cassidy on her heels, Catalina arrived at the northernmost gate under an iron lattice sign stretched between twin beams of oak which read Fino-Espolón Ranch. At the threshold, a pit was dug with cement foundations on each side and inlaid iron rails spanning the gap. Lina's mare hopped across the cattle guard followed by the bay. By the time Diablo caught up, they were riding past a row of sorry sod huts and corrals built on the edge of a brushy creek.

In the distance, near a gray shed with a tin roof and a weather vane, something glinted in the sun.

"It's an automobile," said Lina. "Do you see it, Cassidy?"

"I'm not surprised," said Mary. "It's obvious Fino doesn't spend his money on corral fences." She sniffed. "I expected better."

"1910 Willys-Overland," said Cassidy.

Lina questioned him with her eyebrows.

"It's just something I've picked up on," he said. "Like some people know about horses. I know about automobiles."

"I can't imagine a more useless thing to know about," said Lina. She turned her horse and brought it in close to more readily speak with the others.

"I'd sure enjoy going for a ride in a car," said Mary. "American, isn't it? Have you ever seen anything so beautiful?"

"Can you drive this Willys car?" said Lina. "If the situation warranted?"

Cassidy smiled and gave a wink as he said, "Is the Pope Catholic?" Then he removed the cork from his flask and took a drink.

"You've been saving that line until Adeline wasn't with us, haven't you?" said Mary. "Hell's bells, she is absolutely going to drive me to drink."

Cassidy held up his flask, and Mary reached down from her bay to retrieve it.

"Don't mind if I do."

Lina swatted her hand away with her leather reins. "Leave it. You too, Marshal. As much liquor as you've poured down, I'm surprised we're not lugging you along in a pail."

"How many flasks do you have, anyway?" said Mary.

Cassidy's expression was stoic. "That is none of your affair."

"Understood. I've had a few affairs of my own."

Cassidy winked at her. "When this is over, we go somewhere? You and me?"

"I have an idea where you'll both end up," said Lina. Then to Cassidy: "Enough prattle. You lead the way, Padre. There's an old man with a straw hat up there near the gate. Present us as emissaries of his royal eminence, Monsignor Andronicus of Santo Tomas. Tell him we were sent to present the honorable General Fino with a gift in honor of the auspicious sacramental event unfolding today."

"What gift?" said Mary.

"I don't have one," said Lina.

"But, you just said—"

"What needed to be said to get us through the gate," said Cassidy.

"What are the bride and groom called, anyway?" said Mary. "I know it's Fino's son, but do we know their names? Won't it look suspicious if we don't know their names?"

"This isn't going to work, Catalina."

"Just say the words," said Lina.

They rode up beside the tin barn wood building with its tin roof and weather vane. A painted board sign advertised free drinks in honor of the holy matrimony. One per customer.

The gatekeeper with the straw hat was named Tully.

Lina's plan didn't work.

"I'm sorry Father," said the ruddy old drover as he wiped the sweat from his hairless scalp with the sleeve of his shirt before replacing his straw hat. "You're strangers to Nuevo Piño, and the General said absolutely no strangers allowed."

Cassidy flashed Lina a scowl. *I told you so.*

Diablo snorted and lunged at Tully like he planned to eat the fat of his belly for lunch. The cowboy jumped back, nearly losing his balance.

"You all just turn around and go back where you

came from," he said.

Cassidy turned the donkey around and the rifle boot with its carbine swung out and back like a pendulum.

Lina walked her mare into the space between Diablo and Tully. If the gatekeeper couldn't be buffaloed, maybe he could be bribed. "We come bearing gifts," she said.

"He already said that," said Tully. "It don't matter none to me."

"We have gifts for everyone. You too, friend. " Lina twisted the gold band off her middle finger and tossed it into the dirt.

Tully picked the ring up and polished it on his shirt. He gave it a studious look, squinting his eyes to examine it. Finally, he handed it back.

"Now I know you ain't what you claim to be. No bride o' Christ sworn to poverty would wear such a ring."

"You misunderstand, cowboy," said Mary.

"I don't misunderstand nothin'," said Tully. "Now turn around and git."

Catalina's patience was wearing thin. On the other side of the open gate, at the end of the long driveway, the red Willys automobile was parked under a green and white striped awning near a three-story white stone mansion. Adjacent to the house was a large cathedral built in the same fashion. A red and gold striped circus tent dominated the luxurious green lawn fronting both structures, and children rode ponies and a camel.

Under the awning, three men stood next to the

car. One of them wore a light gray suit and had a bushy red beard.

McKenzie.

Dawson couldn't be far away.

To trek as far as they had through heat and hardship only to be stopped within smelling distance of the enemy was too much.

Lina's eye caught a ragged instrument leaning against the side of the makeshift cantina. She remembered it from the night she faced Dawson in front of the hotel, when McKenzie had watched from the porch.

She took a chance.

"Isn't this Mr. McKenzie's umbrella? Or what's left of it?" she said, eyeing the tatters.

Tully didn't bother to turn his head. Instead, his voice was calm and measured. Lina could tell she had his attention.

"You know Mr. McKenzie?"

"We're friends of his," said Cassidy.

"I don't know," said Tully. "I'm still not sure why you'd show up now and not on the train. It all seems a little peculiar."

"It's very peculiar," said a voice, and Lina turned to see Adeline riding the buckskin between Mary and Cassidy. Veronica, the girl from the village sat between the nun and the saddle horn, and an equally skinny boy rode behind on the cantle. He had his arms wrapped around Adeline.

In the horse's wake, more than a dozen children and a handful of old men and women followed.

"We arrived in town earlier, but as you can see, we've been tending to the sick and needy." Adeline flashed Tully a smile. "It's what we do."

"General Fino said most of the folks from town was already here."

"Ride the horsy," said Verónica, pointing across the field.

"Most, doesn't mean all," said Adeline. "Some of the more desperate families need special consideration. Not all the children are as healthy as others. Shouldn't they see the wonders of the General's hospitality, too?"

Verónica clapped her hands at the sight of the circus animals.

Tully hooked a callused finger against his lower lip and brushed his whiskers. Then he looked at Cassidy. "I'll need to take the carbine you're carrying. Just until you leave. The General said no firearms."

The marshal withdrew the rifle from its boot and turned it over to Tully.

"It's a good thing you're doing. Why didn't you tell me about this before?"

"Modesty stilled my tongue," said Cassidy.

"Modesty isn't usually the Father's strong suit," said Adeline. "Nor my sister's."

She held Lina's gaze as she rode past Tully and, with a smile, led Cassidy, Mary, and the broken, starving families of Nuevo Piño through the gate onto the grounds of the sumptuous ranch.

CHAPTER NINETEEN

Inside the circus tent, Adeline set about gathering food and drinks for the families in her wake. The townspeople already in attendance didn't appear to be any more healthy than the peasants Adeline had brought to the festival, meaning everyone was thin and pasty as wallpaper. All the youngsters gathered together on their haunches around the ring of colorful jugglers and agile acrobats — paeons and privileged alike. The smiling expressions of the children were indistinguishable one from another.

A durable man, not more than three feet tall, with a pompadour and a long waxed mustache wore white pants and an open shirt with huarache sandals. He led two similarly coifed and dressed men on guitar and harp. A fourth man, wet with sweat, clanged two cymbals together between each song, a kind of informal martial punctuation.

The music they played had been a favorite of Aquiles Rivera. Called *son jalisciense* or *mariachi* in Guadalajara, the lively tunes planted themselves in Lina's breast. Buds of melancholy to be watered by tears.

Lina forced herself not to listen.

Inside the tent, four long tables were laid out end to end. Covered with white linen, the tables overflowed with bone china plates, every plate offering white cakes or peach pie, cherry cobbler or mounds of rice pudding garnished with mint leaves. At the middle of each table was a glass centerpiece filled with flowers.

Clowns with white faces and red noses worked as servers, filling glasses with lemonade they dipped from wooden barrels. Another set of clowns worked chipping blocks of ice in red wagons with painted black tongues.

Lina accepted a cup, raised the drink to her lips and froze. In line behind her, standing casually beside a table chewing, with chocolate cake frosting all over his cheeks, was Paco.

When he saw her looking at him, the corners of his mouth twitched with mischief before resuming his typically aloof demeanor. "Hola, prima," he said.

"Hola, yourself," said Lina, putting a firm hand on his shoulder. "How did you come to be here? You should be in Santo Tomas. Mother Mercy will be worried."

Paco's toothy expression was full of candor. "The big 705, she is fast. I have been here more than a day."

Cassidy swept three oatmeal cookies from a platter and shared them with Lina and Mary.

"He stowed away on the train," said Cassidy with a smirk.

"Mother won't even notice I've gone," said Paco.

"Did you leave her a note?"

Paco's smile betrayed him. "Si. I left her a note," he agreed.

"You still should not be here," said Lina. "We have work to do, and there may be danger. I can't watch out for you."

The boy's eyes sparkled. "You are mistaken, Catalina Cristiana Rivera. It is Paco who watches out for you." He drew her ear down to his lips. "I was mistaken. Charles McKenzie is no hero."

Outside, the band played Jarable Tapatico, the Mexican Hat Dance. While Lina, Mary, and Cassidy regained their mounts and walked them into the shadow of the grande villa, Paco stayed inside to help Adeline with the children.

Fino's tremendous stone house, built in the French belle epoch style had no shortage of ornamentation. Its three stories of large arched windows looked out over semi-circular patios edged in curved wrought-iron rails. Below the ground-level doors were framed with ornate stone carvings. Thick green hedges had been meticulously pruned into perfect geometric shapes along the façade and the steps leading to the enormous entrance shone like polished glass.

Next door to the house, the church had been designed in a similar style, its stucco walls decorated with ceramic tiles and indented with narrow stained glass. The high, round-roofed bell tower was topped with a gold tile dome, and the courtyard laid in between them, was a garden full of European extravagance. Lina wondered who watered all the green growing plants and shrubs. In the arid climate, it would be a full time job.

"This man, Adrian Felipe Fino, does well for himself," said Cassidy.

"When we arrived, I saw him go into the house with McKenzie and another man close to where they parked the automobile. There is a side door there," said Lina. "The men were deep in conversation. Not the happy idle chatter as normally befits a wedding."

"I'd like to know what they're talking about," said Mary.

"A business deal no doubt," said Cassidy.

A proper young man in a military uniform bowed to Catalina and Mary, then offered to take their horses to a nearby stable. Playing their parts as women of the church, they smiled and blessed him.

When the man walked past Diablo, the donkey huffed, and Cassidy said, "The donkey stays with me." A look of relief passed on the man's face, and he quickly moved on.

They watched the soldier lead the black mare and bay gelding down a sloping road of crushed white rock to a long barn situated several hundred feet down the hill. There were more soldiers milling around there, some with rifles slung over their shoulders. All wore the dress uniform of the Federales.

Mary whistled low to herself. "I just love the sight of men in uniforms."

"I just love the sight," said Cassidy.

The vast sweep of the rancho was almost overwhelming.

Situated on a high plateau, the surrounding country was visible for miles, dark greens and burnt umber fading to rugged gray-blue mountains on the horizon. It was a panorama only a few could afford.

"I'm curious as to what the wedding party is wearing," said Mary. "I've never been to such a high-falootin' wing-ding before."

"I'm more curious about McKenzie and Fino's conversation," said Lina, shading her eyes from the sun as she scanned the house. "What's the best way to get inside?"

"Let's walk to the church," said Mary, shoveling cookie crumbs into her face.

"Seems a logical place for a couple of sisters to go," Lina said. "Perhaps we could light a candle in thanks for our safe journey."

"Perhaps we'll catch a glimpse of the bride or groom," said Mary. "I'll bet her dress is fabulous."

They walked past a series of tall whitewashed poles, each of them flying a series of red, white and green flags. At the church, sheathes of flower bouquets decorated the wrought-iron railings of the stone stairway leading up to the broad, oaken front doors.

The left door cracked open, and a handsome young man in a blue uniform festooned with medals came out onto the top step and conversed with three other men dressed in military regalia.

Mary stopped a vibrant young woman with a blue ribbon braided through her long, ebony tresses and asked about the young man. "It is Fernando Angel Fino, the groom," the girl replied.

"The General's son?"

"Si," said the girl.

"Who is his bride?" said Mary.

"The lady Alejandra waits inside," said the girl with a giggle.

"I'd give a cat's three whiskers to see her wedding dress," said Mary. She clutched Lina's arm. "Let's walk around to the back of the church. Maybe we can sneak inside?"

"I think we—"

The words were suddenly charcoal in Lina's throat, dry and hard. She tried to speak, but could only taste ashes as she caught sight of a man walking back along the way they came.

Sauntering along, away from the house and the circus tent, his hands casually stuffed in his pockets and wearing his damned Confederate campaign hat, Tut Dawson made his way toward the cantina. He wore dark green canvas dungaree pants and a loose fitting beige blouse that fluttered in the light breeze. At roost on his head, the Confederate cavalry hat.

Cassidy saw him too, and raised an eyebrow, looking at Lina in silent question.

Yes, she nodded. *There is your man.*

With a steady tic in his cheek, the marshal deliberately looked away, back across the open country.

"What's wrong?" said Mary. "What is it?"

"Tut Dawson. He's walking back down the way we came, toward the cattle corral and the gate. Toward the cantina"

"Where is he?" said Mary. "I don't see him?"

While Mary stood on tiptoe and scanned their surroundings, Catalina checked off her options.

Follow Dawson or find McKenzie?

Learn what the railroad man had in store for Santo Tomas, or avenge her family?

She ground her back teeth and damned her luck.

"Watch Dawson," she told Cassidy. "Don't let him out of your sight. He doesn't know you, so you'll have the advantage. I'll join you after Mary and I find McKenzie and learn what there is to learn from him. Then we will make the butcher pay."

"I told you before. I'm not here to kill him," said Cassidy. "We will take him alive."

"We'll take him together, damn you," said Catalina. "It will be Dawson's choice whether he lives or dies."

She held his gaze until the marshal blinked. "You may damn me, Catalina, but I fear in doing so, you damn yourself."

"Damn your philosophy too, lawman. Either stand with me, or stay out of my way."

"Back at the convent, Mother Mercy suggested you were the weakest of us three. You talk loud for such a weakling," said Cassidy.

She watched the marshal depart with Diablo before turning to take Mary by the arm.

"We've lost enough time sight-seeing," she said. "Let's see about getting into the house."

Mary whistled. "Shall we try knocking? But what will we say when they answer?"

Lina wrinkled her brow with an expression of concern. "I do believe you're a bit flushed, dear. Are you sure you're feeling all right? Let's get you inside where it's cool."

Picking up on Lina's play-acting, Mary fanned herself with her hand and agreed. "Oh, my yes. Let's do find us some shade."

They circumvented the front of the house with its chattering guests and passersby to slip unseen past the polished red automobile under the green and white striped awning. Behind the Willys, a small garage built of white stone with hinged wooden doors sat open, its bay littered with car tools. Lina saw a lever-handled railroad jack, a wood-spoked rim with no tire, and three empty oil cans. The smell of gasoline permeated the area.

They turned to the side of the house, a polished wood door with a brass handle stood slightly ajar.

They stepped into a small washroom furnished with a porcelain basin and heavy ceramic pitcher full of water. A fluffy pink towel hung from a brass rail on the beige stone wall and a tan upholstered daybed peeked out from an adjacent alcove.

Lilacs and peppermint were a welcome relief to the driveway's stink of gas.

Immediately, a bean pole with combed back white hair wearing the rank of major met them.

Even the hired help were military. Lina noted the butler had only a single medal, a sky blue ribbon pinned directly over his heart. "May I help you, sisters?" He wasn't any older than Lina, but his back was stooped and his voice frail and cold like morning window frost.

Leaning heavily on Lina's left shoulder, Mary slumped even farther and let out a groan.

"I don't think Sister Mary is at all good," said Lina. "I fear the poor dear's been affected by the heat."

"I'm Tooms," said the man. "Let me help."

Lina allowed Mary to fall into Tooms' arms.

As he walked her to the daybed, Lina cracked him over the head with the pitcher.

Lights out.

Together, the women folded Mr. Tooms in half and lowered him to the cushions of the daybed, then gathered up the pitcher shards from the floor. The tired man looked like he had decided to indulge in a quick afternoon siesta.

"Let's go find some shade," said Lina.

They left the washroom for an open foyer devoid of life. By itself, the round room was bigger than most of the shacks in Nuevo Piño. Green-cushioned stools with gold-leaf covered legs lined the walls under an ornate wooden chair rail. In the center of the room, two flights of red carpeted stairs with a curved white railing led up to a second floor loft. On silver chains, an elegant five-tiered crystal chandelier dangled between the stairwells from a glass skylight. The sunlight caught the crystals, and the walls were awash with rainbow reflections.

Just behind the stairs, under the second floor walkway, French balcony doors opened from the foyer onto a terracotta brick lined courtyard. Lina heard a murmur of male voices.

Lina and Mary crept around the stairs until they

saw Charles McKenzie sitting at a glass-topped table with Fino and another man who had blonde hair and was dressed in a black suit.

Fino poured coffee from a silver carafe as he spoke.

"It's something of a personal nature for me," he said. "I hope you understand."

Parked on the wall beside the open doors, an ornate free-standing walnut closet wardrobe gave Lina an idea. Trimmed with hand carvings, the top of the wardrobe was otherwise open to provide ventilation. Lina crept up to the cabinet doors, clicked them open and was met with the stale smell of old linen and a single white shirt on a wire hanger.

Lina ushered Mary into the wardrobe. "I think we've found our shade," she said, and crawled in behind her before shutting the door.

Inside the closet it was musty and dark, but the conversation on the patio was most illuminating.

******

Charlie Mac had finished only half a cup of Fino's exquisite Columbian coffee when he realized he'd been had. Cautious, he asked Fino to clarify his last statement. The General refilled his cup.

"It's something of a personal nature for me," he said. "I hope you understand." He put down the silver carafe and laced his fingers together on the table place in front of him.

Across from McKenzie with his back to the open foyer of the house, Mr. Gündelfinger stared at him from under expertly clipped blonde bangs.

"I'm afraid I don't understand at all," said McKenzie. "I thought we had an agreement. I need working capital to buy out the property owners of Santo Tomas and hire a work crew to begin the new spur line. As a silent partner, your investment assures you a place at the top of my board of directors."

Fino dabbed at the corners of his mouth with a napkin. His expression was one of sour embarrassment. As if McKenzie had belched or passed gas.

Charlie Mac continued, "When the Santo Tomas spur is a reality my company will own land for more than ten miles on either side of the track." Charlie Mac cleared his throat. "It's not so much about transportation, gentlemen, as it is about securing the real estate and owning the mineral rights."

"We understand what your endeavor is about, and we applaud your foresight," said the German.

"Which is why you'll find a handsome honorarium in the envelope there." Fino sipped his coffee. "I'm not ungrateful for the gift of your rails, your engine, the luxury passenger car you've given to me."

"Pullman, isn't it?" said Gündelfinger.

"Given you?"

"As a wedding gift for Fernando and Alejandra. We're forever grateful." Fino fluttered his hand in apology. "I know it will be difficult to explain to your contractors. I'm sure they don't understand the finer points of international friendship the way you and I do. I'm sure you'll find a way to explain it."

Charlie Mac picked up the envelope and opened the flap. He counted the bills with his thumb.

One hundred dollars. American.

When a million had been promised.

McKenzie labored to respond. What to say? How to say it?

"Why, this is…"

The entire situation was ludicrous — would seem comical if it weren't so bloody serious.

The German spoke slow, as if to a child. "I believe in America this is what is known as a hostile take-over." His English was impeccable.

"Santo Tomas is close to my heart," said Fino. "I have good reason to desire her. To hold her in my hand. To own her." He held out his open palm. "When I was young, I drank from the eternal springs, and loved Santo Tomas with all my heart. I pledged myself to her."

Abruptly, he hand snapped shut, into a hard, white-knuckled fist.

"She spurned me," he said.

Charlie Mac nervously emptied his cup, and pushed himself away from the table.

"Jetzt zerstöre das Dorf," said the German.

"What? No," said McKenzie.

"May I refresh your coffee?" said the German, picking up the carafe.

"Let Tooms handle it," said Fino, snapping his fingers. "Tooms? Tooms?"

"You're mad," said McKenzie. "Did you hear what he said about Santo Tomas? You can't simply steal my train, appropriate my track…"

"I have stolen nothing," said Fino. "If you'd care to

wire your bank, you'll find my business colleagues here have made all the necessary property transfers with your company. Forgive me if you weren't notified in advance."

"The General hates to be the bearer of bad tidings," said Gündelfinger.

"The Sioux City and Orient company," began McKenzie.

"Has been paid in full," said Fino. "All you owed, with interest. By me."

McKenzie's shirt collar constricted his airways, his suit coat seemed too tight. All his dreams. His plans for the future. All he aspired to be.

Stolen out from under him by this Mex sonuvabitch and his European lapdog.

Charlie found himself laboring to breathe and his vision was blurred.

"We…had a deal." It was all he could think to say.

"And you have my thanks for upholding your end of the bargain. You've rid the land of the Riveras."

"But the people of Santo Tomas?"

Gündelfinger tsk-tsked with his lips, then delivered several sentences in German to Fino before he switched back to English. "I look forward to seeing it and reporting back to the Emperor," said Gündelfinger.

As Fino's chest expanded, the medals on his tunic glinted in the sun and he raised his cup high to toast his colleague. "I look forward to showing you. I value the empire's friendship."

"As Wilhelm values you," said Gündelfinger.

McKenzie blinked twice, trying to comprehend

what he was hearing.

Gündelfinger looked at his pocket watch. "Oh, my, General. I believe it's nearly time for the nuptials to begin."

"Si, si," said Fino. "We mustn't delay. This is the happiest day of my son's life. I must not keep him waiting." He tossed his napkin to the table. "We will leave for Santo Tomas immediately after the wedding. This is going to be a day to remember."

"For many reasons," said the German.

McKenzie's face burned and the ache in his stomach spread like blood on a cotton blotter.

Fino read his eyes and nodded. "Do feel free to ride along if you wish." He showed his line of straight, white teeth. "There is no charge for mi amigos."

McKenzie watched the two men stroll into the foyer of the house and disappear behind the great curving staircase before opening the front door to walk outside.

With no one to hear him, he held the napkin to his lips and sobbed.

CHAPTER TWENTY

Catalina left the cupboard like she'd been shot from a cannon, banging the door, marching across Fino's marble inlaid floor to blow through the main entrance hot on the men's heels.

She didn't care if she were seen or heard or later recognized as the famous executioner of the pig-nosed bastard General. She wanted to see Fino on his knees, her razor-edged urumi around his throat — begging for mercy.

Begging to keep his head.

Outside, the crowd was flowing across the grass toward the open doors of the towering church, and two acrobats dressed in orange and pink helped Adeline corral roving hordes of happy, laughing niñas y niños.

"Lina, wait," said Mary, hurrying to keep up as they bounded over the threshold. "It's not good. This isn't the place. Don't—"

"Didn't you hear? This is the man who paid McKenzie and Dawson to take my family."

"I heard, yes. I heard, but there are children here, this isn't the way." Mary's feeble protests were dust in Lina's windstorm of rage. "There are more important things. Didn't you hear what the German said?"

"I heard a lot of gibberish, but I understood the tone well enough."

Mary grabbed Lina's hand and refused to let go. "Sister," she said, as two nearby villagers gave them an odd look. Mary placed her other hand on Lina's shoulder and held her fast. "Sister, please listen. You brought me because I understand the German language. Listen to me, now."

Lina accepted Mary's directive. "Speak fast."

"At one point, you'll remember Charles McKenzie asked about Santo Tomas and the German answered in his native language. What he said was the people of Santo Tomas will be as swiftly ushered away as was your family. He said McKenzie would see how efficient thirty armed men on thirty trained horses can be."

"They are planning to simply sack the town in one night?"

"Even worse," said Mary. "The German said it should hardly take the entire night."

"It's hard to believe Fino would cross the border on a whim? Risk an American reprisal?"

Mary said, "But they won't see Fino. They will see men dressed like Garcia and Denver Three-Moons. They're taking a page from McKenzie's book. The German said so."

In the ancient myths taught by her brothers, such base villainy was commonplace. Theresa, her mother, had stoked Lina's warrior spirit with the *Iliad* and *Odyssey*, had excited her imagination with *Henry V* and *The Tempest*. In those stories, heinous blackguards were commonplace, the order of the day.

In real life she'd known drunks, philanderers, thieves, even killers. But never had she known such a ruthless proponent of mass slaughter.

Fino's broad backside, covered by his navy blue military tunic sauntered slightly ahead of Gündelfinger's skinny frame as they casually merged with a group of local well-wishers who bowed and doffed their caps in deference. Fino beamed, nodded, and preened. He put his hand on a girl's head, bent to kiss a withered grandmother on the cheek.

At the sound of Lina's approach, the German turned first, his fingers curled around a thin, tan cigarette. He nudged the General.

"Adrian Felipe Fino," said Lina. Fists clenched, her fingernails dug into her palms. Her heart raced.

The General turned and faced her. "Sister?"

"I am Catalina Cristiana—"

"Romero," cried Mary, darting between Lina and the big man. "We are sisters Catalina and Mary Romero."

"Romeros, the both of you? Sister sisters?" said Fino, drawing back with an amused expression.

"Get out of my way, Mary," said Lina.

At the sound of her voice, Fino's head leaned to one side. "Do I know you, querida?"

"Querida?"

Darling. Cherished one.

Lina raised her eyebrows. The word forced her to

step back. Something in the General's voice silenced her tongue.

Again, "Do I know you?"

He waited, searching her face for an answer.

Mary remained between them, a rock.

The German nursed his cigarette and a curl of smoke drifted from his lips to dissipate on the wind. Finally, he put his hand on Fino's arm. "Perhaps if the sisters will excuse us," said Gündelfinger.

The men turned to funnel into the church.

"Fino," said Lina, and the General was attentive one last time.

She put as much menace into her voice as she could. "You don't know me. But you will."

Fino's eyes sparkled with curiosity, but he didn't smile, and Lina saw him glance over his shoulder twice more before disappearing into the church.

Mary spun on her heel and pounded Lina's shoulders. "What kinda piss-for-brains idea was that? You could've got us both slung up on the rack."

"He'll pay for what he's done to my family," said Lina.

"Right. Sure. Caw, caw, caw, says the blackbird. The mighty Rivera with her silly sword-thing. Fino will pay. Dawson will pay. It's all we've been hearing from you for three days straight: pay, pay, pay."

"I've got to find Charles McKenzie," said Lina, retracing her steps back toward the house.

"You need to find more than just him, Black Rose."

Lina stopped. "What do you mean?"

Mary marched ahead to face her at the entrance. "Do you hear yourself? The way you talk tickles me pink, but you're thick as these stone walls. Mother Mercy sent four of us down here, not one. We need to pick our battles and then work together. It's not always about you."

Lina felt her breast swelling with emotion. Her breath came in shallow, rapid succession. Up until now, Mary had been her stalwart companion. If Cassidy seemed reticent or Adeline too preoccupied with matters of faith, Lina thought she could rely on Mary.

Now, she wasn't so sure.

"You don't know what it's like...," said Lina.

Mary put a gentle hand to Lina's face. "I do know," she said. Her voice was calm. Soothing. "Oh, honey. I do know what it's like."

Lina jerked away and looked past her to the tent. Adeline was there with Paco, still riding herd over the children, mopping at their faces, gathering them into groups to lead them to the church. The nun lifted a screaming infant from the arms of an elderly woman, caught sight of Lina, and waved with a wide smile. Paco ran toward them.

Lina shifted her focus back to Mary. "I have to find Cassidy," she said.

"Hola, sisters," said Paco.

"Just who I needed to see," said Lina. "Do you know where the marshal is?"

"Si, si," said Paco.

"Show me," said Lina.

Paco picked up her hand to lead her away. "You ain't gonna like it," he said.

*****

Deep inside the ranch cantina, Cassidy sprawled over a table of scattered, cracked poker chips and dog-eared cards. Spilled liquor stained the wood and made the floor sticky and rank, and Catalina held her breath as she walked past a fetid silver spittoon filled to the brim.

A fat man, rank and damp wearing a tiny black sombrero, its crown taller than the diameter of the brim rounded the bar to intercept her. When he spoke, his jowls flung drops of sweat and spittle into the air like a kitchen drudge shaking out a sponge. "Hola, señoritaaaa," he drew out the vowel. "You wanna something cool to drink, seeeester?"

"You make a mistake, Javier," said an older Mexican sitting in the corner. "She no wanna cool. This one, she wanna something hot."

"Zat right, niña? You wanna hot?"

"I wanna you get out of my way," said Catalina, refusing to slow her pace as she brushed by the letch. At the sound of her voice, Cassidy stirred, lifted his head a few inches and raised his eyebrows.

"Bitch nun," said Javier. He spit and the old man rocked back in his corner chair with a howl.

"You lose today, Jefa," he said. "Maybe next time, eh?"

Lina stopped two feet from Cassidy's table and stared down at the wreckage he'd made of himself in such a short time. The old man's cackles died away, and the fat man waddled back around to his place behind the bar.

Outside, the wind picked up and buffeted the barns wooded walls, sweeping the floor of dust, rattling the shutters and shaking the cloudy window. Inside, there was no sound except the tick-tock of a heavy mantel clock perched on a thin shelf behind the bar.

"Look at you," said Catalina. "A United States marshal."

This time, Cassidy didn't bother to raise his head. Instead, he rolled his face away from the surface of the table and merely cracked his eyes. "Deputy," he said.

He pronounced it, *deppitty.*

The tall clear bottle on Cassidy's table was two-thirds air, the liquid at the bottom an odd shade of rusty orange. His empty tumbler mimicked his head, lolling on its side. Catalina set it upright with a forcible impact.

"You wanna drink from his bottle, you go 'head," called Javier. "You pay me when you leave. The padre, he no pay me."

Again, Lina ignored the barkeep and addressed the marshal. "You were going to watch Dawson. Where is he?"

The reply was little more than a murmur. "Tut-tut," he said. "Dunno no tut-tut."

Catalina shoved the table aside, its splintered legs scraping the hard wood floor.

When Cassidy lurched forward, she caught his cassock with her right hand and levered him backwards, his rickety seat protesting with a squawk. "I said, where's Dawson?"

This time Cassidy opened his eyes, and Lina saw the reluctance there.

"You're afraid," she said.

He licked his lips, moved his head to the side. "Not how you think."

CHAPTER TWENTY-ONE

Keeping her face to Cassidy, Lina spoke to Javier. "Make some coffee," she said. "Strong and hot."

"You no pay, I no make—"

Lina stopped the rebuttal with a loud clearing of her throat. Then, gently. "Make the damn coffee…*amigo.*"

"Best hop to it, Jefe," said the old man, a chuckle in his voice. "Hop, hop, hop."

Javier set to work with a string of curse words under his breath.

Cassidy kicked out a boot, hooking a nearby chair with his toe. "Rest yourself," he said.

"I'll rest when we've done what we came here to do," said Lina.

Behind the bar, Javier banged and clanged conspicuously. The clock continued to tick.

Lina looked around the interior of the place. It was nothing more than a frame shed of rickety boards sided with knotty grey wood. Gaps in the timber were wide enough to stick her thumb through, and

Lina sneezed on the dust sifting through from the nearby corral. The bar in front of Javier was nothing more than two wide rough-cut boards balanced on two beer barrels. In the corner of the room, Cassidy's polished walking stick was propped against the wall.

It shared the same color and complexion as the marshal. It might have been as whiskey-soaked as its owner.

"Where's your rifle?" said Lina. "Don't tell me you left it with Diablo?"

"Sold it to the fella who took it when we rode up," said Cassidy. "Tully."

Lina sat on the chair, smoothing her dress over her knees.

"I see. You sold the rifle." The words were tough as iron, as rotten tasting as the musty smell of the closet where she and Mary hid.

Eventually, the warm, burnished aroma of roasting coffee filled the air.

"I wasn't always like this, y'know," said Cassidy. "There was a time the only reason I'd traipse into a squalid hole like this was to pull out a snake."

Something about his voice tugged at Lina, inspired a wave of compassion. "Billy No-shoulders?" she said.

"Yeah. Heh. Billy No-shoulders. First in a long line of sinners." He poured a measure of rusty booze into his glass, then pushed it away. He seemed to enjoy looking at it, relishing the anticipation of pouring down his gullet. "You need to walk out of here, Lina. Get your friends and go home."

"What about you?"

"Forget me."

"What about Dawson? The reward?"

"Hell with the reward."

"Fino's leaving for Santo Tomas tonight," said Lina. "He and Gündelfinger are going back on the train with soldiers and horses. Maybe Dawson too, if we don't find him first."

"To hell with it all. It's none of it my fight."

Lina reached across the space between them and gathered the front of his tunic in her fist. "You son-of-bitch," she hissed. "For just a second you made me care about you."

"Only one second?" he grinned. "Sweet niña, I could show you many such seconds we would stretch into hours and hours."

She shoved him back hard. "Just like that, you give up? Why did you even bother to come?"

Cassidy buried his head in his hands. "I've been thinking. Trying to work it all out."

"If you won't find Dawson for me, or for you, you ought to think about the little ones."

"What little ones?"

"Paco, for one, and the other children of Santo Tomas," said Lina. "Did you hear a word I said? They are going back to raze the village. Tonight! Who will take care of the little ones when the mission is in flames? What will become of them all when the springs are under Fino's control?"

"You don't understand, Lina. It's the children I think about every day. It's them who stop me."

"You're right. I don't understand."

"Your coffee is cooked," said Javier with a grunt.

"I told you she wanted hot," said the old man.

Catalina rose up and took two steps toward the geezer. "I've had enough of you, old man," she said. "Get out." She swept her leg through the frail spindles holding the chair up, breaking them to kindling, dumping the man onto the floor with a crash. "If I see you again, I'll make you swallow your teeth." Lina picked up one of the spindles to use as a club and make good on her threat.

The old derelict scurried ahead of her as she strode to the bar. Once there, watched him scamper out the door. Javier opened his mouth to say something, but after looking at the stick in Lina's hand, he thought better of it and clammed up.

Tucking the spindle under her arm, Lina picked up two steaming mugs, one in each hand, and carried them back to Cassidy.

"Drink up," she said.

He sipped at the lip, grimaced at the heat. After a while, he said, "I'd been a deputy marshal for twenty-three days when I came to Martha's Well, Texas. I was just passing through. Thought I'd take a short-cut back home to La Noria mesa. Horse was tired. I was tired. I decided to spend the night."

It was a preface to whatever burdened him and Lina sipped at her bitter cup, nodding her encouragement. His hair was a matted patch of grass and his cheeks and chin had sprouted a day's layer of mossy whiskers in a single afternoon. Or maybe it was just the light.

"The hotel at Martha's Well was run by a bird

named Jeckel, a broomstick of a man. Trembly and jaundiced. He sold me a hot bath and a cigar, then left me for dead on a straw mattress stuffed with walnuts." Cassidy chewed his lip at the memory. "I slept, but not for long." When he looked at Catalina, his expression held an odd sense of apology. "You can understand, right? It was the mattress, you see."

Lina nodded, and Cassidy continued to tell his story.

"I wandered downstairs and found Jeckel in the middle of a card game with two men from town, a banker and a shopkeeper. They weren't any of them much bigger than the other. Put 'em in a jar and stir 'em up for a pint. They asked me did I want to play?"

"Did you?"

"I played a few hands. For matchsticks, mind you." Cassidy ran his hand through his hair. "I don't think anybody in Mary's Well had more than *uno* pot to piss in." He looked around the cantina. "Just like here. Just like Santo Tomas.

"These three hombres," he said, "These three… cobardes — they tell me about a man bulling around town, doing whatever he likes. He steals from them, pushes them around. He's running the town, pulling it out from under everybody else. The more they tell me, the more it seems they expect me maybe to do something about him."

"This man have a name?"

"Polk," said Cassidy.

"They knew you're a marshal?"

Cassidy nodded. "Finally, the shopkeeper asks me to talk to Polk. Tell him to back off."

"Did you?"

"I should've went back to bed. I should've told them to kiss my ass, and I should've mounted up and rode out of town. But I was tired, and I couldn't sleep." He spread his hands.

"The mattress," said Lina. "I remember."

"Jeckel and his friends led me over to the saloon, where Polk is drinking at the bar. They pointed him out through the window. Brawny hombre with blonde hair. El toro — getting frisky with a local girl called Jennifer Moore. Thirteen years old."

"Funny you remember her name," said Lina, "her age."

"No," said Cassidy. "Not funny. Not at all." The timber of his voice broke in the middle of the declaration and his last few words came out strained. "Before I walked in, I polished my badge with my hanky."

Cassidy's grin was terrible and grim. "I polished the damn badge, Lina."

"What happened then? Did you confront Polk?"

"I was so sure of what the men told me. So sure of my judgement."

"This man, Polk," said Catalina. "He was no good?"

"Quien sabe? *Who's to say?*" He put the mug of coffee on the table, and his voice trembled. "I called Polk out. I told him we needed to have words. He shoved the girl away." Tears brimmed Cassidy's eyes and spilled out. "He reached behind his back."

Lina fought against it, but the sorrow she felt in her heart pushed through. She had seen grief in her life, felt its bone crushing weight firsthand during the past week, but here was a vile burden carried for too long, and its poison had spread through Cassidy as sure as any snake's venom.

"Polk reached behind his back. I assumed he had a gun. I pulled my six-shooter and fired."

"Did you kill him?"

The marshal squeezed his eyes shut tight against the dark memory. "I killed somebody. Not him."

Then Lina understood, and the realization rocked her to the core. "Jennifer Moore?"

"Polk's sister. She ran in front of him even as I fired." Cassidy caught his breath. "I didn't see what I thought I saw. Innocent horseplay…"

"You thought was something else."

Cassidy nodded.

"Jeckel and the others, they goaded you into it, and he did draw on you."

"He didn't have a gun, Lina."

"You said he reached behind his back."

"To retrieve a kerchief. A hanky. Like the one I polished my badge with."

"What happened then?"

"A few hours later, Polk threw himself in front of a train." Cassidy picked up his mug and gulped down three big swallows of coffee. "The townspeople wanted to pin a medal on my chest. Not a damn one of them cared about the kid. They just wanted Polk gone and I was the dumb sucker with a badge who made it happen."

"It was another time," said Lina. "Another place." She stood up, pushed the chair away, and went to him. Kneeling at eye level, she held his hand in her own. Her words were sure and strong. "This is not the same. Now is not then. You might not be what you are dressed as—a holy padre—but you are on a holy mission."

"I haven't been able to trust myself since that night in Mary's Well. I haven't been able to trust anybody else. I don't have faith in anything or anybody."

Catalina squeezed his fingers. "Then come along, my whiskey priest. I will have enough faith for both of us," she said.

CHAPTER TWENTY-TWO

They walked together from the cantina into bright sunlight.

They walked into vast silence and the thick aroma of cow hide and dung.

Where before there had been the squeals of happy children coming from the lawn and the rousing music of courtyard cymbals, now only the breeze whistled through the building behind them. The wedding party had moved inside the church.

The weather vane creaked a steady rhythm. In a far pen, a cow mooed.

A square of rusty loose tin banged on the roof.

At the hitching rail, Diablo shifted his weight from one side to the other, snorting.

Tut Dawson came around the corner of the cantina.

His heavy lace boots were scuffed and his jaw worked a plug of tobacco. His right hand and wrist were wrapped in a tattered, yellowing bandage. One look told Lina he wasn't taking care of his wound.

The skin around the wrapping was cherry red, bloated and shiny with a damp, yellow shellac. She sniffed lightly at the air. It was a wonder she didn't smell gangrene.

But it would come, and as it was, the hand would be sore.

Especially if struck.

In spite of his handicap, Dawson seemed amused to see Lina and Cassidy standing in the doorway. Under the shadow of his gray hat brim, his eyes were inscrutable, but his lips were playful and smirking. He let fly with a stream of brown juice which pooled at the toe of Lina's boot. Sand fleas skittered here and there.

Cassidy stumbled, but gripping his walking pole, righted himself.

Dawson's tone was mocking. "Too much to drink, padre?"

Lina whispered in Cassidy's ear. "Draw his attention. Get him in the open."

Cassidy nodded and narrowed his eyelids. He took two steps, reared back, and jammed his pole at Dawson's face.

Not exactly what Lina had in mind, but it got the job done. She could work with it.

Cassidy parried the drunk marshal's blow, but his attention was fully engaged.

Too engaged.

The stick clattered to rocky earth, and Dawson's cheeks cracked into a full-fledged smile. "I sure am glad you did that, pard. I been just itching for something man-like to do in this froofy hell-hole." His approach was slow and menacing. His face, pock-marked and tough, featured a pink crescent-shaped gash on the cheek surrounded by mottled blue and yellow bruising.

The slow healing result of Lina's whip-sword.

Dawson came crashing in, pinning Cassidy to the shadowy side of the cantina shed, cracking the frail, weathered siding. "I let you have the first one, padre — now it's my turn." Dawson rocked the marshal with a left handed slap. Incredibly, Cassidy stayed upright, reeling into the roadway.

His dark brimmed hat spun away to land flat beside the corral. In the pens beyond, guarded by a triple barbed wire fence, and grieving over the violence, the black white-faced cows lowed mournful and long.

"Now we go downstairs," said Dawson continuing to advance, slugging the marshal once, then twice in the guts. Cassidy shuffled around and faked a right, then landed a balled-up fist, but it glanced harmlessly off Dawson's jaw.

Blood dribbled from Cassidy's lip as he stuck his tongue out and wiped at his forehead with his long dark sleeve. To his credit, he kept punching, teetering on the precipice of oblivion.

He was no coward. But it was hopeless.

Cassidy should've concentrated on Dawson's weakness — should've focused on the bad hand and arm. Make him block with it. Pound on his pain until he became careless.

He would've been more successful if he hadn't spent the past hour trying to wipe away the pass with a liquid eraser. Instead, Cassidy was continually on defense, frantically trying to catch his breath. He put both fists up in front of his face and stepped backwards as Dawson approached.

Another step back and they were at the dusty round corral, Cassidy's back flat against the split rail fence. Again, Dawson battered the man's midsection until he slumped into a crouch, both arms crossed in front of him.

"You ain't even giving me a reason to spit," said Dawson, working on his cud until he spewed a vile wad into his victim's face. Cassidy pitched to the right and once more Dawson punished him with a cranking left hook.

If the Virginian had any concern about the nun watching from behind, he didn't show it. Catalina was sure he hadn't recognized her. She had kept her face down. Here, in a different time and place, Dawson wouldn't see the vengeance he had coming.

She picked up Cassidy's pole and moved forward in a silent glide. Her breathing was easy as she brought the hickory around in a swooping arc, intent on batting off the top of Dawson's skull. It would've worked, but for the warning of the fat old toad Lina had chased from the cantina.

"Cuidado!" croaked the man from where he leaned on the far side of the corral fence.

Like a flash of lightning, Dawson flinched away, raising his right arm to take the brunt of the impact, momentarily forgetting about his bloated, feverish hand. When the pole crashed down, his scream was deafening.

Would they hear it in the church, over top of the

communion mass?

Dawson fumbled with his left hand for the flat, iron .45 automatic at his waist.

If he triggered an explosion of lead, would the sanctuary organ be drowned out?

Lina stepped back with her left foot into a ready stance, then pivoting on her right, she spun, smashing the stick into Dawson's fingers even as the big gun cleared leather.

The automatic spiraled through the air to land at the edge of the corral with a whump.

Cassidy hurled himself at Dawson with all he had left, raking the air with his fingers, kicking up dust with his boots. He knocked off the campaign hat and wrapped his arms around the bigger man's neck. Dawson complained like a bear in a coon trap, snarling, raging, flexing his muscles.

The struggle was short-lived. Bending at the waist, Dawson jammed his elbow hard into Cassidy's ribs, loosening the hold on his neck. Behind him, the marshal fell back against the fence and sunk to the ground.

The old man was running for Dawson's gun. "Goody, goody, goody," he cackled. A wormy raven coveting something shiny.

Lina raced him to the revolver, reached for it, and was knocked aside.

The ringy old bastard almost had it. Flat on her back, Lina kicked the gun through the dirt, then jumping into a crouch, brought the stick around and walloped the fat, bald head. The drunk buckled over sideways with a squawk, and Lina was on her feet, the pole spinning across her shoulders from right hand to left.

Cassidy was down and out at the barbed wire fence.

Across the road, Javier leaned against the canti-na's doorjamb, watching a figure gravitate down the white rock driveway from the house. The red beard and lavender vest were unmistakable. The man's gait was wobbly, but determined. After the news he'd been given, he no doubt opted for something stronger than the wedding mass communion wine.

McKenzie.

Lina clutched the pole in one hand and welcomed the new spectator as Dawson stalked her, keeping his right hand out of range.

"Watch how vengeance is delivered," she said.

Then Dawson was upon her. She sidestepped his wide haymaker and jabbed his knee with the heel of her boot. He grunted, but kept his balance. Lina whirled the pole through the air like a fan blade.

This time, Dawson caught it with his left hand. The man's dexterity was astounding. With one rock-solid grip he jerked the weapon away and sent it sailing into the corral.

Lina twisted around in the long blue habit and pounded ground, putting distance between them. At the back side of the corral, she mounted the fence and perched on the top rail in a crouch. Adjacent to her, a long rail gate opened to the corral rattled on its hinges and jerked up and down. Lina glanced down into the pen. A black angus bull, two tons of snorting animal fury, stared back at her.

From the maze of penned cattle beyond, a tall

man in dark jeans and a blue shirt appeared. He wore a gun and a yellow haired kid ran along beside. "Say, now," he said, "get down from there 'less'n you wanna get hurt. We just got this critter back home."

Two more onlookers.

"Stay out of it, Miguel." Dawson's eyes were round and on fire with exertion. The challenge, the pain—he was enjoying it all too much. "Keep your kid back, too. Y'all just see how we deal with pissants back at home."

Lina ignored the cowboy and leapt into the arena.

Let Dawson enjoy his partial triumph. Let him revel in his audience.

With his jubilance would come pride and over confidence. Lina had fought the man twice before. She had learned from their previous encounters, and she knew his weakness was hubris. More, she knew how he moved, what tactics he used, how he telegraphed his intent. It was one more advantage she had over him along with his festering hand.

Any second now, he'd try to distract her with syrupy Southern charm.

"You got something familiar about you, girl," he said, "and an old boy in my line of work don't know too many nuns. Maybe you and me met before? Maybe before you said your vows and was free to know a man." His teeth were long at the root and spattered with tobacco leaf. "I mean that in the biblical sense."

She had less than a minute, maybe mere seconds, to rip away the veil and habit and get to her urumi.

Praying Mother Mercy would forgive her, she tore at her outer garments and cast them into the dirt.

CHAPTER TWENTY-THREE

She unwound the urumi from her waist. With a slight flick of her wrist, the blade propelled itself to its full length. The afternoon's cool breeze had crept away to die, but without the uniform of the Sisters of Señora Maria, the heat was tolerable. She wore her sheer, black blouse and ebony leggings. Her braided hair, though still pinned back, was free to breathe.

She was free to breathe. Free to face Tut Dawson one last time.

Not the Black Rose now, but Catalina Cristiana Rivera.

"As it should be," she said.

Dawson squatted down to pick up Cassidy's hickory pole. Spun it around his wrist with his left hand, then planted the blunt, hard end into the red sandy soil of the paddock. He let out a gust of air, followed with a chuckle of delight. Shaking his head, his blue eyes dancing with recognition, Dawson used the top of the pole to tilt back his hat. "I'll be go to the devil," he said, his words filled with mirth.

"You are the devil," hissed Lina.

"If I might just ask you a question, Miss Rivera? How the hell did you come to be here? And dressed up like a holy ball of blue sky?"

Lina sent a tremor through the urumi and it hissed along the ground in the late afternoon air.

"You ain't feeling too awful talkative, eh?" Dawson edged closer, keeping his weight on the stick. "I can understand. What with all you been through." He held out his stinking right hand, a frayed tendril of wrapping hanging from his wrist like a spider's web. "I been through a lot too. But, I'll tell ya, my invitation still stands."

"What invitation?"

"I'm willing to let by-gones be by-gones. I'm willing to kiss and make up."

He took another step closer.

Lina sneered at the brute's predictability. He hoped to distract her with platitudes until he was close enough to strike.

Turns out, she had the reach on him.

Her arms were a whirl, and the steel snapped up through the air on a trajectory of death. She aimed to take Dawson's head in one fell swoop.

And then he caught the edge of the urumi with the pole.

Biting deep into the wood, the impact sent a shock back to the hilt, and Dawson jerked to the side, a trick he'd tried before when the urumi was buried in his hand. But Lina was ready and twisted with the momentum, wrenching the whip-edge free. Again, the urumi again sailed into a series of spiral arcs.

"I'm gonna wrap that thing around your pretty little throat," said Dawson with a growl.

"Tell me more," said Lina, taunting him. "Tell me how you're going relish my screams."

Deep inside, she felt calm spreading through her body. She wasn't afraid of him, and he knew it. He wasn't used to it, and it angered him to distraction. Yet another advantage she had.

The urumi soared past the hickory and split Dawson's dirty bandage, slicing a deep groove into the pus-filled flesh of his arm. Recoiling as if shot, the man spasmed backwards, dropping the pole with an agonizing scream.

Lina pulled back on the urumi for a killing strike.

Gunfire echoed through her ears, forcing her around to face Miguel. He leaned over the top rail of the fence with a laconic look on his face, the barrel of his Colt .44 pointed at the sky. "You wanna fight, you fight, but I ain't gonna bear witness to murder in my pen, lady."

There was no arguing with the gun.

Lina crouched low and flung the urumi above her head, sending it out with a hard snap, a steel rail creased the cowboy's palm and loosened his fingers. When he dropped the gun, the towhead leaned toward it. "Leave it," said Lina.

The boy froze where he was.

"What kind of woman are you?" said Miguel.

Lina told him her name.

******

Rivera.

The tumblers in Charlie Mac's head dropped into place. He'd finally dialed a successful combination. The awful predicament Fino put him in would resolve itself with Catalina Rivera. The vault would open back up. Once more, he'd access a fortune.

But he had to be shrewd.

From where he stood outside the corral fence, watching the fray between Dawson and the girl, he could hear the hooves of a dozen horses clopping down the road from the church livery. When Miguel sent a gunshot skyward, a few errant whinnies erupted from the troupe.

McKenzie saw the soldiers coming in the corner of his eye, the first of thirty men and their mounts, a caravan making their way into Nuevo Piño. Once there, they'd be loaded onto the train — his train — tucked in, fed and watered for their impending ride north. There was nothing he could do to stop it.

Then again, maybe he didn't need to.

He turned away from the convoy of soldiers, some wearing full army regalia, some dressed like Garcia's peasant army.

Maybe McKenzie would just let things play out, and then at the right moment, play the trump card God had dealt him. Fino wanted the Riveras out of the way. Nay — needed — the Riveras out of the way. It didn't take a head-doctor to know Fino feared them.

What if, at the climax of his triumph over Santo Tomas, at the very brink of conquest, McKenzie could convince the General the Riveras yet lived? With Catalina in his power, he could do just that.

With her in his possession, he'd have a bargaining chip.

He'd get more than a paltry hundred dollars. Who knows how far he could leverage the General's fear? He might even get his railroad back.

There was a roar of anger from inside the corral. Tut Dawson, the fool, was trying to kill Charlie Mac's last hope!

He stepped up onto the fence and held his breath.

Again Dawson had blocked the girl's peculiar weapon with his wooden staff. McKenzie was intrigued by the long steel foil. It wasn't a sword, but neither was it a true whip. No matter what one called it, it obviously took tremendous skill to wield. But it wasn't a weapon for close combat, and using the Miguel's gunshot as a distraction Dawson had worked inside the blade's perimeter.

Rivera's flying boot lashed out to slam into Dawson's knee. It was the third such blow McKenzie witnessed, and he was beginning to understand the girl's strategy. She didn't need sharpened steel to kill her opponent with a thousand cuts. She herself was the weapon, whittling away at Dawson's defenses, methodically hitting the same spots again and again, repetition increasing the pain.

Behind them, on McKenzie's side of the fence, the cowboy Miguel sat on his haunches while his boy wrapped his hand, staunching the river of blood gushing from the wound. Next to them, aroused by the violent action in front of him, the big angus bull crashed into the gate and bellowed with derision.

Rivera belittled Dawson with equal scorn. "You talk like a man, but chico, I just don't think you've got what it takes," she said. "You keep promising to kill me, but you can't deliver. Make a woman wonder what else you wouldn't be able to deliver on."

Insane with rage, Dawson lunged for her throat, and she slammed her forehead into his nose. There was a pop and a burst of blood decorated the ground. "I should've guessed."

The continued badgering was taking its toll. Dawson was getting sloppy and tired.

But McKenzie knew him, had felt his rage first hand. Catalina Rivera was one mistake away from the full bore of Dawson's fury.

He had an idea.

He crawled down from his position and crept along the fence, keeping an eye on the deadly skirmish.

As predicted, Rivera made her mistake.

Tripping on a pile of blue garments in the middle of the arena, she lost her footing and tumbled to the ground. She rolled to her back, but Dawson crashed on top of her. He outweighed the girl times three, and knelt over her torso with his left hand clamped around her throat.

McKenzie arrived beside Miguel and smiled. "That's some cut," he said.

The cowboy grimaced as his son continued to wrap the wound.

Over the kid's shoulder, Charlie saw the iron bolt

he was looking for. Again, the bull bawled and careened into the gate. The latch bounced at the heavy jolt. The gate rattled. One turning motion would set the animal free.

McKenzie looked over the fence, then back into the ring at the ongoing battle.

Remarkably, the girl had escaped from Dawson's embrace and once again had the upper hand.

Still on his knees, Dawson took the brunt of a boot to the face, falling backwards into a lolling daze. Above him, Rivera pushed heavy strands of loose, blood-dampened hair away from her dirt-stained face. As she crouched over Dawson, McKenzie was reminded of Comanche warriors he'd seen, or cats with mice.

Dawson struggled to push himself up while Rivera waited.

McKenzie was through waiting. He reached past Miguel and unlatched the gate.

Quickly he mounted the fence. "Catalina, run!" he called.

Dawson looked up.

Fino's angus bull plowed headlong through the open gate straight for him.

The Rivera girl made the fence and rolled underneath to safety.

Dawson's screams were cut short under the clamor of hooves and the bray from a full ton of enraged bone and gristle. Soon Dawson made no sound at all.

CHAPTER TWENTY-FOUR

Catalina tightened her right arm around Raul Cassidy's waist and wrapped her fingers tight around his belt. His left arm sprawled across her shoulders and he struggled to hold up his head.

Charles McKenzie pointed Tut Dawson's gun straight at them. "You so much as twitch, I'll put three bullets straight through the both of you."

"Don't...don't let him...win," said Cassidy, blinking.

"I've already won."

"You okay, Mr. McKenzie?"

"Fine, Miguel. How's the hand?"

Lina turned her head and saw the cowboy hold up his wrapped injury. "I'll live." He gave McKenzie a salute. "You want us to keep Mr. Dawson's body down here?"

"Thank you, yes. Poor soul."

"May he...burn in hell," said Cassidy.

"I honestly thought he'd be able to escape the bull's charge." McKenzie clucked his tongue. "Such a tragic fate for a man in his prime."

"May he...burn in hell," said Cassidy.

McKenzie waved the gun in the direction of the cantina road. "Let's go," he said.

Lina walked ahead of the railroad man, up the road, back toward Fino's house. Cassidy had his feet under him and moved more easily on his own. They were both banged up, would be aching and sore for days.

But they were both alive.

"No thanks necessary for saving your lives," said McKenzie. "Following my instructions now will be gratitude enough."

Lina scoffed. "You saved nothing except your own skin. What's the matter? Was Dawson going to sell you out? Maybe he knew something you didn't want Fino to hear?"

"I assure you, it was nothing of the sort."

"What then? I thought you two worked together."

"No. I barely knew the fellow. Can't you accept the fact I simply couldn't bear to see him kill a woman in cold blood? A beautiful woman?" Charlie came up close behind Lina, bringing his lips to her ear even as the cold steel gun barrel prodded her spine. "An incredibly beautiful woman, indeed."

Had she not been shepherding Cassidy along, she might have tried for the gun. Even bruised she was more agile than this old goat, Lina was sure of it. But if the gun went off, even if by accident, she didn't want the marshal's blood on her conscience.

And there was more to it, of course.

Since Raul's story about Mary's Well, she'd felt her heart fluttering with a strange new rhythm. And she'd started calling him Raul in her mind.

"Where...you taking us?" said Raul.

"Not far," said McKenzie. "A quick walk up the road, and then you'll have plenty of time to rest."

"I know about Fino and the German," said Lina.

McKenzie stopped in his tracks.

"What do you know?"

Cassidy pulled away and moved to the side of the road to sit. Lina turned to look at the bearded Texan.

They were half-way to the towering stone estancia.

The red Willys waited under its striped awning in front of the garage, and the air carried the delicate notes of *Ave Maria*.

How much longer until the service was over? During the fight with Dawson, Lina had been aware of the parade of horses into town. Even now they were likely loading the train with supplies, filling the water tank and stoking up the fire.

She eyed the red Willys automobile.

Again, McKenzie asked, "What do you know?"

Lina walked straight into the gun, allowing the barrel to press into her abdomen. "I know they betrayed you." She whispered the words, slow, let them fill with admiration and respect before letting them fall from her lips to Charlie's eager ears. "I know how much it hurt."

"How?"

"I was there. Listening. Back of the doorway. Inside a closet."

McKenzie's face filled with blood. "How dare you?"

Had she overplayed her hand? Lina touched his

beard. Came close, put her lips to his cheek. "I dare because I admire you."

She kissed him.

"I admire what you've built. What we might still build." She let her lips linger below his ear. "Together."

McKenzie chewed the inside of his cheek. "What about the marshal?"

"What about him?"

"You were with him."

"We came for Dawson," said Lina. "Now that Dawson is finished, our relationship is finished, too."

"I suppose he'll want to take Dawson back to Texas?"

"No, there's not enough left of him to take back."

"Will he claim the reward?"

"Whether he does or not is no concern of mine." said Lina. She let McKenzie gaze into her passion filled eyes and ground her breasts into his suit coat. "But as soon as he leaves, we'll be alone."

Charlie Mac quickly seemed to warm to the idea. "Yes, yes. Okay, very well then." He pointed the gun at Cassidy, but spoke to Lina. "Explain it to him."

Lina knew she only had a few seconds. McKenzie was befuddled by her overture, but he wasn't stupid. She had to play everything to the hilt. She only hoped Raul would understand.

"I'm staying with Charles," Lina told him. "Take your bounty and go back to Texas."

"Señorita?" said Cassidy. "I don't understand."

"I've got business with Charlie No-shoulders at the house," she said. "You understand that kind of business, don't you?"

Cassidy's attention shifted from Lina to McKenzie's gun and back. "I do," he said. "But do you?"

"Of course."

"What about our companions?"

"Take him home too," she said.

"Him?"

She tilted her head, motioning toward the house. "I'm sure Willy will help you."

Up until now, the color had been flowing back into Cassidy's face. Suddenly he showed a wave of green. "Oh, no…no, no…I don't think so," he said.

Catalina nodded.

"No, no, no," he whispered.

Lina closed the distance between them with two quick steps. "You have to. Now, before the service is over. Nobody will stop you. They'll think McKenzie gave you the okay. Take the automobile and flee."

"Do you know what you're asking — of course not! You've never driven one of those things. They run out of fuel and water all the time. The tires go flat. They…they…well, they just aren't a substitute for a good donkey."

"You told me you knew how to drive it."

"I do. But knowing how to do it doesn't mean I enjoy it."

"It will get you back to Santo Tomas twice as fast as Diablo. Maybe faster."

Cassidy tightened his jaw. Rubbed a hand over his face.

"They are planning to take the city. If you leave now, you have a chance to arrive before the train."

Cassidy swallowed hard. "How do I...," he looked into her eyes. "How do I know you will be all right?"

She cupped his hand in her chin. "You don't, chico."

He stood up and let Catalina lead him to McKenzie.

"Will you have the men take care of Dawson's remains?" he said. "I will prepare my burro."

McKenzie kept the gun handy while signaling Miguel's boy. The towhead joined them in the road, and McKenzie gave the instructions.

Cassidy accompanied the boy back down toward the corral, and Charlie Mac put his arm around Catalina's waist. "We will get to know each other better now, eh?"

Lina kissed him hard on the lips, then pointed at the gun in McKenzie's hand. "I'm hurt, amado." *Beloved.* "Is this still neccesito?"

Charlie let the gun fall limp by his side and they walked arm and arm to the house.

Once there, Lina led him into the washroom where they discovered Tooms still unconscious on the daybed.

"Typical," said McKenzie. "Though I don't blame the poor rotter. I imagine it's been a long day."

Lina loosened Charlies' tie. "Let's both freshen up." She kissed him again, and he dropped the gun into his wide suit coat pocket.

"I like the way your mind works, dear."

Lina bowed her head. "I told you I was eavesdropping earlier."

"Yes?"

She moved to the heavy porcelain wash basin and dipped a sponge into the pool of water. "I heard how they took your train away. How they bought the rail out from under you."

She ran the sponge over his forehead.

"It's a disgraceful betrayal," she said.

Charlie closed his eyes and relaxed. "It is indeed."

Lina moved back to the basin. She dropped the sponge and put a hand on each side of the basin. "I heard it all. Disgraceful is absolutely the word."

"Mmm-hmmm," said McKenzie, his eyes still closed. "Let's stop talking now?"

******

"Did you hear me, Charlie?"

He opened his eyes. "I will if you will?"

"I heard. Every. Word. Including the words about what you did to my family."

She picked up the basin and tossed a gallon of water into his face.

McKenzie fell backwards, sputtering. "Now, Lina, please understand. You don't know the entire story. You must—"

She brought the empty basin down on top of McKenzie's head, cracking him hard enough to split the basin into two pieces.

As promised, Charlie Mac stopped talking.

CHAPTER TWENTY-FIVE

They got the red Willys automobile started, and Cassidy stopped long enough at the cantina to get some extra water for the car in case it overheated. "Straight to Santo Tomas," said Lina, standing on the sideboard. "Follow the tracks as much as you can, but avoid the soldiers in Nuevo Piño. Drive around the village."

"I know the way," said Cassidy. He gripped the steering wheel, looked back at the Fino-Espolon ranch. "Are you sure the three of you will be okay?"

"Paco is here," she said. "How can we not be?"

"Bring Diablo back to me."

"If he lets us."

"I will tell you his secret." Lina bent low. "He likes a shot of tequila. Gift him with a bottle, and he will be your friend for life. He is a burro with a very long memory."

"I'll remember."

"Lina?"

She bent down and kissed his cheek. "Go," she

said. "Before they catch us both."

"Vayo con dios," he said.

Cassidy levered the car into gear and touched the accelerator. With a rumble and a noxious black cloud of spent gasoline, he clattered away down the road.

"He sure is some kind of priest," said Tully, joining Lina in the road, "and you're some kind of nun. Are you sure you two ain't been communionized?"

"You mean excommunicated?"

"That's what I mean, right there," agreed Tully. "Kicked out."

Catalina began to walk back to the church to find Mary, Adeline, and Paco.

"To be honest, old man, I don't think they'd ever let us in to begin with."

She spent the entirety of the walk trying to decide how best to explain her disheveled appearance if anybody saw her.

******

Nobody did.

Catalina crept behind the garage, along the walls of the house and church, keeping to the lengthening shadows. Grateful for the long wedding mass, she scurried to the church livery stable. The barn was long with an open central breezeway of oak stantions and square pens to either side. Loose straw littered the dry floor, and the heavy smell of livestock clung to her nostrils.

The aroma carried Lina back to the remuda at Rancho Rivera, the long afternoons she spent training her dark chocolate brown Andalusian mare, Verny and the endless afternoons riding the open range with Carlos or her mother. The Rivera stock was undiluted and could be traced directly to 15th century steeds on the Iberian Peninsula. Would that she had Verny with her now, she would ride across the desert, swiftly overtaking the 705 engine and Raul Cassidy's automobile alike to warn the village of its impending doom.

It suddenly dawned on her. This was what the Sisters of Sorrow foresaw.

Mercy had explained how they rarely appeared, but during Lina's short time at the convent, she regularly heard the mournful chants and long haunting melodies far into the night. So much so the dark intonations were lodged firmly in her head, repeating endlessly.

Endless as death.

Overcome by the audacity of Fino's plan, Lina steadied herself on a rail at the first open stall. The pen was filled with straw piles and old tack, smelling of leather and dust. A pair of leather riding gloves had been thrown carelessly to the corner of the hard packed floor. She picked them up. Old and crusted with dirt, they'd likely been forgotten years ago. The gloves were narrow, with short fingers, as if for a child. She turned them over and saw a thread-stitched set of initials on the cuff: FAF –Ferdinand Angel Fino.

Lina placed the gloves on a shelf against the wall.

It was hard to imagine. While she was riding Andalusians in the Texas wild, the handsome young groom saying his vows next door was busy with his own mounts on the Fino-Espolon. She wondered what he had been like, this heir to so much extravagance, this beneficiary of evil. Would they have been friends? More? Could it be her taking the place of Lady Alejandra at the altar? Such was the twist and turn of fate.

Even now, was Ferdinand aware of his father's nefarious plans? If so, would he join him? Or, like Catalina, would he rise up to defend the holy springs?

A familiar whinny came from a stall at the other end of the stable, and Lina hurried to the black mission mare. Adeline's buckskin was there too, along with Mary's bay. They had been brushed, fed, and watered. To Lina's relief, their saddle bags and gear were safely ensconced in a tidy alcove next door.

With nobody around to watch, Lina took time to wash her face, comb out her hair, pin it back up, and change into new clothes. She had arrived with only one habit, coif, and veil, and there was nothing left of those but tattered remains, fit only for burning.

Burning.

She reached into her pocket and removed the black rosary she had been sure to preserve. Mercy had yet to teach her any prayers to accompany her handling of the beads, but just holding the string in her hand brought a sense of comfort, of strength.

She opened her bag and dressed in the only wardrobe she had. A black tunic with wood carved clasps, scarlet piping and button loops, flared sleeves and laced leather gauntlets.

Black leather pants with nickel conchas and leather tassels running down the outer seams.

Knee-high, lace-up boots.

Overall, the long, flowing cloak with its dark cowl.

Other than the cookie Cassidy had given her, Catalina hadn't eaten since breaking camp in the morning outside Lohman Siding. She was famished.

From her provisions, she found half of a lard-sandwich and a round of bacon.

Catalina walked her mare to the opposite end of the stable and casually ate in the doorway she had entered. Chewing slow, she washed down her meal with clean spring water from her canteen.

Almost immediately there was a rush of applause and a loud cacophony of organ pipes, guitar strings, and cymbals. Far up and to the left, at the back of the cathedral, on an open stone patio, a group of church men in black stood together, followed by acolytes in white robes and a party of soldiers and women in lavish dresses. Cheering and clapping, all eyes were on the young couple in the center of the mix, Ferdinand and Alejandra.

He was everything a dashing young groom should be. Handsome and regal. She was the consummate Edwardian bride, resplendent with little makeup, her black hair pinned in a fashionable Gibson Girl pile at the top of her head with a long veiled hat trailing behind. The bodice of her majestic white gown was covered in frills, and her wide, puffy sleeves tapered to the forearm. A high neckline and collar gave Alejandra a noble air. Her smile was sublime.

It was like Catalina had been thrown into a vast game of chess.

Dawson had been a pawn.

McKenzie too.

Here at last was the royal family.

Just inside the door to the livery, a heavy charcoal stick, used for marking horses sat beside a coal oil lantern and tin of lucifer matches waited for dark.

For the briefest instant, Lina entertained the mad desire to light the lantern and carry it near the patio on the mare's back. Once there, she'd fling fire into the proceedings and call the wanton destruction divine providence.

Vengeance is mine, says the Lord.

"And I will be his right hand, and his terrible sword," whispered Lina.

But not this way.

She watched the pretty bride with her ebullient smile bend down and offer flowers to a little girl in a yellow summer dress. Did they also deserve to die in the fiery wrath of the Black Rose?

Lina picked up the charcoal stick and rubbed it against the inside wall of the barn. It left a black smudge. For several minutes she worked the charcoal back and forth on the surface of the wood, pressing hard to leave an indelible mark.

"Catalina, Catalina!"

Lina heard Paco calling before she saw him, and dropped the charcoal.

She pressed back inside the barn at his approach.

"Hush," she told him when he appeared. "I mustn't be seen."

"All eyes are on the lovely bride and her groom.

Why would anybody notice you?" Paco scoffed. "Just say you are with the circus."

"I must ride to Santo Tomas," said Lina. "Now, while there may yet be time."

Paco picked up Lina's somber tone and listened close while she told him what she knew. "Find Mary and Adeline. Tell them to follow as soon as they can."

"Sister Adeline has decided to stay in Nuevo Piño for a fortnight. She desires to give the children aid."

"She doesn't know about Fino's plan."

"This would make little difference to Adeline," said Paco. "You don't know her like I do. She's stubborn. If she says she will stay here, then here she will stay."

Lina chewed her lip and gave a moment's thought. "It doesn't matter," she said. "All that matters is I get back as soon as possible."

"On horseback you will not beat Charlie Mac's big 705. Not even with a head start."

"It's not Charlie Mac's engine anymore, Paco," said Lina.

"I was wrong about him, wasn't I, hermano?"

"We all were," said Lina. "It doesn't matter now."

"Only one thing to do. You want to get home fast, you will ride back to Santo Tomas with me."

"With you?"

"Si, señorita," said Paco. "The adventure of a lifetime. We ride back on the train. It leaves tonight."

CHAPTER TWENTY-SIX

With scores of boisterous Nuevo Piño residents, Catalina marched with Paco, Adeline, and Mary in plain sight down the white rock road behind the wedding party's wagon. At the gate beside the cantina, they broke away from the crowd and watched the parade of noisy well-wishers. Young and old, drunk and sober, smiles and tears, all of life was on display.

"General Fino will drive his son and daughter-in-law around the perimeter of the town several times and the crowd will follow, singing the anthems and folk songs of the clan." Paco pulled a silver pocket watch from his trousers. "We have at least an hour to board the train."

"Unseen," said Mary.

The western skies were a deep ochre shot through with smears of purple and pink below the evening's first stars, guiding lights in the clean indigo firmament. "The dark will help," said Paco. "We'll wait under the supply car. As it is loaded, the doors are kept open and often left unattended."

"I don't like cramped spaces much," said Mary. "But we do what we gotta do."

"You're not going with us," said Lina.

"Excuse me? You wait just a minute—"

"I'll move faster without you," said Lina.

"You're just rude," said Mary.

"But it's true," said Paco. "The Black Rose, she is like the quicksilver."

Mary stuck her tongue out. Then she jerked a thumb toward Adeline. "What about her?"

"I'm staying put," said Adeline. "Never in my life have I seen such poverty. At the wedding ceremony, I had the opportunity to visit with the parish pastor and an assistant nun. In spite of Fino's riches, there is an overwhelming need here. I feel a true calling to stay, if only for a few weeks."

"The children of Santo Tomas might need you as well. Especially after tonight," said Lina.

"Mine is not the gift of prophesy, sister. Neither do I think is it yours. We do what we do based on what we know at any given time. What I know is I'm needed here for now."

Lina didn't argue. Instead, she told them about Dawson, and how Cassidy had started back to Texas ahead of them with the General's car. "If his noticed it missing, I haven't seen any sign."

"Preoccupied with the marriage," said Mary, "and with his mission of vengeance."

"We have you to thank for the knowledge," said Lina. "Without you, the German's words wouldn't have made sense."

"You've been a great help," said Adeline. "If you would stay, I'd welcome your company."

Mary appealed one last time to Catalina. "You're sure?"

"If Adeline is staying, then I believe you ought to stay with her," said Lina.

"On the other hand, I'm certainly capable of taking care of myself," said Adeline.

"That's not the point," said Lina.

"I spent an entire trapping season with a camp in Montana," said Adeline. "We'd go out in the morning snows and get stranded one away from the other for days on end. You either learned how to survive on your own, or you didn't. And them's that didn't ain't here to talk about it."

"Can't tell you how good your words make me feel," said Mary. "You sure you don't need somebody else under those train wheels, Lina?"

After another few minutes of discussion it was decided. Mary and Adeline would stay at the Fino-Espolon rancho for two weeks, endeavoring to aid the local church in its relief efforts.

As night settled in, the Black Rose and Paco stole across the desert, cutting through the bleak wilderness to arrive at the train opposite the town.

The heavy 705 idled in its spot under a squat water tower, snoring like a tremendous bear in hibernation. Wafts of steam rose from its bulk. Men scurried around the slumbering edges like insects.

"Bring those ponies down this way." A familiar voice.

"Tully," said Paco.

"Hell if this one ain't got a bum hoof."

"And Miguel," said the Black Rose. "The soldiers have them handling the horses."

They crouched behind tall spidery strawberry cactus and blooming ocotillo, not daring to make a move for fear of being seen considering the sparse cover. At the train, seven box cars parked behind the Pullman and a second passenger car were open. With fine saddles, halters and breastplates, the cowboys tacked up their war horses, leading the heavily equipped mounts up reinforced doors which doubled as ramps.

"They are making a tight fit, eh, Señora? I don't think it wise to ride with the animals."

"We'll ride in the supply car," said the Black Rose. "At the end of the train, where they are tossing the canvas bags and loading ammunition."

Paco narrowed his eyes in the heavy dusk. "Ammunition?"

"I recognize the markings on the side of the crates. You see — the tall letters on the one they are delivering into the car right now?"

Paco nodded as he watched a man carry a box into the freight car and set it into place with deliberate care.

Extremely. Deliberate. Care.

"It's dynamite."

"Ay caramba! You can't expect me to ride with the dynamite."

"The adventure of a lifetime?"

"I had hoped for a few more years to tell of it."

"You will tell of it, chico. If I know you, not even death would stop you spinning tall tales. Your ghost would haunt the scribes of penny novels and western adventures for generations."

"Don't joke," said Paco. "You'll upset my stomach."

They continued to watch the soldiers and cowboys load horses and supplies. When the darkness was complete, lanterns flared to life and pinpricks of glowing red cigarettes showed the back and forth transit of men and beasts.

"Perhaps we can sabotage the train here?"

The Black Rose considered Paco's suggestion. "Set off the dynamite?"

"Why not? Would that not stop them?"

"It would cerntainly destroy the last two cars, perhaps kill some soldiers, and needlessly injure several innocent horses." She played the scenario through from in her mind. Finally she said, "But no, I don't think that would stop them. We would need to destroy the locomotive itself, and we simply don't have the time."

With a creak of pully and rope, the men closed each car in succession. Once a door crashed into place, a heavy crossbeam bolt strapped with iron dropped into place, locking it tight.

On the Pullman, electric lights sprang on, and Paco gasped. He gouged his partner's ribs and pointed across the open field. "Señorita, loooook. It is Charles McKenzie."

The boy was right. Framed in one of the square glass windows, McKenzie's red beard was plainly visible surrounding his ruddy dough-like face. The top of his head was swaddled in white bandages. "The baron is more thick-headed than I surmised," said the Black Rose.

"A pity," said Paco. He made a show of spitting onto the ground.

With his hero falling from such a tall pedestal, the boy's pride had suffered a blow.

The first of many, thought the Black Rose.

Then: "The end car is still open," she said, "but unattended. We go now, or stay behind."

Without a backwards glance, they ran for the train. Arms pumping, legs churning, Paco kicked up the sand with the jerking leaps of a desert cottontail while the Black Rose fell into the fast, easy gait of the wolf. It was a close race.

Paco narrowly won, but only because of his height — he was able to skid to a halt under the boxcar ahead of his opponent.

Together they waited, struggling to stay quiet as they steadied their breathing. Two sets of military uniformed legs stomped along the side of the car.

One of the soldiers called inside. "All clear, amigo?"

"Si," came the reply as the man clomped down the ramp. "We have one more box to bring on."

The men walked away, up along the line of the train and after a count of ten, Paco put his head out from under the carriage. He looked both ways and waited a moment. "Now we go," he whispered, and led the way up the ramp and into the warm dark confines of the car.

The inside of the boxcar smelled like leather and fresh pine wood.

The Black Rose pulled a tin of matches from her pocket and struck a light.

At the back of the car, pine wood crates, stacked two and three high were packed into the space and belted in with webs of hemp and burlap straps. Two rows of hinged travel trunks, stacked on atop the other stood six-feet tall. They were slid together at the front and secured with a trio of braided rope looped through open eye screws fixed in the boxcar's frame. The space in the middle was filled with towering stacks of blankets heavy tarps.

The car rocked and groaned as, farther up the line, heavy horseflesh moved and shifted in their transport cars.

Like a squirrel, Paco shot up the side of the canvas mountain. "The beasts are packed like pickled fish, while we ride in luxury," he said.

As the match light burned away, The Black Rose picked a ground level spot in the shadows, between two trunks. Crouched low and with her cloak enveloping her, she would only be seen by the keenest eye.

In spite of what Paco said, Lina thought they were packed in like pickled fish.

"They must be planning for quite the celebration," said the Black Rose.

"Why do you say it?"

"There are six crates of dynamite and twelve barrels of black powder. And there are two stacks of crates with whisky too. Also wine and cheese."

"Will you show me the cheese? When we are underway, will you open the crate?"

"Surely you're not hungry after feasting all day long?"

"Surely, I—"

"Una momento," said a gruff voice outside, and Paco went still as a rabbit waiting for a coyote to pass. "I thought I heard a voice."

The train rocked back and forth under the weight of the horses, and the trunks and crates inside the car creaked and groaned.

From her hiding place, Lina saw the soldier standing outside on the track smoking a thick cigar that looked like a drooping dog turd from his lip. He wore a scowl on his face, and his nose played host to a fleshy black mole. His uniform, untucked at the waist, showed he held the rank of sergeant.

He plodded up the ramp and stood in the door-way, smoking and moving his head one way, then another. Finally, like a teamster hauling a freight of heavy lumber, he swung his backside around and pounded down the ramp under the pull of gravity.

He waved at his unseen companions, and within minutes they had raised the door and bolted it shut, Catalina breathed a slow sigh of relief but they continued to wait in silence.

Locking Paco and the Black Rose inside.

They waited with only the ticking gears of Paco's watch to keep them company.

"We can't leave without the Generalissimo," he whispered.

"The couple, Ferdinand and Alejandra. Do you

think they will be happy, Paco?"

The boy seemed surprised by the question. "Why not?"

"Their fortunes are built on shifting sand."

"I do not understand?"

"Fino, the Revolution. Change is in the air. The future will be worse before it is better. The Sisters of Sorrow have said it."

"Bah," said Paco, spitting again. "Forget the Sisters of Sorrow. Soon, these nuns will have you praying to the blue ghost of the springs. Listen — Paco lives for the moment. Why? It is in the Bible. Live for today, said God. You might think I'm making this up — I'm not. The Black Rose should maybe do the same?"

She considered his words without answering.

Then there was a series of small explosions, almost like cannon shot, and the car lurched ahead and settled into a steady roll.

They were on their way.

CHAPTER TWENTY-SEVEN

They rode for what seemed like hours.

"These tracks, they are not so smooth, eh?" said Paco from the darkness above.

Catalina steadied herself between the shifting trunks, anticipating another heaving move to the left or right. She stood tall, holding on to one of the straps, tried to stretch away the muscle pain building in her calves, lower back and shoulders. Slowly she breathed in through her nose and out through her mouth to help combat the nausea growing in her stomach.

"I could wish to be on the Pullman with Fino," she said. "We would end this debacle here and now."

"And it would be more comfortable."

"It would be more comfortable," she agreed.

Lina had tried to rest, but the jerking and lurching of the car made sleep impossible.

She found the tin of paint in her hip pocket and smeared her fingers in the oily dark tallow of one side. Then she drew the cross on her face, from forehead to chin, across both closed eyelids and the bridge of her nose. She colored the rest of her face with the crimson Apache dye, admitting the smell of it compelled her to action, enjoying the slick sense of it on her skin.

She imagined what she would do when they reached Santo Tomas. It would be well after midnight when they arrived.

The question weighing most heavily on her mind, was when would Fino unleash his army? Would he wait until dawn? Or would he strike in the deepest hours of slumber?

Likely it depended on how much the General had to drink. At the patio reception she'd seen him quaff a tall tumbler of amber liquid. And there were the cases of liquor riding along with them. She kicked at one of the crates. How dare he frame an attack on innocents as a joyous celebration?

"Help me, Paco."

"What are you doing, hermano?" The boy rolled off the pile of blankets and landed on the rolling floor beside her. "Are we breaking open the cheese?"

"Breaking being the key word." She put her fingers under the lid of the biggest crate and pulled. Continued effort would avail her nothing but splinters.

"Help me find something to pry these lids off."

She lit several matches, but there was nothing.

"I had thought to spoil the bottles of liquor," said the Black Rose.

"I had hoped to eat," said Paco.

They rode on together, sulking in disappointment.

"We have black powder," said Paco. "Are you sure we can't sabotage the train?"

"And blow ourselves up with it?" The Black Rose thought about the horses in the car ahead. She wouldn't risk harming a bunch of senseless beasts. "We will bide our time," she said.

Then, with a surprising jolt, the train braked. Then came another jolt, followed by a chain of steel reports.

"What's happening?" said Paco.

"I don't know." The car came to a shuddering stop.

The Black Rose put her face up to a crack in the door of the boxcar, but could see nothing. It was still dark outside.

She lit a match so Paco could see his watch. "What time is it?"

"Still early. Not yet eleven."

They heard voices.

"Hide between the trunks," said the Black Rose. "I will take your spot." She took a quick step back. With legs like steel springs, she catapulted herself to the top of the blanket pile just as the voices stopped outside.

The graveled throat and bloated words told her who had cracked open the boxcar's door. The ramp fell to the rail bed with a crash, and the Sergeant tromped up the incline swinging a lantern from its wire handle, swearing under his breath.

"Fino es un cerdo — a swine. Swine, swine," said the Sergeant. He put the lantern on the floor and looked around. "Oink, oink, oink."

"Are you finding it?" called another soldier from outside.

"Si, si. Yes, hold on." The Sergeant pulled an iron bar from under his arm, found the crate he was looking for, and attacked the lid. Nails gave way with a shriek, and the wood top popped up and away to reveal a nest of straw.

The Sergeant put down his bar and dug through the bedding until he found a bottle of factory rum. He sat the bottle on a second crate, then reached in for a second bottle. After he had removed the third, he replaced the lid of the liquor crate, banging the nails back into place with his bar.

"The General is waiting," said the outside soldier.

"Let him wait, the swine," said the Sergeant. But not loud enough anybody beyond the confines of the supply car could hear.

"Hurry, they have emptied their last bottle, and I do not want to be the one holding up their party."

"And I have yet to take my first drink," said the Sergeant.

Then a mischievous look crossed his face, and though he thought himself to be alone, he looked around before cracking open the wax-sealed cap on one of the bottles.

With an ornery smile, he hefted the rum to his lips and took a drink.

As he wiped his lips with his sleeve, Paco dropped his pocket watch to the floor with a clatter.

Instantly, the Sergeant spun around. Who knew a man so large could move so fast?

"Who is it?" he said. "Who the hell's there?"

He advanced on the row of trunks and bent low.

Almost immediately his arm shot out like a steam piston to retrieve something hidden in the dark recesses of the car. He pulled Paco out and tossed him to the floor like he was landing a sea bass.

"Ah, so!" he said.

Paco tried to crab-walk backwards away from the ox, but the Sergeant's kick was swift and on-target. A hard boot sent Paco crashing toward the front of the car.

"Teach you to sneak in here," said the Sergeant.

"What's going on in there?" said the outside voice.

"Una momento," said the Sergeant with sadistic joy. "Just getting rid of a mouse."

He unsnapped his shiny black holster and pulled out a heavy revolver.

"Don't you know? The best way to get rid of a mouse is with a cat," said the Black Rose above him. "Not a fat, slobbering ass." She let her cape billow out behind her as she dropped in front of him.

"Gaaah," cried the Sergeant. In the orange light of the lamp, the weird black cross and blood red paint had its desired effect. "What the hell are you?"

"I'm a cat, getting rid of a mouse," she said. He swung his gun up, but the Black Rose took his arm in both hands, twisting, bringing it down across her knee, shattering bone in two place. The Sergeant screamed and fell back, tipping the lantern.

"Fire, Paco," said the Black Rose and the boy was on it, scooping up the lantern to hurl it across the outside landscape.

"What's going on?" The other soldier appeared at the end of the ramp, but the Black Rose controlled the Sergeant at the top. With one hand on his collar and another on his belt, she spun him around to face the door and put her boot on his rump.

The force of her shove drove him straight into the second soldier who stumbled, but immediately regained his balance.

Instead of pressing the attack he ran several yards from the train to where the broken lantern was burning itself out. Pulling his revolver, he fired three shots into the air.

"Dammit, he's alerting the others. Run, Paco."

The boy jumped directly from the car to the roadbed while the Black Rose careened down the ramp, covering the distance between train and soldier before another shot could peal through the air. She launched a flying kick that snapped back his head and put him on the ground.

The soldier rolled, came up on his hands and knees, but the Black Rose was there, driving a fist into the fleshy parts of his face. The edge of her hand came down on his neck, and he fell limp at her feet.

Back at the train, soldiers responded to the gunfire, pouring out of the passenger car behind the luxury Pullman like ants on their way to a picnic. The Black Rose kicked sand over the lantern fire, but the night was lit by the moon and stars, and her shadow was visible crossing the range, just as were the soldiers.

A rifle retort added to the growing chaos. Then another. The Black Rose heard the slugs smack the ground nearby and crouched low, aiming for a thick patch of desert marigolds. With the entire attack force at alert, all she could do was run.

With the odds against her, there was no way to fight and win.

She made the flower patch with a volley of lead tearing through the landscape and the old Sergeant's voice flinging obscenities at her.

More than the fading gunfire or the off color names, the echo of failure dogged her heels as she ran, filling her with distress.

******

"Vengeance has left me where I started, Paco, alone in the desert. Just as I found myself on the morning of Dawson's raid — with death behind me and enemies lying in wait ahead of me."

The night air was cool and still. Lina carried the cape and cowl of the Black Rose in a bundle under her arm. Her leather gauntlets and boots creaked, reminding her of night time noise from childhood. "Crickets and junebugs," said Lina, looking toward the black shadow where the stars abruptly stopped, a miles wide range where the train had finally vanished from the horizon.

"Vengeance is mine, sayeth the Lord. I've certainly made a mess of things."

Paco put his hands on his hips and cocked his head. "Estas loco en la cabeza?" he said. "You got part of what you came for. Dawson is dead. Aren't you at least happy about that?"

Lina inhaled the smell of mesquite and prickly

pear, caught a whiff of coyote scat and heard the train whistle far away. People said it was a lonely sound, but she'd never thought of it as such. Not until now. Not until she walked across the desert hardpan with nothing.

Not even a sense of satisfaction.

"No," she said, "I'm not happy. Are you?"

Paco swung low and picked up her hand. Holding it high, he danced in a spiral, kicking loose gravel across the caliche. "Of course," he said. "Dawson is gone. The Riveras have been avenged. Justice is done."

"Vengeance and justice aren't always the same," said Lina.

"In this case, they are."

"I don't think so."

Lina squeezed the boy's hand and he stopped his jig. "Explain it to me?" he said.

"We were so focused on Dawson we let McKenzie and Fino go free." Her laugh was bitter, and she could see her breath as cloud in the crisp, moonlit night. "I told Cassidy that killing Dawson was a holy mission."

"Wasn't it?"

"I'm starting to doubt it. Mercy and the people of Santo Tomas are alone, unaware of the evil descending upon them. Now, we are alone, Paco, here — without water, without help."

"You forget we have each other. Neither of us is alone." It was Paco's turn to squeeze Lina's hand. "I have lived for weeks on the open range. I will find water, food. You'll see, Catalina Rivera. You'll see Paco tells the truth. Don't lose hope."

"I should have killed McKenzie when I had the chance. Fino, too."

True to his word, Paco found water nearby. It would take hours to fill even half of Lina's canteen from the trickling spring. Enough to keep them alive through the next morning. The afternoon sun would suck the water from their marrow and bleach their bones. The desert would leave them as dead husks to crumble in the wind.

By then Santo Tomas would be a smoldering ruin. Mercy and the other sisters, killed or driven off.

Lina imagined Andronicus opening the wine cellar for the triumphant Fino, drinking a toast with Ned Sedgewick and Carlyle, the mayor.

"This is all my fault," said Lina.

"If you want someone to blame, blame Paco. It was I who dropped the watch and made the noise."

"I should not have put you in danger in the first place. I should have made you stay behind with Mary and Adeline."

Paco scoffed. "You are too much concerned with yourself, prima. It is a hazard of your family. You want to be everybody's savior."

"Sister Adeline would say the position has already been taken," said Lina.

"You seek vengeance, but you're not satisfied when you get it. You want to see justice. But when it comes, it's not enough. You think you can be all things to all people. You want to be servant, leader, follower, and teacher. You are twelve different people all at the same time." He flicked the cloak in her arms with his fingers. "You are certainly two people, at least."

He was wise for his age, and he was right. But at the same time, he was wrong.

Catalina Rivera was not twelve people, or even two.

There was no Catalina Rivera. Not anymore.

That girl died the same morning as the rest of her family.

Now there was only the Black Rose.

Twenty minutes later, they found Cassidy's abandoned Willys automobile.

Almost immediately they were surrounded by horsemen.

CHAPTER TWENTY-EIGHT

The 705 roared into Santo Tomas after midnight, wrapped in a swirling cloud of steam with a fearsome blare and a squall of screaming brakes. Whirling cyclones erupted in its wake, tossing pea gravel and grit high in the air, tearing at the boards of the merchant loading bays. The train split the night like a white hot meteor, crashing to rest with a booming jolt, waking the sleeping village from its slumber.

At the convent of the Sisters of Santa Maria, Mother Mercy Justice was already awake for the clamorous eruption. Both evenings since Catalina and the marshal left, she'd had trouble falling asleep, and tonight the Sisters of Sorrow had again taken up their dirge.

When the first thunder hit her ears, she imagined a pop-up rain was on its way and crawled out of bed, dressed quickly, and slipped out to her garden to cover the flowers. Then she realized the rumble she heard was the train, the steel monstrosity slamming into town.

She rushed to the south side of the mission and somebody on the community side of the wall pulled the alarm. Bells in the gable above tumbled one over the other, ringing out the alert. Shouts came from the village square. People hollered with excitement.

Bare-headed, her hair pulled back in a tight bun, Mercy hurried to open the heavy gate. Two sisters were already there, Sofia Lee and Carolyn. She nodded her thanks as they helped open the way as Andronicus joined them. The Monsignor was pulling on a long black coat over red underwear, and wore light cotton slippers. "What's going on, Mercy?"

"It's the train. Coming in fast, unexpected."

"I should say unexpected." The priest's hooked nose flitted back and forth like a stunned buzzard. "Nobody notified me of any such arrival."

Then a new wave of sound came from the tracks. A big, booming crash, followed by another, and then a third. The bawling of horses and pounding clatter of hooves.

Gunfire erupted.

Cries of anticipation became screams of terror.

Mercy ran to the street ahead of the others.

A dozen concussive blasts were followed with grievous wailing and a spattering of gusty shouts.

And ugly heinous laughter.

A man came out of the mercantile building, pulling at his boot with one hand, holding a rifle with another. Two doors down, a woman poked her head out of a window, saw the gun, and screamed. Two men waddled out of Lloyd's batwing doors to see what the fuss was about.

More gunfire, and Mercy saw an orange glow blossom at the gin house behind the hotel.

"Sister Sofia. Sister Caroline," The two nuns flanked Mercy on the brick paving, waiting for instruction. "Santo Tomas is under attack."

Mercy spun on her heel and brushed past the Monsignor, leading the others back into the mission. What she had feared for so long was coming to pass. She had tried to deny it. When the Sisters of Sorrow appeared, she told herself it was about the Riveras. When Catalina showed up on her doorstep, she assumed there would be time to make plans.

She had sent the Black Rose on a reconnaissance mission. If Cassidy collected the bounty on Tut Dawson, so much the better. But she had not expected trouble with Fino so soon. Yet, here he was. She could sense his presence, an evil riding the night air.

An explosion cut through the night, accompanied by screams and the barking of dogs.

Inside the common room at the convent, she brushed woven placemats to the floor and put both hands on the big wooden table.

The twenty-four sisters of Santa Maria flowed in through the door from their quarters. Awkwardly awakened, they had responded to the bell, dressing in mere minutes, appearing before Mercy, ready to serve.

Beyond the walls of the convent, the noise of battle settled in. The din of repeated blasts, the cries of surprise and confused anguish. They only had a few minutes before the first casualties came in.

"We will not shirk our duties during this time of need," said Mercy. "The facts of this assault will become clear with time. First and foremost, we must look after the infirm. The very young and the very old. We must aid the wounded and bring comfort to the dying."

Now dressed in full vestments, Andronicus barged into the room, interrupting Mercy's speech. "It's chaos out there. Chaos!" He slammed his fist into the palm of his hand. "Why does this have to happen now? The mission is precariously poised. We're waiting on our new pastor, waiting on new revenue from his eminence the Bishop. Why now? This will make a shambles of everything I've worked for."

"It's hardly the time for self-pity," said Mercy.

"And you," he said, looking around the room, wild-eyed and mad, "you women stand here clucking like a flock of spring chickens. He flung his arm out to indicate the battle. "Can't you see what's happening out there?"

"We were just addressing our duties, Monsignor."

"Address them more quickly."

A rapping sounded at the nearest outside door, and two of the nuns hurried to respond.

"McKenzie will answer for this," said Andronicus. "Mark my words, if he won't answer to me, he'll answer to the Almighty."

"Charles McKenzie?" said Mercy. "What does he have to do with it?"

The startled expression on Andronicus' face was the guilty look of a schoolboy with his hand in the church offering plate. He fumbled through a series of words with his answer, finally settling on, "Why, the train, of course. It's his train. It's obviously being turned against us by savages."

To Mercy, it was clear the priest knew more than he said, but she didn't press for answers. The man was aggressively self-serving, but it was clear even he hadn't foreseen what was happening tonight. He rushed from the room as the two sisters from before carried in a young man, mortally wounded.

"Lay him on the table," said Mercy. At the sight of the man's shattered, open ribcage, she crossed herself. "Sofia, Caroline, come with me."

The sky above the mission wall was a glowing, angry red. In front of the north gate, the seven Sisters of Sorrow patiently murmured under their breath, waiting for the Mother Superior to activate them.

Mercy stood with her adjuncts at each shoulder. "You who have sung of such dire circumstances, must now act," she said. "First and foremost, the Sisters of Santa Maria are an order of peace. Tonight the peace is shattered, and I'm asking you to rise up in our defense."

Sofia Lee was of Spanish descent. In her mid-30s with close-cropped black hair, she was slim, muscular and athletic. She had come to the convent after a life on the street. She was a master of blades, and a student of Creole fencing. Mercy had never asked her to revisit those talents.

Until now.

Sofia's brown eyes never wavered from Mercy's face. Her devotion was complete. "All things in

God's time," said Sofia.

Caroline Harp was an African woman, younger than Sofia, but harder and more mature. Since her days as a child in South Carolina, she carried a star-shaped edged throwing weapon handed down through her family. They called it a Kpinga, and she didn't lay it down even after taking her final, permanent vows of peace. Mercy hadn't asked her to. "His will, not ours," said Caroline.

In the flickering light, Mercy addressed the women who stood before her.

"I had hoped for the return of the Black Rose and a good report. Over time, I had hoped to think things through. We, who stand here, are different than the other sisters. We see the world differently, with different values. The others will act as caregivers. I'm asking you to be warriors."

She paused to gauge the reaction of the women.

"Understood," said Sofia. Caroline nodded.

Stoic, the seven sisters waited for instruction.

"The man I fear is behind tonight's battle has a long history with Santo Tomas, and with me. His name is Adrian Felipe Fino, and he is a monster."

Mercy addressed half the line. "Four of you guard the west wall and the pilgrim's wading stream. If McKenzie's train carried an army, it's likely they have explosives. We must protect the springs."

The shrouded women bowed and hurried through the garden gate.

"The rest of you take positions in the street to the south, north, and east. Welcome the wounded, relieve the distressed, protect the charity work of the other sisters." Mercy's voice was like ice. "Defend the holy order, without quarter. To the death if need be." She turned to Sofia and Caroline. "Come with me."

The three advanced into the street and were immediately met with two men on horseback, firing their rifles indiscriminately.

The one on the black horse with a white blaze wore a shaggy sweater over Federales trousers and spit-shined boots. Laughing with glee, he shot a man who appeared in a window of the cantina. The victim fell backwards with a crash through one of the plate glass windows.

The sloppy sombrero on the rider's head was tied around his chin in a way no one familiar with the hat would wear it.

The second man, whipping a gray steel dust stallion, was dressed as a peasant with cotton clothes, but he also wore tall leather boots. Mercy wasn't fooled.

The costumed soldier was busy pumping rounds of lead into the mercantile building when the nuns appeared. "Come out, come out," he yelled. "Pigs for the slaughter."

Through the shop windows, Mercy saw the proprietor and his family ducking behind the counter, hiding amongst the shelves.

"Shut him up, Sofia."

The young sister sprang forward, closing on the gray horse from the rider's blind side. The Spanish fighting knife she produced from her sleeve was called the navaja, a folding weapon with a long

curved blade. The ancient design was augment-
ed with a modern, tempered steel spring set in a
polished stag's horn handle. Sofia propelled seven
inches of razor-keen death.

"Pigs for the slaughter!"

As the kill-crazed rider brought his rifle around,
Sofia ducked beneath it and made a crisscross motion
with her arm, lacerating the tendons behind his knee.
The soldier howled and fell toward the wound, grasping
it with both hands, allowing the nun to spin around the
rear of the horse and cut the other leg as well.

Mad with pain, the rider twisted in the saddle,
lost his balance and, slipping, tried to hang on to his
horse's mane. Sofia met him halfway to earth, driving
her blade up through the fleshy underside of his jaw,
pinning his mouth shut with an expulsion of blood.

"Nothing more to say?" Sofia jerked back her
blade and slapped the steel dust away, turning to
face the first rider as he circled back.

From the saddle of the black horse, the soldier
cackled, pointed his rifle with one hand.

Sofia dodged to the side, and Caroline was
immediately behind her, crouched low, her arm
outstretched, the Kpinga throwing-edge already
on-course, flickering through the firelight.

Two of the weapon's five steel points buried themselves deep in the soldier's lower throat just between
the collar bones, and he fell sideways, almost taking
his black horse with him. The animal reared up,
dumping its rider full to the ground. Mercy watched
the animal race away toward the mission.

Caroline stepped on the dead man's astonished face, bent, and retrieved her weapon.

She crossed herself and joined Mercy in a charge toward the rails.

The Mother Superior issued her commands. "Caroline, secure the hotel. There will be more wounded than the mission can hold. We will need beds. But be careful. Don't take any chances. Don't trust anyone. There are those in Santo Tomas who will be against us."

She drew the shiv from the crucifix around her neck. "Sofia, you're with me. We must take the battle to its source. We'll make our way the train."

Sister Caroline cut left to the hotel and hurled her Kpinga into a pair of gunnies on the porch, Shane Ricketts and Clem Ruiz. Immediately, one of them fell over, clutching his arm.

"Dammit to hell," said Shane, blood running through his fingers as he tried to apply pressure to his blood-soaked sleeve. "Aced by a woman — twice in three days."

"What the hell's the world coming to?" said Clem.

He leveled his gun at Caroline, but his grip was hurried, his hands slick with sweat. She cartwheeled over the, steps and her impact sent him flying into a support pillar.

Caroline bashed Clem in the teeth with the butt of his own revolver, then stood tall and sent Mercy a salute.

"There are more troops coming," said Sofia.

She was right.

Mercy counted six horses with troops in the saddle tramping down the last box car ramp. Beyond them, four men stood beside an open crate, tossing small packages up to the horsemen as they rode off the train.

One of the men took off to a spot behind the hotel, holding the package close to the lit cigar in his mouth.

Seconds later, the village was rocked by another explosion.

"It's wanton destruction," said Mercy. "They have no strategy, no plan."

"The strategy is terror," said Sofia. "The plan is to raze the town and everyone in it."

"They're not expecting any real defense," said Mercy, studying the train. Behind the steaming locomotive and its tender, there were two long green Pullman passenger cars, and seven open box cars. "Let us disappoint them."

One of the passenger cars was lit from inside with electric light, and a man sat inside, his face in shadows, drinking from a tall mug. At first Mercy thought he had white hair, but then she saw his head was a mass of bandages. When he turned into the light, she recognized McKenzie's red beard.

Suddenly, they were discovered. "Best get away, Señoras!"

The man at the dynamite crate levered three rapid fire shots in Mercy's direction. She flinched, and the two nuns deliberately went to ground hard with slugs chewing up the earth around them.

"Watch out for stinging bees, eh? They fly everywhere!" The man went back to his business of distributing explosives, and Mercy rolled to her feet, helping Sofia with the same movement.

A young man with a waxed mustache and two sweaters stepped between the cars from behind the Pullman. He was buttoning the fly of his trousers with one hand, carrying his carbine carelessly pointed at the ground with the other. Mercy showed him her stiletto. "Drop it," she said, and he complied. She beckoned him back toward the hotel and Sofia retrieved the gun.

"How many men are with you?" said Mercy.

"Mi no tellin' you shiit," said the soldier.

Whisper soft, Sofia put an arm around his chest and held the tip of her navaja to his throat. "Answer the questions," she said.

The soldier's face held firm, but his fear was manifest in the growing wet stain below his belt. "I guess you weren't quite done back there," said Mercy, glancing at between his legs. "I'll ask you again: how many?"

"Trienta y seis. Cuarenta. More."

"Thirty-six," Mercy translated. "Or forty. All with carbines? Dynamite, too?"

"Si, si."

"Why? What's your mission?"

The man shrugged. "No mission. We kill everybody we see."

"On who's order?"

The man shrugged, this time with a wide smile of defiance. "I see now you are holy sisters. You no kill me in cold blood."

Mercy nodded, and Sofia clubbed him in the back of the head with the rifle stock. He went down in his own stink with a heavy groan.

"I hate it when they're right," said Mercy.

A new volley of shots pinged around them from the town's square, and they dived for cover along the side of the hotel.

Rifle blasts splintered white washed pillars, and the punched into the corner siding.

They pushed themselves to the ground.

The last horse soldier to leave the train galloped toward them, guns blazing.

CHAPTER TWENTY-NINE

With Sofia beside her, Mercy buried her face in the dust between the hotel and the railroad tracks as smoking death pinned them to the ground. She felt the heat from the bullets and nettles of chaff kicked up on impact to scratch her face and hands.

Trapped between a volley of fire from the street in front of the hotel and a horse soldier bearing down with two six-shooters, it was only a matter of time before the heavy percussion signaled their end.

Then came a swift whistling and a heavy, wet thud.

Mercy lifted her eyes to see the horse rearing up, wavering as the soldier fell backwards, tugging at an irregular piece of steel protruding from his chest.

"Caroline," said Mercy, seeing the nun lean down from the corner of the roof above.

The rider took the horse sideways and both collapsed in a pileup that left the soldier crushed to a pulp. While the horse disentangled itself, Mercy helped Sofia to her feet and caught a glimpse of

Charles McKenzie watching them from inside the Pullman. He seemed agitated and confused. A second man appeared behind Charlie, a trim gentleman with clipped blonde hair wearing a dark suit.

Mercy turned her attention back to the horse. "We could use a good horse."

Sofia ran past the passenger car and caught the frightened pony near the front of the tender. Mercy's heart caught in her throat as a second mount, a roan gelding, appeared around the nose of the 705. But the man in the saddle was dead, collapse over the withers of his horse, a lit kerosene lantern still in his hand. His shirt was spattered with blood. She recognized him from town, one of the few villagers who had given Fino's army a fight.

Sofia led the soldier's gray stallion to Mercy's side, and the two nuns removed the dead man from the roan's saddle. "His name was Sloan," said Mercy, identifying the bartender in the dim light cast from the Pullman. Quietly she knelt beside the body, whispering a prayer, drawing a cross in the air over his still features.

"Let's us ride, Mother," she said. "We can do nothing for the dead. Maybe we can encourage the living"

Mercy nodded and stepped into the saddle.

"There are four hundred people in Santo Tomas," said Sofia. "Where are they?"

"Where we should be. Holed up inside, away from all the fighting," said Mercy.

"Afraid?"

"Why not?"

"There are more of us than there are of them."

"There is a festering rot in Santo Tomas," said Mercy. "From the sheriff to the Monsignor. From the mayor, Carlyle, to half the business men. They have been plotting for months to sell this town, piece by piece, to Charles McKenzie."

"Surely this kind of destruction wasn't in their plan?"

Mercy agreed. "Somebody miscalculated. They didn't believe it would come to open destruction." She pursed her lips in disgust. "Of course, they don't know Fino."

She held the reins and kneed the horse around to the left. "Take me to the homes and the jacallas. Let's raise an army to fight this madness."

Sofia steered her horse alongside Mercy's roan. "What if the people won't fight?"

"Then they will die," said Mercy. "But I will first make damned sure they die ashamed."

The locale around the business district was littered with spotty settlements, shacks, barns and acreages their owners called farms during the rainy times that came around every two or three years. Communities of thatch-roofed huts, walls made from sticks and mud, decorated the landscape between Santo Tomas and Rivera territory, and soul-crushing poverty lived side-by-side with brick-house splendor.

Raiding parties from the train, gone ahead of Mercy and Sofia had already blasted much of it into oblivion. At each stop along the way, Mercy prepared to deliver her inspirational pep-talk, only to be stopped by the sight of dead patriarchs and wounded children, pillars of flame and pyramids of wreckage. The living were too busy grieving to fight. The dead didn't care.

As they approached a pebbled lane beside a burning hut, a woman screamed and Mercy led the way. Around the corner of the bonfire, one of Fino's men, dressed like a revolutionary, held a young girl's bare arm behind her, forcing her to the ground.

When he saw the horses coming toward him, he shoved the girl away.

Sofia was an angel of death. Swooping in on Mercy's right, she swung her arm into an underhanded arc and buried her navaja to its hilt in the soldier's chest. The girl screamed as her attacker dropped to the ground, vomiting blood.

Mercy quickly dismounted to cradle the sobbing girl in her arms. "You're saved," she said. "The danger is past."

"Mother Mercy?"

"I've got you."

"My parents…they…they are…."

The girl flung both arms around the nun, and they held each other beside the fire.

"I understand," said Mercy.

"These people are not built for war," said Sofia.

Mercy nodded. "Forgive me," she said.

"Some of us can stand up, some can't."

"I hope there's enough of us who can."

"The world is changing, Mother Mercy. I fear all of us will be forced to make such a choice sooner rather than later."

Mercy helped the girl to her feet and onto the back of her horse. Then she mounted the saddle behind her and wrapped an arm around the slender waist. "We'll take you to the Sisters of Santa Maria, where you will be safe," she said. "Do you have a name?"

"Lucia."

"God has blessed you, Lucia."

"I don't think so, Mother."

Mercy held the words in her heart. She whispered, "I don't think so either, niña."

******

Other than the purring rumble of the 705 and the crackling of flames, the town was ominously silent when they rode back around the square.

Hoof beats echoed off the mission walls as the gray and the roan carried Mercy, Lucia, and Sofia onto a main street lit by bonfires. There — that used to be a print shop. Here was what had been a lawyer's office. On the corner, what remained of a clothing store. The air was hot as midday, and everything flickered with an eerie orange glow.

They were met by a congregation of business owners on the boardwalk outside the cantina led by Ned Sedgewick and the mayor. Carlyle carried a mesquite branch with a white sheet attached to it as a makeshift flag of peace. Andronicus stood behind him. On each side, three of Fino's soldiers, all holding rifles, fenced them in.

"What's this?" said Mercy.

"We're offering a truce," said Sedgewick. "We're outgunned, outmanned. It's over."

"You think so?" said Mercy. "What are the terms of surrender?"

"Unconditional," said Andronicus.

Mercy turned in the saddle. "Where are my nuns? Is the mission safe?"

"The Sisters of Santa Maria are busy inside the mission caring for the wounded, just as their vows require," said Andronicus. "At least they care about the masses, even if you've decided to play cowboy."

"Had I not played cowboy, I can't imagine where this poor girl would be now."

Andronicus appraised Lucia with a sneer. "You would sacrifice an entire village for one girl?"

Mercy ignored the question. "What about the springs?"

"The springs are under the hand of God," said Andronicus. "To rise up or die as he sees fit."

"You and I will have words, Monsignor."

"No," said Andronicus, holding up his hand. "Not now, Mercy. I understand you're upset." He smiled. "It's a trying time for all of us."

"This way," said Sedgewick, leading the way across the street to the hotel.

"And if we don't?" said Sofia.

One of the soldiers brought his rifle into line with the nun.

Sofia chewed the inside of her cheek. Then looked at Mercy.

She nodded, then dismounted and led her horse to

a hitching post beside the cantina. Mercy followed suit, helping Lucia do the ground.

"Who are you going to see?" she said.

"Whoever's in charge of this army," said Sedge-wick. "I think it's Garcia and his Injun."

"It is not Garcia," said Mercy.

"It don't matter what I think anyway," said Sedge-wick.

"That much has always been true," said Mercy, "for as long as I have known you."

She and Lucia fell in line behind the others with a single rifle escort bringing up the rear. When they arrived at the hotel porch, the soldier walked ahead to hold the door, and Mercy looked at the train. Again she caught sight of McKenzie and the blonde man inside the Pullman. Something had changed in the time since she saw them last. This time Charlie Mac was angry and working his mouth in defiance of the grim blonde who sat near him.

When Mercy turned back to the hotel steps, the bald rosary maker greeted her in English. "This is for Lucia Walters," he said.

He hadn't been there a moment before. Now he waited, as relaxed as ever, dressed lightly, and free of distress. For the carefree expression on his face, he may as well have been sharing a cup of tea during a pleasant spring morning.

In his hand was another black rosary.

Like the others, it was made of wood, but rather than being stained black or crafted from some dark variety, it was burned. Mercy accepted the gift and marveled at its integrity. Burned, yet it was strong as new. Except for the color and the faint smell, it was undamaged.

"Please do not think we're ungrateful," said Mercy, "but we have a bit of a crisis here at the moment." Something in the old man's smile made her explanation seem foolish. "Surely you've seen what's happened here tonight."

"There is no crisis, Mercy. All proceeds according to His divine plan."

"Forgive my doubt, friend," said Mercy. "But, honestly—look around you."

"You look around. Behold a pale horse, and the name that sat on him was death." The rosary maker smiled. "There, the Black Rose comes."

Mercy glanced into the street.

"I don't think—"

When she turned around, the rosary maker was gone.

"Where did he go?"

"Who, Mother?" said Lucia. "Where did who go?"

Mercy felt the weight of the evening press down on her shoulders. With a heavy heart, she picked up Lucia's hand and placed the black rosary in her hand. "Keep hold of this," she said. "Always remember God is with you." She laced the girl's fingers between her own.

The soldier at the hotel door was impatient. "Move," he said with a wave of his gun barrel.

She ushered Lucia into the hotel lobby ahead of her.

The businessmen of Santo Lucia stood in a clump in the center of the room, looking up at the staircase. Mercy watched a broad shouldered man descend the steps slow and steady. Smiling. Triumphant. Full of himself.

Two soldiers in full Federale regalia walked behind him, rifles at the ready.

A fat cigar in one hand, a glimmering drink in the other, Adrian Felipe Fino singled her out of all the people in the lobby.

"Hello, Louise," he said. "Madre de Dios, it's good to see you again."

CHAPTER THIRTY

The Black Rose rode through the night like she was thirteen years old again, without a care in the world. The Andalusian beneath her wore a doma vaquero saddle with no pad and glowed with the color of fresh tilled earth in the moonlight. Surefooted, strong, and sparkling with youth, the vitality of the horse fed the rider.

She held the reins easy in her hands, the firm comfort of her gauntlets, boots and jodhpur pants giving her confidence in the face of what she had supposed was absolute defeat.

The desert breeze was cool, but not frigid, and her dark cloak carried behind her on the wind.

To her left, Paco rode a swift paint pony.

To her right, Raul Cassidy sat astride Denver Three-Moon's mare, Dahteste, which meant "warrior woman" in Apache. It suited him better than his donkey, Diablo. Was she wrong hoping Adeline and Mary would leave the beast at Fino-Espolon when they came home.

If there was a home to come back to.

The Black Rose pushed the morbid thought from her mind. The two women were moved by their convictions as much as Catalina Rivera. At least Adeline was. There was no reason to suppose they wouldn't cover this same ground in a few weeks. She hoped when they made the journey, Santo Tomas would still be there.

The steeds running directly in front of her climbed a rocky ledge and motioned for her to join them. Paco and Cassidy slowed, cutting circles in the roadbed before holding up their hands to signal the trailing legion of horse soldiers to rein in. Clouds of dust and strings of foul oaths built up before the team finally settled down.

"Them bowlegs are half drunk, I think," said Paco.

"Them bowlegs saved your life," said Cassidy.

"How is it you got them to ride to Santo Tomas in aid? Garcia is not known for his benevolence."

"I appealed to his vanity," said Cassidy.

"There is much there to appeal to."

"I offered him a trade to make him an important man in his community. More important than he already is, I should say."

"What do you have that's worth so much?"

"A red Willys automobile," said Cassidy.

On the hillock, the Black Rose put the nose of her horse between Denver Three-Moons and Manuel Michael Garcia. "Why do we stop?" she said. "Santo Tomas is just over the next rise. You squander time, Garcia. "

The revolutionario pulled a long face and picked

at his gold teeth with a stem of jackweed. "My corrida, my rules."

Dressed in the traditional charro fashion of his people, Garcia wore a rust-red bolero jacket adorned with rose blossoms and an intricate maze of thorny vines embroidered with metallic gold thread. His pressed shirt was white and clean with a red silk tie around the collar. His tight pants were decorated on the outside with silver conchas and leather tassels. He wore a wide brimmed sombrero over a swatch of wild, dark hair and his eyebrows were wide and dark, as if painted on with greasepaint.

"Have a care, señorita," said Denver Three-Moons. "Only Garcia commands the horsemen."

The old Apache spoke the truth, and there was a gentle timber to his voice, strong, but easier than before. The experience with Ben Cain at Lohman Siding had forged a kind of bond between them. If the battle for Santo Tomas did same for her and Garcia, the Black Rose would have a powerful ally.

"I apologize, Don Garcia."

Garcia leaned over the horn of his saddle as if sharing a secret. "I'm only doing it for the car," he said.

"Fino will count on the element of surprise to shock the villagers into a state of confusion and retreat. Once they've shut themselves up inside their squalid shacks, they will be easy prey," said Garcia. "That is what I'd do." A slip of paper appeared in his fingers like magic. With his other hand, he withdrew a pouch of tobacco from his jacket and sprinkled out a stack of leaves. He rolled the quirly with one motion and held it out for Three-Moons to light.

The old man struck a match, and Garcia lit up, breathing in deep and peering across his horse through the curls of smoke.

"I am sorry about your family, niñita. Whatever differences we had in the past..."

"Are still differences, viejo. But not important today?"

Garcia's laugh was authentic. "I begin to like you, Black Rose. Yes, I begin to like you very much."

"In Santo Tomas, your men will take care of the soldiers and the train?"

"And you and I will find Fino," said Garcia. "As we agreed."

The Black Rose urged her mount clockwise to address the restless army below. When they saw her, the men stilled their horses. Paco gazed up from his pony, his face eager and full of pride. Cassidy appeared completely sober for the first time since she'd met him.

"Whatever it is you think you fight for today," said the Black Rose. "You are wrong. If you think this is about honor, or glory, or...an automobile..." She glanced over her shoulder at Garcia's pleased expression, "you're mistaken."

One of the men coughed, and a string of comments were passed back and forth among the men.

The Black Rose continued. "The men we fight are conscripts of evil, their leaders driven by motives of black hedonism and lust. They take from those who have less simply because they can. Show them no mercy, because they surely will show none to the women and children they slaughter." She raised her voice in challenge. "Are you with me? Do you ride with Garcia and the Black Rose?"

The men lifted their arms as one, and in each hand was a rifle. Around their chests were bandoliers crammed with bullets, and most of them wore sabers on their hip. The cheer arising from their lips shook the clouds and rattled the moon.

"It is good," said Paco.

"We ride," said Cassidy.

"For justice," said the Black Rose on her flint-rock footing, and her Andalusian's iron-shod hooves struck sparks in its turning.

"I'm doing it mostly for the car," said Garcia, pitching his cigarette to the plains.

The army cried out, and like a rippling wave, grew in strength and resolve until its front line rushed past the idling train and galloped into the village square.

******

Santo Tomas was an inferno.

The Black Rose had never seen such destruction, not even on the morning her home was sacked. She rounded the front of the train at gallop, arriving in the street in front of the cantina with Cassidy and Paco at her side.

Behind them, Garcia's men yipped and hollered, and the first counter-attack began as gunfire erupted on the other side of the box-car string.

They broke for the mission espadana and were met with wails and cries of pain under the four bells. "The walls are truly too thin," said the Black Rose.

It was impossible to take in the horror all at once.

Three city storefronts had collapsed into burning heaps of slag, and the flames were spreading through the alleys and walkways. A handful of old men carried gallon pails full of water from the direction of the pilgrim's wading river, spilling most of their cargo along the way.

Hopeless.

Like trying to snuff a live volcano with tears.

Bodies littered the boardwalk in front of the mercantile, and of the buildings not burning, only two still had unbroken glass in their windows.

"Paco, stay and help the sisters with the wounded."

"Where will you go?"

The Black Rose held her urumi in a coil near her hip. "To retake the town," she said.

"Not alone you won't," said Cassidy, showing her the carbine in his hand.

"No," she offered him a grim smile, "not alone. Not anymore."

They turned and were immediately met by four of Fino's cavalry rounding the far end of the mission. The lead man was tall and wore a silk stove-pipe hat. The Black Rose didn't take time to ponder the odd chapeau. Instead, she dodged the oncoming rifle fire in a whirling display of horsemanship, nudging the Andalusian to canter sideways before driving ahead into the fray. Stovepipe held fast to his carbine, levering a pattern of continuous fire sure to cut the Black Rose in half were she content to stay in the saddle. Giving her steed its head, she slipped down to hang from the bridle, keeping the horse's body between her and the gunman, bullets sizzling overhead.

She swung herself back up into the saddle at the last second and let fly with the urumi. The tactile steel shimmered through the air, then cleanly slicing through Stovepipe's neck. He died without a sound, tumbling to the ground in a clumsy display, and the whip-sword curled back around to take the next soldier's arm.

Cassidy stood motionless in tough leather stirrups, eyeing Fino's men through iron sites. He was all efficient motion, tapping the trigger, levering a second shell, tapping again. The soldiers went down to either side of him like a parting of the Red Sea.

The Black Rose and Cassidy convened at the cantina boardwalk, and they saw three of Garcia's men give chase to one of the invaders. Upon meeting a formidable resistance, the soldier didn't appear to have the stomach for war. Crouched in the saddle, the soldier scurried away down a side street like a morning wood roach. They watched the three men in pursuit disappear from view, but three simultaneous shots signaled the inevitable outcome.

"To your right," said Cassidy, and the Black Rose twisted in her seat to see a soldier swinging a lasso in the air, looping the rope in her direction. With her between them, Cassidy couldn't get off a safe shot, and it was too late to duck out of the way. As the noose came down on her shoulders, she did exactly what the wrangler didn't expect and spurred her Andalusian into his lesser steed. The slim brown mare buckled under the heaving weight of the big warhorse, but she took the soldier and the Black Rose down with her.

They hit the ground barely six feet apart, the Black Rose with the hemp firmly squeezing her arms to her side, him desperately hanging on to the coil in white-knuckled grip. The Black Rose was first to her feet, and again she charged, not letting up for an instant.

"Stay still, witch."

"Like hell," said the Black Rose, performing a daring pirouette she wrapped even more of the slack around her arms before levering a sidekick into the bully's left kidney. The soldier bent back in misery and Cassidy wheeled around the pileup of complaining horses, looking for a clean shot.

The Black Rose struck again, this time stomping the back of the soldier's knee, sending him into a devastating face-first collision with the edge of the village boardwalk. When he tried to recover, Cassidy shot two holes through his chest.

Dead fingers let go of the rope.

"We've got to ensure the safety of the outer village," said the Black Rose, shucking out of the lasso. "The people there will be confused, frightened. The children—"

"I'll go," said Cassidy.

"Find Three-Moons, round up some of the men."

Cassidy nodded and rode toward the train. He rounded the engine and was gone. The Black Rose watched his progress, then darted back to the steps of the hotel where a familiar figure stood in open defiance of someone inside the doorway.

"Mercy!"

The Black Rose bolted down the street toward the Mother Superior even as the older woman backed slowly toward the steps. Did she have a young girl by the hand?

Who was Mercy talking to?

A man's voice gave a garbled command and Mercy denied it.

Mercy denied him. "I won't have any part of it. Now, if you'll excuse me, I'm taking this young lady to the convent where I will find her some food and proper clothing. There's no reason for her to endure your gloating half naked."

The Black Rose stopped less than thirty feet from the steps, waiting for Mercy to turn around. A soldier stood in the doorway, his rifle at the ready.

His English was flawless. "You haven't been given permission to leave," he said.

"I don't need permission," said Mercy. "I'm going regardless of what you say or do. Shoot me if you will, but I'm going to preserve something of this poor child's dignity."

With the girl in tow, Mercy turned on her heel.

The soldier triggered a terrific blast, cutting her down in mid-stride.

CHAPTER THIRTY-ONE

Surrounded by velvet soft cushions and wood paneled splendor, Charlie Mac nursed his whisky and wondered how and where he'd lost it all. Certainly his financial accounting wasn't as scrupulous as some. Maybe he'd relied too much on the good will of his creditors. Maybe he'd taken on too much, too fast. On the other hand, weren't industrialists all across the nation leveraging comparable fortunes in grand bids to build their empires? Wasn't Charles McKenzie cut from the same cloth as the Morgans and Rockefellers?

He said as much to Gündelfinger, as if the stupid Kraut was intelligent enough to recognize the common traits McKenzie shared with the barons of high finance.

The German offered a glib smile and pulled the stopper from a fresh crystal decanter. "Rockefeller? Well, look what happened to him. Your own country only just recently turned on him, yes?"

"If you mean the Sherman Anti-Trust fiasco—"

"Your mistake, Herr McKenzie, was trusting too much in paper and pen." Gündelfinger's eyes glinted as he leaned over the table they shared with an offer to top off his glass. "General Fino and I — we don't trust paper and pen."

McKenzie gulped the remainder of his drink and held out his glass.

While the German poured, he compared Fino and himself to Bismark. "We believe in blood and iron." He wagged his finger at Charlie, scolding, berating. "One day you may learn enough to join us."

But the withering look he offered Charlie was full of doubt. "You foolish idealistic Americans have yet to understand the world."

Gündelfinger's words bounced around Charlie's head like a billiard ball. He put a hand to the bandage on his head.

Turning to the window, he watched the horses running up and down the street in front of the hotel. He became momentarily enamored with the sharp, quick flashes of light synched in perfect rhythm with a dozen booming explosions. Each bullet fired was another rail tie ripped from the ground of Charlie's future. Each explosion, like a sledgehammer blow to a rail spike between his eyes.

He rubbed the bridge of his nose between thumb and forefinger. When he opened his eyes, he saw a pompous foreigner viewing the spectacle outside alongside him, but with the contemptuous idea it was for his benefit and not Charlie's.

The world tilted on its axis, and McKenzie felt a

surge of bile rise into his throat.

No, he told himself. He wouldn't show weakness. Wouldn't let the bastard get him down.

Both men watched through the window of the Pullman car as some of the villagers came together in front of the cantina waving a white flag of surrender.

"Gott im Himmel," The German clapped. "They are like sheep in their simplicity."

Quickly, a group of soldiers surrounded the men and began herding them toward the hotel. It was at then McKenzie recognized the blue habit of two nuns on horseback riding to intercept the group.

His eyes felt scratchy and full of sand, and his skin was greasy and raw. His head pounded and he clenched his jaw in time to his trip-hammer heartbeat.

If only he had a bargaining chip. Some sort of leverage he could use against Fino to get his train back.

If he hadn't fallen for that damned Rivera woman's tricks, he might've been able to offer her up in trade.

Instead, he had nothing Fino needed. A fact the German knew too well and decided to use now to humiliate Charlie Mac one last time.

"Fino spoke true. These dummkopfs can't even defend themselves. What kind of men are they, not to stand up for their homes? Their families?" Gündelfinger swirled his drink with deliberate goading. "But then, I guess you would know all about what it means to be a coward, eh Charlie?"

McKenzie's reply was a rumbling slur, hardly loud of enough to be heard. "I know where you can put your big talk," he said.

"What was that, Charlie? Did you have a comment? Something you wished to say?" Gündelfinger sat back in his seat and continued to watch events unfold outside. "Once you've finished your drink, you may be excused."

"Excused?" said McKenzie.

"Yes, Charlie. I'm asking you to leave the train. For good. Once and or all. Your betters are in control. It's simple."

In the street, the crowd of villagers marched with armed guards and downcast eyes toward the hotel. The nuns too had joined the procession, but unlike the others, they held their faces high. McKenzie wondered at the shortest of the two, an attractive older woman who walked with her arm around a young girl. With sheer defiance, her chin jutted out toward the soldier beside her, and her walk was hardly the stride of a discouraged paeon. She said something to the rifleman, and the look on her face was a mixture of pride and anger.

The fact a nun such as she would stand up when Charlie had so readily laid down was shameful.

"Did you hear what I said, Charlie?" said the German, combing through his yellow hair with his fingers. "Finish your drink and leave our train."

Our train?

"No, not your train," said Charlie with little more than a whisper. "My train." All the long days growing up under his father's whip came back to him. All the long, seemingly endless days of ranch work. All the times his father had cussed him and called him stupid. All the nights after his mother died and his dad drank himself to oblivion.

Charlie Mac had risen above it all, first buying a few cows of his own, then acquiring property. He'd taken out loans and made good on them. What he couldn't get through perfectly honest means, he'd been able to acquire through shading the truth and manipulation. He became a master of rhetoric and an expert at sharing his vision.

He'd accomplished so much, and now he was being told to walk away without so much as a gun to his head.

The gun was implied, of course, but the German bastard considered himself above such crude behavior. Charlie, on the other hand, was a Texan. Crude behavior had been his stock and trade for years.

Watching the rigid nun defy her captors filled Charlie with purpose. He wouldn't give up his train.

He'd see it destroyed before he'd give it away for free.

As the company of prisoners gathered at the hotel steps, McKenzie turned to the German and slammed down his tumbler. Keeping his hand wrapped around the glass, he said, "You can go to hell, Kraut."

Then he leaned over the table and splashed the contents into Gündelfinger's face.

Before his adversary could do more than sputter and reach for a linen napkin, McKenzie was up and staggering toward the Pullman's rear door. For the first time since Tooms found him in the washroom where Catalina Rivera had left him for dead, Charlie had a plan. The girl hadn't worked out, but this would.

This time he wouldn't take any chances.

Pushing through the rear door, he was out of the car and stepping off the platform before he heard the German lob a string of high-pitched curses his way. Careful not to fall, he took the steps to the ground one by one, gauging his distance, holding tight to the stair rail.

The air was filled with acrid smoke which dried his nostrils and burned the back of his throat. A random gunshot rang out, and the clatter of horses hooves echoed back to the railroad tracks. Charlie heard the German shout one last obscenity and decided the Kraut wasn't coming after him.

So much the better.

Charlie wanted him to enjoy the Pullman for all it was worth. Now, more than ever, he hoped the arrogant son-of-bitch would revel in his success.

"Enjoy it while you can," he said, as if he were speaking directly to him. "Enjoy it for the rest of your life."

The fresh air had a sobering effect on Charles McKenzie.

Always a man who held his liquor well, his new-found sense of purpose honed his senses and cleared the fog from his mind. Like a hawk, he turned to spy up and down the train line. All the box cars were open, including the final car holding the army supplies he needed. Nowhere did he see a single soldier.

If Fino was anything, thought McKenzie, the Mexican was overly sure of himself, of his plans. Leaving the train unguarded showed as much. A quick jog put him near an open wooden crate, its discarded top pried loose and cast aside. The side of the crate confirmed its contents.

Danoso — *harmful.*

Explosiva.

McKenzie bent over the rim to rummage inside. If only there was enough to do the job.

He remembered Fino's boasting as they had traveled through the starlit void to Santo Tomas. Not only was there enough dynamite in the supply car to level the village, but the General had brought along barrels of black powder too. The information hadn't been offered simply as a way of passing the time.

Fino had *bragged* about it.

It would prove his undoing.

McKenzie could barely contain his joy.

Clutching a paper-bound package of explosive sticks in each hand, he set to work, placing a bundle under the frame of each car. Once finished, he planned to string the dynamite together with a trail of powder, saving an entire barrel for the engine.

He only prayed he could roll it to the front of the train without being seen.

As he worked, he thought about the expression he imagined he would see on the German's arrogant face when, after dropping a lit cigar into the works Charlie would jerk open the rear door of the Pullman just so he could watch him die.

It would be glorious.

CHAPTER THIRTY-TWO

It didn't surprise Mercy when Fino singled her out of everybody else in the hotel lobby. It would have surprised her if he hadn't targeted her.

"The attack on Santo Tomas is nothing but revenge, Adrian," she said, addressing him by his first name. "This entire atrocity begins and ends with you, personally." Since taking her vows, she had never cursed or spat in public. Now she did both, "Why the hell bring these innocent people into it? They're nothing to you."

Halfway down the stairway, the General didn't bother to deny it. Instead, he rolled his cigar between curving lips and spread his arms wide. If he wanted, he could have jumped over the railing, flapped his arms, and flown around the room.

He was just that confident.

"*These* people?" he said. "These people? Your sheriff, a man who crawls out of a bottle once a day to piss? Your mayor and his merchant friends who, months ago, signed letters of intent to sell everything around the mission to the Sioux City and Orient Railroad? Your own Monsignor, who—"

"We have heard enough," said the Monsignor from the front row of villagers. "We came in good faith to hear your demands, not receive an accounting of our sins."

"I find it interesting you would have sins in this regard to account for, Andronicus," Mercy said to the priest. "Perhaps you'd care to enlighten me?"

Fino's voice again took center stage. "Ah, Louise. Dear heart, there is no reason to quibble. And this is no way to hold a reunion." He stepped to the side of the stairway, making a path to the second floor. "Come, upstairs. Let us catch up with one another. I have an open bottle of the Russian Molokan wine you used to love so much."

"I shan't go anywhere with you. Not until you call off the killing."

Fino's smirk was exaggerated, his disappointment inflated for the sake of his audience. "Call off the killing? Why, we're just getting started." Hasty instruction put the soldier on Fino's left at attention. A second command set the butt of his rifle to his shoulder. He tugged the trigger, sending fire into the crowd, putting Ned Sedgewick down with a thrashing squeal. The crowd spasmed back in shock, then broke for the door. Three guards took up residence in front of the door, shooing everybody back into place.

"I pity you, Adrian. Almost twenty years, and it's still so important to you. So important you would squander your soul in order to have the final say."

"You of all people should understand, Louise. You know firsthand what the Riveras took from me. From both of us." He puffed his cigar and gazed down at the dead sheriff. "Move him into the next room." Fino nodded at two of the soldiers near the door, and they hastily complied with his order, one grabbing the dead man's shoulders, the other taking his feet.

"If your plan is to kill us all, then please get on with it," said Mercy. "It would be a joy to meet my savior today.

"Say now," said Carlyle. "She don't speak for all of us."

"That's for damn sure," said Clem Ruiz. "We're willing to negotiate for whatever it is you want. I mean, if you want the nun, you go ahead and take her."

"Just leave what's left of our village in peace," said Carlyle.

"I think it's the pleading I enjoy most of all," said Fino. He raised his eyebrows. "Admit it, Louise. You enjoy it too, no? It is why you became a bride of Christ? To listen to the endless pleading? To revel in the enumeration of sins?"

Mercy tightened her grip on Lucia and turned her back on Fino.

With the girl under her wing, the Mother Superior brushed past the rifleman, pushed open the hotel door and stormed out onto the porch.

"You can't leave, Louise. I won't allow it," said Fino.

Mercy's defiance was on display for all to see.

"Arrogant, stupid little man. I won't have any part of it," she said. "Now, if you'll excuse me, I'm taking this young lady to the convent where I will find her some food and proper clothing. There's no reason for her to endure your gloating half naked."

"You haven't been given permission to leave," said the soldier at the door.

"I don't need permission," said Mercy. "I'm going, Adrian. The end. Shoot me if you will, but right now my only concern is to preserve something of this poor child's dignity."

She turned to go, and heard the explosion even as her legs went out from under her and the world turned black.

******

"Mercy, no!"

The Black Rose landed at the foot of the hotel steps in a flurry of dust, her long black cloak spread into the night like the wings of an enormous raptor scooping up its prey. Her urumi sparkled in the light from the lobby.

At her feet, Mercy rolled onto her back, an ugly blotch of red spreading at her waistline through the blue fabric of her habit.

The soldier made as if to fire again.

With a spiraling sideways toss, the Black Rose caught the gunman under the arm, with her whip-sword, ruining tendon and bone even as it rent the cloth of his uniform. With an awful grunt, he fell to his knees, pitching the gun forward. Still smoking, his rifle landed on the steps with a racket.

A shout came from inside the hotel. "Stop her! Stop her now!!"

The Black Rose ignored Fino's cry and cradled Mercy in her arms.

"C-catalina?"

"I'm here, Mother."

"Y-you h-have the rosary?"

"I carry the black rosary, yes. Always. Just as you instructed."

Mercy turned her head toward the porch where the girl in the spare nightshirt squatted in terror. "Lucia."

"I will watch over the girl."

Mercy squeezed her eyes shut as the blood continued to spread down the skirt of her habit. She struggled against the pain to swallow. "The springs."

Of course. The healing springs of Santa Maria.

The miraculous touch of the Blue Nun.

Mercy may have thought she was giving the Black Rose her final instructions, but the words were more than that. Legend said the springs could heal any hurt, cure any sickness. If Mercy had any chance at all to live, the Black Rose knew it was through the power of the springs.

If only they could reach the pilgrim's wading river.

At Fino's command, two more soldiers dashed out of the hotel lobby. Crouching at Mercy's side, the Black Rose quickly wrapped her urumi around her waist, then slipped both arms under the trembling nun. Muscles rippling, she lifted Mercy away from the line of fire as the men started blasting. Bullets kicked up columns of debris, stitching a hem of death at her heels.

With an evasive pattern of footwork, the Black Rose managed to round the hotel and make the side street across from the mission. Behind her, Fino himself joined in the pursuit, barking out orders to his men.

His frustration at losing Mercy was curious. The previous afternoon, Mary and Catalina had over-heard Fino's plans for McKenzie's railroad and the region's valuable real estate. Such ambition could be explained by simple greed. What didn't make sense were his ruminations on Santo Tomas.

As is the village was something more than a village. Something like a lover.

"Santo Tomas is close to my heart. I have good rea-son to desire her. To hold her in my hand. To own her."

The Black Rose remembered Fino's words.

"When I was young, I drank from the eternal springs, and loved Santo Tomas with all my heart. I pledged myself to her."

And then.

"She spurned me."

Who spurned him?

A salvo of shots slammed into the side of the hotel from the two directions, nearly catching the Black Rose in the crossfire. The single break in her concen-tration meant she hadn't noticed the gang of gunmen coming at her from the direction of the springs.

To her left, a horde of Garcia's men hurrahed a ragged column of soldiers past the cantina and up the mission street. Now there was more gunfire echoing through the town than when they had first arrived. The desert horsemen were salvaging the town, but it did little to help get Mercy to safety.

Another blazing hail of lead showered the street as the shooting party advanced, but the Black Rose was helpless. As long as she carried Mercy in her arms, she couldn't use the urumi at her waist. All she could do was try not to be shredded by insistent battery.

All she could do was run.

She made it to the corner of the hotel and, slinging Mercy over her shoulder, she reached up and began to climb the side of the building as she had on the night the Black Rose was born. Gripping the bricks in her callused hands, working for every toe-hold, the ascent was arduous, the strain, tremendous. Every muscle and sinew screamed in protest, the joints of her fingers threatened to lock in defeat.

Ten feet.

Then twenty.

Fighting the fierce pull of gravity with each renewed effort.

Her burden was so quiet. So still. If only she'd been able to reach the springs.

But she hadn't, and there was no use in thinking about it now.

A man's shout interrupted the shooting. "There she is."

Then another: "Bring her down."

As bullets pinged off the structure around her, the Black Rose was grateful she climbed in the shadow of the hotel, away from the night's bonfires. In the dark, the rifleman couldn't see what they were aiming at. The more they fired, the more they missed.

The more they missed, the more they cursed.

Their frustration fed her courage.

Thought her final effort left her spent and exhausted, the Black Rose mounted the roof with Mercy tenderly in tow. Swiftly, she positioned them at the side of the glass skylight where she had once dropped down on Tut Dawson.

It may have been only a few days ago, but to the Black Rose it seemed like a lifetime. So many terrible things had come to pass in such a short time.

Now Santo Tomas was a smoldering ruin, and 705 engine Fino had swindled from Charlie McKenzie, complete with its luxury cars and boxcar army transports, idled below.

Mercy's cries were soft and filled with pain. But there was more at work than physical duress. Mercy's eyes fluttered open to reveal turmoil rising up and spilling over. Tears rained down her cheeks, the product of an intense emotional storm.

The Black Rose took off her cloak and bunched it up into a headrest. Careful not to disturb the wound, she arranged Mercy's habit and made the nun as comfortable as she could. At the hotel wall, gunfire gave way to conversation. Then came the scuffle and scrape of somebody attempting to scale the wall.

"Stay with me," said Mercy. "Must...tell you..."

"We are besieged, Mercy. Forgive me." The Black Rose covered the space between the skylight and the corner of the roof in seconds, timing the momentum of her kick to strike the first man whose head popped over the edge.

With a sickening crack, she sent a soldier hurtling into space.

Again, a torrent of gunfire plagued her, and the Black Rose was forced to retreat.

"Don't leave me again, Lina," said Mercy. "Please… don't leave."

"I'm here, Mercy. I will stay."

Huddling in the center of the roof, under the stars as they moved in their heavens toward dawn, Mercy flirted with death, and the Black Rose heard the sister's story.

CHAPTER THIRTY-THREE

"We were oh, so young my sister and I," said Mercy, "and the Texas frontier was wide open in those days. It was a splendid time to be alive. The air was full of endless possibilities, but Dad wanted to raise cows." Her lips cracked at the memory and her eyes gently closed. "It was always about those damn cows. To this day, I hate cattle…unless it's dead and roasted."

Presently, she opened her eyes and continued. "Victoria and I were born in the old Irish country, but father wanted a better life. We were seventeen years old when we came over on the boat."

The Black Rose found Mercy's hand and held it to her lips. "Such an adventure…," she said.

"It was wondrous. Everyone we met was filled with the same kind of ambitions, the same lofty dreams. Dad bought into a real estate deal, was offered a few hundred Texas acres near here." She nodded in the direction of the mission. "For nine idyllic months, we lived just outside Santo Tomas." Mercy's face hardened and her fist clenched. "Then Fino came."

"He attacked your ranch?"

Mercy shook her head. "He came as a friend. He came…courting. Had he simply razed the Byrne homestead, like he's done to the village tonight, it would have been more honest. Would've save us all so much time." Mercy tried to sit, but the pain forced her back down. "You must understand, the border country was wild in those days, less organized than today. There were dozens of bandit gangs, and raids on settlers were not uncommon, though we never experienced the violent incursions we heard about. Adrian Felipe Fino was a gentleman bandit. He brought candy, gifts, and small tokens of affection for everyone in the village. Victoria and I looked forward to his frequent visits."

"You were young and smitten," said the Black Rose.

"Then, as now, Fino was larger than life and always surrounded by his men." For a moment, Mercy was lost in the past. "He was more than a little charming, and before long, he offered to take Victoria and me to his burgeoning rancho across the border."

"Your father allowed it?"

"My father refused." Mercy's voice reflected the pride she felt. "He wasn't alone. Several men in Santo Tomas denied Fino their daughters."

"He wanted to take…more than the two of you?"

"Many more. I think there were fifteen or sixteen of us. He called it his Summer Garden Excursion."

The Black Rose tried to understand. "Was he finding wives for his men, or outfitting a harem?"

"He was outfitting a whore house."

"What happened?"

"Some of the men stood up to Fino, including my father. They were killed."

"Your mother?"

"Shot by his side."

The Black Rose felt her heart sink. She knew too well what Mercy had been through, and she squeezed the older woman's hand with empathy, silently encouraging her to continue her story.

"Once across the border," said Mercy, "Fino took us to a hacienda with a lovely, bubbling stream. On one side was a beautiful, white-washed frame estancia. On the other, across an open field, was a long, barren bunk house. Most of us were kept there, to live in squalor. To do the devils work, servicing the men with all we had." Mercy smiled. "Except for Victoria. Fino had admired her from the start. He treated her like his princess."

"He took her for his own?"

"Yes," said Mercy. "She was to be his and no one else's. He is an evil black-hearted bastard. And after stealing her daughters and forcing them to become prostitutes, Fino had the gall to return to Santo Tomas and wed my sister at the mission here in front of the entire village. Andronicus performed the mass."

"Under duress, I'm sure," said the Black Rose.

Mercy acknowledge the sarcasm. "Of course. Andronicus does not change."

"Where were you?"

"By the time of their marriage, I was hundreds

of miles away. Fino had sold me to another gang of bandits who had their fun with me. After they were finished, they sold me to a brothel in Chihuahua."

"How is it you came to be here?"

Mercy's breath came in ragged gasps. "Eventually, I escaped. Barely. There was...much blood."

"You had to fight to be free?"

"Had to fight," agreed Mercy. "Had to kill. So much blood. I came to the springs to wash it clean. My sins...will never be washed clean."

The Black Rose cradled Mercy in her arms, hushing her, telling her everything would be alright. Doing her best to comfort her.

"I took the vows," said Mercy. "Louise Byrne became Mercy Justice. I tried to forget. But then came word from across the border. Fino was at war, and skirmishes were blowing up all across the region."

"You must've been worried about your sister."

Mercy nodded. "No time," she said. "No...time..."

From the corner of the hotel came the sound of new assailants. The Black Rose turned and saw a man climbing onto the roof from the top rung of a ladder. His eyes searched the darkness, presumably for her, his words were directed at the men below him. "I'm there, I'm there, hold your horses, dammit."

The way he walked was familiar, the way he talked, all the more so.

Without her cape, the Black Rose surged up, lean and prepared to fight. Her grim visage stalled Trask's advance as two more men cleared the ladder to take positions on the roof behind him. These weren't soldiers, but neither were they with Garcia. One was wall-eyed with a bowler hat plopped on his head the other was bare-chested with a heavy beard. Trask took a step back in fear, bumping into them. "Aw, hell no," he said. "Not you again."

The Black Rose whirled like a saw cutting into timber. Alert to her skill, Trask dodged the attack by falling flat to the tar-covered roof. His men weren't so lucky.

Bowler went first, lobbing a wide open haymaker punch. Whether he meant to connect, or simply block her attack, the Black Rose had no idea. Either way, the clumsy swing was ineffectual and only served to throw the dizzy man off balance. He slipped, wind milled into a spiral trying to right himself, and met a roundhouse kick to the side of the face. He fell off the roof backwards, clearing the way for his shaggy friend to advance.

The Black Rose judged her brawny opponent to be more dangerous than Bowler or Trask. His bare arms, chest, and back were a damp landscape forested with thick matted hair, and his breath came with a series of wet growls. Hunched low, he circled her like a rabid dog, darting in to taunt her, flinching away at the last possible instant, looking for the precise time to strike.

Then Trask was back on his feet, flanking her. Together, the two men had her turned around and now they crouched between her and Mercy.

"You working for Fino now, Trask?"

"Soldiers say clear the roof, me and the boys figure why not?"

"You really think you can?" said the Black Rose. "You couldn't stop me when you worked for Cain. Why should now be any different."

"Because I didn't have Walnut with me then."

"Walnut?" said the Black Rose. "You're joking? What kind of name is Walnut?"

"Hard to crack, you stupid bitch," said the shaggy man, trying to take advantage of the distraction. He came at her full bore, head down like a bull, arms out to either side. He meant to knock the wind from her, wrap his tree-branch arms about her ribs and squeeze her like a casing of sausage.

Instead, the Black Rose parried his advance, dodged the arms and came up behind her attacker. Her fists were like steam pistons crunching into his kidneys, contributing to Walnut's own momentum, sending him over the edge of the roof after his friend. When he hit the ground there was a sickening wet splash, like a melon split with an ax.

"Not so hard to crack after, all."

Suddenly, Trask realized his predicament, and his Adam's apple moved up and down as he pleaded for clemency. "I'll just...I mean, I'll go on back down if it's all the same to you, Missy."

"In the short time we've known one another, I've grown rather fond of you, Trask." The Black Rose walked toward him. Seductive. Alluring. "I'd rather you stayed."

Trask backed away, first one step, then another two steps, more quickly than the first.

"I don't wanna fight anymore, Miss...uh...whatever your name is."

"Hasn't anybody told you my name?"

"No, ma'am. Down below, they just said they'd give us fifty pesos if'n we cleared you off this here roof?"

"Fifty pesos." The Black Rose pretended to mull over the news. "Split three ways?"

"Split ten ways," said a voice.

During the fight, the soldiers had found two more ladders. One had been propped up against the rear of the hotel, where the voice came from. A third was seven or eight feet farther along, close to the opposite corner of the building. Soldiers filed onto the roof, all of them open handed, each of them falling into position around her.

There was nowhere to run.

With dozen soldiers surrounding her, the Black Rose took stock of her position.

"No guns? Why not shoot me down?"

"Fino wants Garcia's woman alive," said the first soldier.

"If he thinks I'm Garcia's woman, he couldn't be more wrong."

"It doesn't matter. He said to retrieve you."

"Retrieve? Like a lost child, perhaps? Or a missing lamb?"

"Whatever you say, lady," said the soldier.

"He'll have to come get me himself," said the Black Rose, bolting into action. Using the soldier's momentum and taking a quick side step, the Black Rose helped him over the edge of the roof.

Upon his collision with the earth, the talking

soldier fared no better than Walnut.

Two more soldiers attacked.

One of them carried a ten-inch blade in an ivory handle, and openly boasted, "Alive don't mean uninjured." He wore a heavy blue tunic and smelled of lilac toilet water. Unlike the others under Fino's command, he wasn't wearing any kind of disguise and wore the rank of a corporal.

He came at her torso, thrusting forward with the skill of a veteran knife-fighter. The Black Rose unslung her urumi, blocking the attack with the steel coil, using it as a bludgeon to swipe back at the impact. Warily, the corporal came in again. He was good, better than anyone the Black Rose had yet faced on the roof of the hotel, and after so many skirmishes, she was getting tired.

"Not so much to say eh, senorita? Where's your smart mouth? Please? Share with me your lip?"

The corporal came in sideways, bending at the waist, slashing up at her breasts. The Black Rose blocked, parried, lashed out with the spiraled urumi like she would use a bronze shield. They came together again, clashing steel against steel, the other soldiers closing in the circle around her. She couldn't let them grab her, couldn't let them overwhelm her with numbers. Her weapon was the urumi, but in close quarters it was awkward to use, and the corporal pressed the attack.

"You are tired, Rosie. Give up now, and who knows? Fino may let you live."

But the Black Rose was not about to give up. A

warm cramp of pain, and she realized the Corporal had cut into her thigh. A blow to the arm, and her wrist went numb. She moved the pain aside and focused on her years of training, her fighting skills no man could casually best.

"If I am to be defeated, I'll see you dead first," she said.

The corporal raised his eyebrows in mock surprise, delighting too much in his perceived victory, too concerned with making a show for his men. "I'd like to see you try."

She reared up high above him, leading him, and he fell for the fake, leaving himself open and exposed. Just what the Black Rose had waited for. Looping back inside, she drove her elbow into his throat, crushing his larynx, collapsing his wind tunnel, and pushing him off the roof. The corporal fell clutching his collar, and the Black Rose unrolled her weapon with a shimmering, swift fling.

The men ran for the ladders, leaving her to stand alone on the roof in triumph.

She returned to the Mother Superior's side, breathing hard, mind a flutter, considering a thousand options for escape, not finding a good solution in any of them.

"Mercy," she said, finding the nun on her side, turning her onto her back. "We need to get you to the springs."

"Forget me, Catalina. Save yourself. I'm so sorry. Fino..."

"What about Fino?"

She looked up and saw the Fino standing on the

roof. He hair was a slab of perfectly sculpted marble, his mustache, a clot of thick, white paste. While his soldiers had fled, the big man had ascended the far ladder to the peak of the hotel.

Apparently he was here to take matters into his own hands.

"Get up, niñita. Face me," he said.

The Black Rose squared herself against the General.

CHAPTER THIRTY-FOUR

That's when Charlie Mac's big 705 went up in a concussive ball of fire.

Whump!

The shockwave was a wall of boiling air hitting with the impact of a padded sledgehammer. Reeling to the rooftop, nearly blind from the white hot blast of the boiler, the Black Rose flung up her arms against two more calamitous blasts. She pushed herself to her full stature and from her vantage point here on the roof watched as men and munitions were tossed into the sky on clouds of orange and black. More peals of thunder ripped into the night.

Fino too had been knocked to the floor of the rooftop, his lit cigar rolling across the tar, scattering chunky loose embers of ash.

The railroad tracks played host to a wall of fire rising above the two-story hotel, mad, dancing flames casting flimsy films of ash and spent wood toward the moon. Ears ringing, throat filled with smoke and choking vapor, the Black Rose fully realized what had happened.

"The train," she whispered.

"What's happened, Lina?" said Mercy.

"No," said Fino, crawling on his knees toward the edge of the building. "I won't allow it." He levered himself up before the conflagration on wobbly legs. "It cannot be."

From below and to the right, a triumphant cheer arose.

Carried on the clamor of racing hooves, the voices announced victory in a battle which neared its end. The Black Rose walked to the front of the hotel and looked down into the street. Cassidy and Garcia rode with five additional men, leading a pack of horses with dead soldiers tied to the saddles. Along the boardwalk and empty street, the residents of Santo Tomas cautiously appeared. People poked their heads around corners and out of windows. Two men meandered toward the fiery devastation. A young couple with a child between them walked down the street near the mercantile.

Cassidy looked up, saw the Black Rose, and waved.

She turned back to the roof.

Fino stood over top of Mercy's huddled form.

Not taking her eyes off the General, the Black Rose addressed the nun. "You said after you took your vows, Fino was at war. You said skirmishes were blowing up all around the region." Her voice went low, as if anticipating the answer. "Who was he fighting?"

Mercy's voice was weak, trembling.

"The Riveras," she said.

"And your sister?"

"I traveled to the hacienda," said Mercy. "Under the cover of night. I...arrived to such destruction. The entire rancho...was on fire."

At the confession, Fino flinched like he'd been slapped. "You...were there?" he said.

"I found Victoria battered, alone under a partially collapsed wall of the house. Everything was...ablaze, but I pulled her to safety...she...was..."

"Dead?" said Fino.

"In labor," said Mercy.

The Black Rose felt a heavy weight roll through the pit of her stomach.

"She died giving birth to the child."

"You lying bitch," said Fino, with a roar. "What you say can't be true."

Mercy ignored Fino's rage and spoke to the Black Rose. "Before she passed, she gave me the burnt rosary. It was her rosary. To pass on to her child. She wanted you to have it, Lina."

The Black Rose let the words sink in.

"My mother was Theresa Estella Rivera. She was the granddaughter of Contessa D'Mores of Madrid."

"I delivered you in the midst of Fino's crumbling home," said Mercy.

When you were born, there was a fire. I was there, in the middle of it. You are, quite literally, a child of the fire.

"I carried you to the Rancho Rivera myself. I put you in Theresa's arms," said Mercy.

"Your sister, Victoria..."

"Was your mother."

Eyes ablaze, Catalina Cristiana Rivera pushed to her feet. "And Fino?"

"Is your father," said Mercy.

The urumi fell to the rooftop with a clatter, and Lina walked away from them both, stopping at the precipice, looking out over the village. The locomotive and tender was a wreck of burning, twisted steel, the Pullman cars burst open like overripe fruit, spilling their blackened guts across the rails and into the street. Another wave of soldiers rode past on the retreat from Garcia's forces.

The battle was won.

But Catalina had lost.

The stink of Mexican bourbon and heavy cigars assailed her senses. Fino stood beside her. Reaching out, he put a hand on her shoulder. "La hija," he said.

Daughter.

Without a second thought, Catalina's arm shot out like a steel bolt, her powerful fingers squeezing tight, an iron vice around Fino's throat.

The General's face turned a deep red as Lina took a step toward the edge of the hotel, holding firm. Fino tried to shake he head, weakly lifted his arms to his neck.

His face was purple.

Lina stood on tiptoe, placed her lips close to his ear so he'd be sure to hear.

The smell of rancid cigar smoke was overwhelming.

"My father is dead," she said.

Then she levered herself into position and pitched

Fino from the roof of the hotel into the burning train wreckage.

With only forty feet to fall, there wasn't much time for him to scream.

CHAPTER THIRTY-FIVE

Inside her quarters in the mission, Catalina sat on her straw mattress, counting the beads in her rosary, trying to remember the first prayer Sofia had tried to teach her. A hazy, weak sun dribbled tepid light through the slotted shutters over her window, and when the bell rang for evening vespers, Lina pretended not to hear it.

"Ave Maria. Gratia…plena." She hesitated. "Dominic…domtum…something, something." She tossed the rosary onto her pillow with a sigh. It didn't matter anyway. No matter how much she had come to respect the Sisters of Santa Maria, she had no intention of taking the vows to become an official member of the order.

As the Black Rose, she already had a mission — from God or the Devil. Sometimes, she thought, it wasn't clear.

She was still sorting it out.

More than two weeks after Fino's early morning siege, Adeline and Mary had finally arrived at the mission with Diablo in tow and scores of stories to tell. "Did y'all know the secret to making good fry-bread is the way you grind the corn flour?" said Mary. "I never knew that."

"The children of Nuevo Pino tell stories of the Black Rose. The legend is spreading far and wide," said Adeline.

"Too bad Prince Ferdinand didn't fall too far from the horse-apple tree," said Mary. "From what I saw, he ain't no better than his papa."

Catalina had kept Mercy's revelation about her parents to herself. She wasn't surprised to learn her new brother retained the dark blood of the General, but the news worried her. If Ferdinand retained the family evil, how much better was she? Aquiles Rivera used to have a saying: *Blood will tell.*

Would it?

And how dare Aquiles tell her such a thing, knowing full well she wasn't his child.

Here too was another puzzle.

There was much to share with them about Santo Tomas as well.

The day after Garcia and Denver Three-Moons drove Fino's army back across the desert with the General's body strapped on a pack mule, the restoration of the village had begun. Carlyle and most of his downtown friends were either dead or chased out of town, and a new group of aldermen had been meeting at the mercantile. Their first order of business was cleaning up the tracks and petitioning the Sioux City and Orient to send a new train.

They would need plenty of supplies to rebuild. They would need help from other communities. Miraculously, none of the springs had been damaged in the onslaught, and the mission was still sound. Mercy said the Lord provided protection, but Lina wasn't so sure. Could have just as easily been dumb luck.

Pilgrims would still come, and maybe more than one of them could be coerced to stay and lend a hand with the village reconstruction.

Catalina brushed stray wisps of lint from her blue habit and walked to a small writing table positioned in the corner of the room. She let her fingers trace the curved engraving on the back of a silver pocket watch, then straightened the collection of four books she had salvaged from her last ride out to rancho Rivera.

Shakespeare, Homer, the *Holy Bible*, and Sun Tzu.

Mary suggested Lina ought to have a dime novel or two to lighten her mood.

She clicked open the pocket watch and cursed the heavy molasses drip of time.

Lina fussed over the books, arranging them three times according to size, then color, then alphabetically. Other than the timepiece and a burnt tintype of Theresa, the bound hardback volumes were all she had been able to save during her visit to the ruined homestead.

She walked back to the bed and chewed her fingernail.

In the hallway, somebody knocked on the wall.

"Come in."

Cassidy pushed the door partially ajar and peeked through the crack. "Am I disturbing you? I heard the bell for vespers."

"It's all right. Come in."

He slipped around the corner and carefully shut the door behind him, making sure not to make any noise. "Visiting you alone in your bedroom would probably not be to the Monsignor's liking."

"What the Monsignor doesn't like, he can roll up and sit on."

Cassidy smiled. "I heard you were getting a new pastor?"

"Father Michael Demetrius," said Lina. "He's here in Santo Tomas, but I have yet to meet him."

"He will replace the Monsignor?"

"Unfortunately, no. Andronicus' request for assignment to the Bishop's detail was denied. He'll be staying with us for the time being."

"I will redouble my prayer efforts for you." Cassidy smiled at his own comment, but remained standing behind the door in a tan suit with a vest and silk tie. His boots were polished, his nails trimmed. He smelled of bay rum.

She realized she'd never seen his face so devoid of whiskers.

"Have you talked with the aldermen, yet?" she said.

"Yes."

"You delivered your speech, just like we rehearsed?"

"Yes."

"You explained about Dawson's demise? About your heroic flight back in the auto?"

"Yes."

Since the night of the battle, talking to Cassidy was like prying a turtle out of a tin can.

He'd remained in town to help with the cleanup, proving himself to be a fine arbiter of disputes. When he was sober, Cassidy was a natural born leader. He was the kind of man the community needed if it intended to recover from the fiesta de balas — the carnival of bullets — it had endured.

But the darned fool could be exasperating.

"Are you going to tell me how they answered your appeal or not?"

"The good and proper gentlemen listened with polite interest to everything I had to say."

"You're teasing me, damn you."

"Now, now, sister. That is no way for you to talk." Cassidy's head remained bowed, but his eyes rolled up to meet hers with a sheepish expression. Casually, he pulled back the lapel of his jacket to show her the silver star pinned to his shirt. "I have accepted the position as constable of Santo Tomas."

It was just the answer she'd hoped for. Lina hurried across the room and took both of his hands in hers. "I am happy for you, amigo."

"I will be staying in the spare room behind the office and taking my meals at the hotel."

Cassidy lowered his eyelids with modesty. "I suppose it is wrong to want to celebrate at the cantina." When he looked up again, she noticed for the first time the beauty of his gray eyes. "I haven't had anything but water and coffee since that night."

He really was quite handsome. Why had she never noticed it before?

Lina leaned in and kissed him gently on the forehead.

"You will be the scourge of the west, Constable Cassidy."

"I won't carry a gun."

Catalina smiled, thinking about the meeting about to take place in the cavern below. She placed a tender finger to his lips. "If all goes well, you won't have need to," she said.

His embrace was awkward and quick, and then Cassidy rapidly scurried through Lina's door and down the hall of the convent. Once he was gone, she engaged the deadbolt on the door, making sure it was locked.

She walked back to her desk and clicked open the pocket watch.

Twenty minutes to go.

Catalina picked up the black rosary and rolled the beads between her fingers and thumb. Finally, still unable to complete Sofia's Latin prayer, she stripped out of the blue habit and sensible shoes. She padded to the end of the bed where she unlocked the leather straps of a humpback trunk Adeline had supplied.

She withdrew her long black cloak and tin of Apache warpaint.

Once she was ready, the Black Rose pushed back her bed and threw aside the rug to reveal a trap door cut into the floor of her quarters. Gripping the heavy iron latch, she pulled it open and descended to the cellar below.

✳✳✳✳✳✳

The centuries-old corridor was believed to have been carved from the limestone rock by the Spaniards under Don Cicero Da Costa before their untimely demise. Mercy said Father Lopez' journals were curiously vague on the subject, but it was clear the old Franciscan knew of the maze under this section of the mission, and made use of the wide vaulted chamber for storing wine. The cool temperature was a comfort after spending the entire day working in the garden, and the news from Cassidy was equally uplifting. The Black Rose was eager to share what she knew with her comrades.

When she had wound her way through the first set of passageways, she came to a locked steel door. She withdrew a silver key from her cloak, opened the door, and entered a second hallway. Here the spring water seeped through cracks in the rock, leaving the mud floor damp and smelling of mildew — not entirely unpleasant.

As the days moved into weeks, the Black Rose had begun to appreciate her surroundings as much as the people who lived there.

Emerging in the open meeting place, she was pleased to see the Mother Superior had arrived before her. The room was a square almost twenty feet on each side with a low ceiling that grazed Mercy's black cowl. In the far corner recess, where the ceiling was little more than four feet high, a bubbling stream made its way along an ancient bed and a silver cup hung from a hook on the wall.

"How are you, Mercy?"

The nun sat in a cushioned mahogany chair decorated in ornamental carvings. On top of the heavy oak table in front of her was a series of compact paper envelopes. Each envelope acted as a place holders in front of seven chairs. The envelopes were sealed with a pressed dollop of scarlet wax bearing the imprint of a rose blossom. In the center of the table, a tall candle provided the cavern's only light.

Mercy acknowledged the Black Rose with a welcome expression. "Forgive me for not standing up," she said. "The gunshot wound still bedevils me at certain times of the day. I'm healing, but slow."

"You're doing remarkably well."

Mercy's sparkling eyes caught the glint of the candle and she gestured at the trickling spring water. "I wash the wound twice a day and pray to the Blue Nun. I'll soon be good as new."

The Black Rose took the woman's easy faith in stride, even if she didn't always understand it. During her time with them, the nuns had proven themselves to the skeptical Catalina Rivera. They were honest and hardworking. They showed discipline and compassion in the correct measure. They had integrity — when so many people in the new century struggled with the very meaning of the word.

If they had a few irrational religious quirks, the Black Rose could overlook them.

"Ah, but here is Sofia Lee and Caroline," said Mercy as the two sisters appeared through the hallway entrance. They nodded and took their places at the table, putting their black rosaries next to the sealed envelope in front of them.

Soon, all seven who were called sat around the table.

After the Black Rose shared her news about Cassidy, Mercy raised herself to a standing position and called the meeting to order.

"Each of you knows I have been following the evolution of Santo Tomas for many years. This is where my family settled after coming over from the old country, and this is where my destiny lies. Heaven has brought each of you here through different circumstances, and heaven will bring more." Mercy's voice took on an ominous tone. "Not everyone who comes will hold goodwill in their hearts."

From her position at Mercy's right hand, the Black Rose gauged the reaction of the other five women. Sofia Lee offered a grim smile of understanding, and Caroline gave a slight nod of her head.

Adeline was the convent's official annalist and acted as recorder for these hidden proceedings as well. She dipped her pen in a glass inkwell and used the brief pause to finish recording Mercy's words in a leather bound volume with crème pages.

Beside her, Lucia's nervous eyes bounced from one sister to the next. Self-conscious, she rubbed at her nose. The Black Rose made an effort to catch the girl's attention and offer her a reassuring expression.

On the opposite side of the table, Mary drummed her fingers on the wood. "I can't help but notice we've all got one of those black wooden rosaries," she said.

Lucia picked up the cross and its burnt beads. "I

don't understand, Mother," she said. "It looks as if it's been in a fire, but it smells of spices and fresh sandalwood, and the black is not soot." She rubbed the cross vigorously with her fingers. "It doesn't soil the skin."

"I'll bet you got yours from a little blind fella, didn't you?" said Mary. "Was he bout so high?" She held her hand at eye level.

"The rosary maker has approached each of us in turn," said Mercy. "With the exception of Catalina."

"Each sister he recruits seems to have a specific skill we need," said the Black Rose.

"Or perhaps it is each individual sister who needs us," said Mercy.

"Yes, of course," said the Black Rose.

"What about the envelopes?" said Mary. She picked up the folded piece of paper. "If it's an invitation to another wedding, I'd like permission to skip it."

Mercy's ignored Mary's ramblings. "We seven have been brought together at this time and place for a reason," she said. "Like the Sisters of Sorrow, our Lord has a purpose for this order." Mercy's scrutiny moved over each of them. "The world has entered a new era of rapid change. Forces are gathering for the good...and for evil. The mission walls have stood the test of time, but it will take added effort to keep them strong. It will take a bulwark against the darkness. Our order is that bulwark."

Lucia raised her hand. "Our order, Mother? You mean the Sisters of Señora Maria?"

"No, child," said Mercy. She spread her arms to encompass the women at the table. Not all the

Sisters of Señora Maria are called to serve in this particular way. I mean the order of the Black Rose."

Mercy's voice reverberated through the cavern, and all the women sat in silence, taking in the idea before them.

Finally Sofia broke the silence and said, "And the envelopes?"

"Our next assignment," said Mercy. She signaled her permission to break the seals.

"Do we all get to wear spooky warpaint and a cloak like Catalina? I'd like to wear a cloak."

"Hush, Mary Rosetta," said Mercy.

The Black Rose reached for her envelope, picking it up with eager anticipation.

All was as it should be.

She appreciated these women of the convent, and in that appreciation felt a sense of destiny fulfilled. Whatever lay in store for them, she was confident in her ability to help guide this new order to become a force for good in the world.

She committed herself to the holy war ahead, vowing to more than curse the darkness. She vowed to fight on behalf of the light — or die in the attempt.

Then just for an instant, she had the odd sensation. Somehow, someone outside the chamber watched her, and the image that came in her mind was of Nuevo Piño and Fino's luxury estate.

CHAPTER THIRTY-SIX

The Andalusian stallion beneath his Mexican saddle was the color of polished walnut wood and brushed to reflect layers of clean, rich depth. The animal's coat was equal to its soul. Never had Ferdinand known a steed so strong, yet supple.

So eager to move, yet so cooperative with its rider.

In ages past, the animal would be the envy of generals and presidents. It was nothing less than a warhorse.

Ferdinand would continue to train it as such.

They crossed the open lawn to arrive at the barn with its central breezeway of oak stanchions and square pens. Dismounting, he kicked at the sloppy pile of loose straw in the doorway and demanded Tully show himself.

"Señor Fino?" said the cowboy, shuffling from a rear pen with a shovel in hand.

"What the hell have you been doing all day, old man? Returning from my ride, I expect to find a tidy stall for Lucifer. Instead, stacks of dirty bedding block the entrance and the floors are thick with dung."

"Miguel is sick with the croup today, just like the Lady Alejandra has been, and—"

"You would blame your sloth on my wife?"

"I only meant to say—"

The heir to rancho Fino-Espolon slapped Tully's face with an open hand. "I never want to hear my wife's name from your lips again. Do you understand?"

Tully slumped as if invisible chains were clamped to his forearms, and Ferdinand jammed the stallion's reins into his hand. "Brush Lucifer down. Feed and water him. Make sure his stall is clean and the bedding fresh."

The old fool fell all over himself with apologies.

"For God's sake, don't grovel," said Ferdinand.

He watched Tully lead the horse away before rotating on the heel of his riding boots.

Running his fingers through his thick, oiled hair and straightening his white cotton shirt, he struggled to calm his breathing. He wore his shirt unbuttoned to the belt where he carried a black target pistol in a patent leather holster that drooped over his white jodhpurs. Placing his hand on his holster reassured him.

"Ferdinand, darling?"

The young man raised his head to the patio of the great cathedral next door. Standing on the patio in the last rays of the late afternoon sun, Alejandra waved. "Maria wants to know about tonight's meal. Do you prefer fowl to roast pork?"

Ferdinand felt his brows drop low and wondered why he was being bothered with such nonsense. First the damned stable was a shambles, now these puckish shrews couldn't prepare a damned meal without quizzing him. "Leave me be, can't you?" he shouted.

Didn't the silly bitch understand he was still in mourning?

It had only been two weeks since his father had returned from Santo Tomas on the back of a swaybacked mule. Even now it didn't seem possible. How could it be true? How could the great Fino have been so dishonorably slain?

Something on the floor caught his eye and he bent to pick it up.

It was an old riding glove from when he was a child. His father had insisted the wrists be monogrammed with leather stitching — FAF. With nobody watching, he tried it on. The fingers were too small, the leather shriveled and dry.

He tossed the glove back onto the floor and raised his head to a sight he hadn't seen before.

A second glove waited on a dusty shelf next to a greasy black paint stick.

Somebody had used the stick to draw something on the wall.

Ferdinand felt his breath come in gulping spasms at the sight, felt his blood race and icy fingers, like the legs of a thousand spiders, crawled up his spine. In fear and anger, his hand jerked for the holster and unsnapped the cover.

He pulled the slim gun and raised it to shoulder level, aiming at the illustration on the barn wall with clasped, shaking hands.

Even as Ferdinand screamed aloud with each tug of the trigger, rending into tatters the old gray barn wood around it, the enormous painting of an intricate black rose seemed to shrug off the bullets and continue to defy him.

A LOOK AT: THE SWORD OF THE BLACK ROSE

The legendary sword of St. Agnes has been found, and the Black Rose is tasked with retrieving it at any cost.

But a resurrected St. Patrick's Battalion, rechristened the Sainted Brothers of Monterrey, want the sword for their own malevolent goals.

An agenda that may have already claimed the souls of two innocent Santo Tomas girls and threatens to engulf the world in fire.

With her razor-sharp urumi whip-sword and the comradery of warriors, Lina's alter ego carves a new legacy in the chronicles of Western adventure.

AVAILABLE SEPTEMBER 2020 FROM A.W. HART AND WOLFPACK PUBLISHING

ABOUT THE AUTHOR

Richard Prosch's western crime fiction captures the fleeting history and lonely frontier stories of his youth, where characters aren't always what they seem and the windburned landscapes are filled with swift, deadly danger.

His work has appeared in True West, Roundup, and Saddlebag Dispatches magazines, and online at Boys' Life. He won the Spur Award from Western Writers of America for short fiction, and his Jo Harper stories have received nominations for the Peacemaker Award from Western Fictioneers. Richard lives in Missouri with his wife, Gina, son, Wyatt, assorted cats, and a Great Pyrenees named Moose.